Is It Time?

(The Caretakers)

By

Roscoe Harman

Copyright © 2020 Roscoe Harman

All rights reserved, including the right to reproduce this book, or portions thereof in any form. No part of this text may be reproduced, transmitted, downloaded, decompiled, reverse engineered, or stored, in any form or introduced into any information storage and retrieval system, in any form or by any means, whether electronic or mechanical without the express written permission of the author.

This is a work of fiction. Names and characters are the product of the author's imagination and any resemblance to actual persons, living or dead, is entirely coincidental.

The views expressed in this work are solely those of the author and do not necessarily reflect the views of the publisher, and the publisher hereby disclaims any responsibility for them.

ISBN: 9798663240826

PublishNation
www.publishnation.co.uk

Foreword

A fictional novel – or is it?

How bist ol' butt?

I live in a time when it seems the whole world is changing.

It all started when I accidentally blew up the house. It was my sister's house. She was not pleased.

Mine was a life of violence; but then I was born into an unjust world and violence is its natural companion.

My name is inconsequential when compared to my tale.

They say that before a man dies a record of his life may be shown to him in an instant.

My Dearest Cousin,

I am acutely aware that I have not contacted you for, oh, my goodness, it must be at least ten years now. Please forgive my tardiness and I trust that our relationship is still as strong as it was during our childhood and early years. I offer no real excuse for my lack of contact other than life is lived at such a fast pace now, that it barely leaves one time to draw breath, let alone put pen to paper.

Having assumed all the pleasantries, like how we and our various families are, I should like to spring straight to my reason for contacting you 'out of the blue' as it were.

I have recently come into possession of some documents which have, quite literally, left me breathless at the thought of their potential significance.

Knowing that you are associated with the University, and therefore have access to its library, (I assume that is still the case?), I could think of no person better to raise the subject of these documents with.

To state that they of universal interest would not be an exaggeration.

I hope this piques your interest sufficiently to respond to this letter at your earliest convenience and with the arrogant assumption that you forgive me, utterly, for my lack of previous contact.

Yours sincerely and apologetically,
Beattie

Dear Beattie,

It was lovely to hear from you. Indeed, you have piqued my interest with regard to your find.

I can assure you that I still hold a position at the University and have free and copious access to the library. Presumably this is of significance in determining the Provenance of your documents?

The family, as you rightly assumed, are all thriving and, as luck would have it, my time is fairly free at the moment, for whatever research you may require, it being the beginning of the holiday period. There are a few tutorials which I must oversee but apart from that I am enthusiastic to hear your tale.

Yours, in intrigue,

Jackie

My Dearest Cousin,

I was so relieved to receive your kind letter that it quite made my day!

This will be no short tale since the documents which have come into my possession span many centuries and have already travelled widely throughout the world as you will discover. Perhaps it will be best if I explain one segment at a time?

I shall call this segment, which is more about me than the treasure, 'My Background', as it explains what has happened to me over the last decade which, in turn, explains how these extraordinary documents came into my possession.

I trust you read the enclosed with an air of patience. Knowing a little more about me and my life is essential to your understanding the limitations in my wisdom.

Kindest regards and gratitude,

Beattie

(Encl.)

My Background

I earn a modest living buying and selling what I'll graciously call "object d'art." To some I might be described as an antique dealer but the reality is, I'm probably more of a junk dealer. Choosing the middle ground, I describe myself as someone who deals in bric-a-brac.

Occasionally I am lucky enough to find an article of some worth, which I then auction through one of the big houses, or sell via one of my esteemed contacts. More commonly I attend Car Boot or Table Top sales to pass on what to me is little more than rubbish, but hopefully, to others is some an ideal collectable. The web has opened up both my tiny business and my limited mind. I must admit, it brings me a vicarious thrill as I watch the deadline approach on an article and two collectors increase their bids to win the on-line auction.

I also have a passion for attending physical auctions. I go to many such events, filled with the excited anticipation of the prospect of "the find" of a lifetime, or at least one which will change my lifestyle.

It fascinates me to watch others casually inspect items prior to the auction, then feign disinterest, when really it is the very item for which they have travelled fifty miles. This attitude of disinterest is merely their misguided attempt to influence others into believing that the item has no value and is unworthy of a bid. I know this because I've employed this same tactic myself.

The other reason I attend these events is for the social contact. Ours is a very insular profession and if one is associated with it for a number of years, as I have been, one can't help but get to know people who make their living in a similar way.

We are usually the ones who are the first to arrive and often the last to leave. We get there first to have the opportunity of viewing the Lots carefully, in order to mark our programme with the top bid we plan to make for any item.

Unfortunately, the decent stuff tends to be in the later Lots, so it is common that most of us are around for the duration. It is during the middle section of the auction that we tend to congregate and swap tales of recent purchases and sales, like peacocks displaying their fan, in effort to exaggerate our instinct, knowledge and importance.

Another source of resalable goods which I love to explore, are in areas outside main cities where markets and small shops exist. These display mostly useless, if pretty, bric-a-back. We professionals, however, know that sometimes in a back room, they possess an article from which we can command a good price in the city.

Whilst not giving away my sources, such places as South Wales and its surrounds are a happy and often prosperous hunting ground of mine. These artifacts I then peddle to dealers in for example Cheltenham, the Cotswold's or even London. The lesser items find their way into a local auction or onto the web.

Sometimes I make a large profit, sometimes a small one. The way I judge my success, is to tally up all the items bought and sold in any month, and as long as, having covered my expenses, I am on the plus side I count this a good trading period. This may not be the way a businessman works but it suits me.

It is in regard to a certain 'find' that I am prompted to write to you for advice on how to proceed, so outstanding and unique is its nature.

As you may remember, writing is not a particular love of mine, nor did I achieve great marks in my English exams at school. However, I felt that the subject matter was sufficiently important, and of such potential interest to so many, that I would break with the habit of a lifetime and put pen to paper – or more truthfully, spell out each word on my computer using at first one finger, and with practice, two fingers.

Copious use of a spell check facility aided me greatly in my endeavours; in fact, so much so that I named it 'Mr Greaves' that being the name of my old English teacher.

It is also relevant that you know that my talents lie more in the 'artsy' things of life. I am a fair painter, which I put to use with minor repairs on paintings; I adore wood and restoring a long-abused article to their original grandeur; and I am good at languages where I count myself proficient in French, Spanish and a salt and pepper shake of German.

Holidays at these destinations keep my proficiency levels at the level of 'adequate'. Although, in France, I did once determinedly seek out an English-speaking shop, a money exchange I seem to remember, only to enquire "oo eh la framage?" Thereby profoundly embarrassing the people I was with, and causing great amusement to the shop staff and customers. By the way, I was kindly and patiently directed to a shop selling cheese, as was my desire!

I once attended an upholstering class; which skills have proven invaluable. There are many, once faded, chairs out there which are now dressed in a fine array of garment thanks to my skills in this area. So, 'artsy' is a good definition as you can see.

I did have a husband for a short while. He was a dentist. Nobody loves a dentist – not even me after two years of marriage. The breakup was amicable. No children. We never got around to them. There hasn't really been anybody else since.

My waistline is the only thing to have suffered from this divorce. I have now reached the universal definition of 'not quite fitting comfortably into a theatre seat'. It is more a case of once wedged into the furniture, not moving again until it is time to leave the theatre, when another struggle ensues.

I have a dog. He is a little rascal of a border collie cross, which is a polite way of describing a mongrel. After six years I am as fond of "Reggie" as I ever was. Reggie beats a dentist for companionship hands over paws. Besides, taking dog-years into account, we are actually the same age. (Early forties being expressed in woman-speak as late thirties!)

Enough about me! Although I must say that it has been a cathartic experience defining myself on paper. I have never done that before. I sincerely hope that you weren't too bored, Jackie. Trust me, it was a relevant explanation for why I find myself in such a quandary now.

To Begin ...

One day earlier in the Summer I was on a quest, in my usual haunts, to restock my now flagging inventory.

As such I set off in my trusty bright yellow Cortina Estate, with Reggie in his usual place curled up on the back seat, and found myself turning off the motorway into the lesser inhabited areas. I eventually found myself in Ross-on-Wye, a beautiful tourist spot. I never buy anything here. Its definition as a place attracting tourists clearly identifies it as a place in which to sell and not to buy. However, from this town I followed a smaller road towards a village called Lydbrook.

The road was beautiful as it wound in harmony with the River Wye along its valley. There was hardly any traffic here and my heart was light and attitude positive. Shortly reaching a signpost that indicated I had arrived at Lydbrook, I stopped the car in a suitable space, and with Reggie, we wandered towards the river bank. Well, *I* wandered, he pranced.

Someone had kindly thought to place a cross-plank, supported by two uprights, here to allow the admirer to sit. I sat. Ahead of me, on the hilltop across the river, stood what looked like a stately home. I learnt later in the village pub that it was, in fact, a monastery.

Having rested peacefully from my journey, Reggie and I set off to walk back along the road verge as if towards Ross. I love walking and a more idyllic spot I could not imagine. It was still early in the day so I had plenty of time left to carry out my purchasing quest so there was no urgency. No self-respecting dealer opens before at the earliest 10.00 a.m. so I had time to kill and could think of no more pleasant way of passing the time.

I hadn't gone very far along this roadside when I realized that Reggie was not with me. Looking around I couldn't see him so, slightly frustrated, I retraced my steps.

"Reggie. Reggie. Where are you? Come here boy."

There was no sign of the little rascal. As I called out after each ten steps or so the rising aggravation I felt inside was reflected in my voice.

"Reggie. Reggie. I'll chop your tail off. Now, come here."

"Reggie."

Suddenly I spotted him. He was, nose down sniffing, engrossed in investigating something in the long grass.

I bent and patted my thighs in the long-accepted custom of dog owners. "Reggie. Reggie. Come here boy." My entreaties went unhindered. Reggie showed no sign of obeying my pleas and that left me with just one recourse, that of going to him and grabbing him by his collar. This I did with not a little frustration.

"Reggie. Whatever have you got there?" My hand grasped his collar and gently pulled. He fought me by pulling back with his little but strong legs.

I looked to see what it was that had led my companion to become so infuriating. I could see nothing. I expected at the very least to see an injured mouse or bird but not a sign of livestock was evident. My patience was flagging so I gently pulled him again. In response he took on an even greater angle with his paws firmly planted before a stone half buried in the ground.

Now Reggie has never been a disobedient animal and this adamant behaviour of his was truly out of character. With this in mind I began to offer some latitude.

"What is it boy? What have you found? Let mummy see." I moved into a position so that I could lift the stone to find out what lay under it which had so engrossed my beloved pet. I pivoted the heavy stone onto its edge, all the while holding firmly onto Reggie's collar with my other hand. My eyes scanned the earth where the stone had lain. Nothing. There was nothing there at all but a solitary woodlouse now scurrying for new cover.

"What is it you stupid animal? Look; there's nothing there."

I was about to let the stone fall back to its original resting place when something caught my eye on the underside of it. I was intrigued, so letting go of Reggie's collar, I used both hands to turn it over allowing it to fall with what had been the underside now showing on top. I really thought that my imagination had taken over and bent to see if my eyes deceived me.

There before me was a flat surface, unlike its other side, and on this was carved in relief the picture of a donkey. Yes, I kid you not! It was a donkey carved into the stone face. What's more, on closer inspection, I concluded that it was an elegant donkey carved by someone with more than a little talent. He truly was a superb animal staring back at me with, (don't think me mad), with piercing but kindly eyes.

"Well Reggie. What have you found here? You clever boy. Good dog, Reggie."

As a child I was an avid collector, as my poor long-suffering mother can attest to. As we would walk through a wood or along a beach, I would spot something of interest, like a pebble or a shell, and insist that due to its magical properties, it was essential that my mother carry it in her handbag until we reached home. This she learned to do without question or complaint, although the more treasures I uncovered and handed to her during the preamble, the shorter the walk became.

My childhood room boasted that no surface was untouched by such collectables. It is therefore absolutely core to my nature that this remarkable picture in stone be taken home. So decided I shuffled back to my car to collect old newspapers I always stored there. Returning to the stone, I placed it onto the newspaper wrapping some of the paper around and over it for protection. Next, returning to my car again, I placed the package into the boot.

The rest of the day was uneventful. I purchased a superb walnut coffee table, a box of Paragon china and a metal statue of the god, Pan. Tired but happy I arrived home some hours later and unloaded the car. By now I had forgotten the donkey residing there and it remained tucked up in its makeshift bed.

The First Clue

It was well into the next morning before I remembered the carved stone and recovered it from my boot. For the first time, over a cup of tea, I inspected the article in detail.

I was utterly amazed to discover that, in the background of the carved donkey, a symbol and words were also evident. The symbol is best described as a circle squashed from the top into the shape of a smiling mouth with no teeth. If you can't envisage that picture, try thinking of a child's drawing of a fish - without its tail.

Can you picture that, Jackie? It is important to hold that image in your mind since it recurs throughout the following documents.

The inscription was as follows:

(Tailless fish), From the Lyd to Ross mark 3 with water. Above it is mine.

(Tailless fish), Therein find treasure of value above gold.

The Visitor

It was my excitement at this discovery which caused my, usually alert, defences to fail me.

As the telephone rang at that moment, I answered it with only half a mind on who might be calling. It was Robin. I shan't use his full name for legal reasons because the criminal court case against him is still pending at the time I write this.

"Hi, Beattie. How are you?" he enquired in a cheerful voice.

I wish people would state who they are when ringing. My mind was diverted to pick up clues from this innocuous statement as to the identity of the caller. How often, even given an unfamiliar or unexpected first name by the caller, it sets my mind into a frenzy of activity trying to identify them?

"Hi. I am fine, thanks." I decided to leave the sentence there since the only thing I knew about this stranger from his voice was that he was male.

"It was great to see you at the auction Wednesday. I didn't get a chance to speak to you then, so thought I'd give you a ring now." Ah, ha! That narrows it down. My trusty brain now recalled those present at that event. I was drawing closer to an identity.

"Annie sends her love by the way." Got you! There's only one man I knew whose partner was called Annie.

"Robin!" I declared with triumph in my voice. "How lovely to hear from you. What are you up to these days?"

Now Robin and I were not friends as such but we were both in the same 'game' and had a passing acquaintanceship. He had sold me some items and I had passed certain things onto him. It was a good working relationship.

"Oh, same old, same old. You?"

"It's funny you should ring just now, actually. I've just come across something which is intriguing me."

"Really? What's that then?" he enquired. I quickly explained how I had come across the picture stone and briefly described the carving therein. Then, moving the receiver to the table, I read him the inscription. There followed a short period of silence on the other end of the 'phone.

"Read that again," he implored. I acquiesced.

"What do you think it means?" I enquired – not so much to him as asking myself the question.

"I'll pop round now," he exclaimed. This pulled me up short. I had in no way expected this reaction. Admittedly he only lived about ten minutes' drive from me but I was in my 'comfy' (scruffy) clothes and slippers and in no way suitably attired to receive a visitor.

"No. No. Really, there's no need."

"It's no trouble. Give me ten." So saying, the 'phone went dead and I was left to resign myself to my self-imposed fate.

With a sigh I prepared to receive Robin having first commented to Reggie in disgust "Some people!" Needless to say, Reggie was little interested and his response was a short glance at me before once again laying his head on his paws and closing his eyes.

True to his word, in a little less than ten minutes my doorbell rang. I welcomed him, far more politely than I felt, and ushered him into the sitting-room. On my invitation to sit, he ignored me, preferring instead to look around the room urgently. On spotting the rock on the table next to my chair he immediately stepped over to it and picked it up. "The cheek" I thought silently.

He produced a magnifying glass from his jacket pocket and inspected the item whilst blithely ignoring me completely. "Who did he think he was? Sherlock Holmes?" I hovered behind him.

"This is remarkable," he exclaimed after a moment. "Therein find the treasure above gold. I wonder what that is?" How typical of a man to find intrigue in the promise of treasure rather than admire the fine artwork of the donkey. It was almost as if the animal hadn't been noticed by him. What a travesty.

"Where exactly did you say you found this?"

"In a village called Lydbrook in the Forest of Dean. Down by the river." I answered.

"From the Lyd to Ross mark 3 with water. Above it is mine. The Lyd, that's Lydbrook surely? Mark 3. What can that be? Three steps, three miles, three…?" His mind was obviously off on its own track and there was no point me offering suggestions.

"With water. With water. That could be the river. The River Wye is around there isn't it? I should think it is, don't you?" For the first time he actually acknowledged that I was in the room by looking at me.

"Possibly." My response was terse but then I wasn't essential to his thought process and I knew it.

"Above it is mine. Above it is mine. If we can find this mark 3, whatever that is, then we need to find out who owns the land above it." I was pleased to have been included in this mental exploration by his use of the word "we". However, my humour was not improving.

"Therein find the treasure above gold." He was back on the treasure again. My tether was nearing an end. I was niggled. I was being ignored – and I didn't even really like this man that much.

"Yes, well. Whatever the riddle means it is most likely just nonsense. Some kids messing about. Anyway, I have things to do, so if you will excuse me, I really must …" I didn't finish the sentence because in spite of my mind running like lightning through the possible conclusions, none of them sounded too friendly.

Robin seemed to lurch into the present and for the first time realize where he was. His six foot two, curly mopped hair and lithe thirty-four years, spun on the spot to face me full on.

"Of course, Beattie. I'm so sorry. It was very rude of me to intrude like this." His ingratiating smile of apology melted my aggravated heart and I found myself appreciating his handsomeness. What? Even a cat can look at a king in appreciation!

"Not at all. It was very kind of you to come round."

"May I just take one more minute of your time so that I can copy the inscription?" Without waiting for reply, he pulled a scruffy looking bit of paper from his jacket, a pen from the same source, and began copying the words.

Having finished he looked at me again. "Excellent. Now I can think about this and let you know if I come up with anything." He, at last, moved towards the door adding "But I'm sure it's just nonsense. As you say; probably some kid who's read too much Enid Blyton." With this dismissive statement he departed.

As I shut the door gratefully and returned to the sitting-room I looked across at Reggie. He didn't like Robin I knew. I hadn't noticed him during Robins visit but now saw that far from curled up sleepily he was sitting upright in his basket like a sphinx guarding the pyramid.

"It's alright, Reggie. The nasty man has gone now." With this, Reggie visibly relaxed again, and whilst he didn't lie down, he at least relaxed the area around his muzzle which had been ready to bark, or attack. I should have trusted Reggie's instincts because I already knew my little friend to be a good judge of character.

Robin didn't call me again for nearly a week. After this time, I contacted him to see if he had come up with any revelations about the inscription. He assured me that he hadn't and that he was now convinced that it was some prank by children. This explanation didn't ring true, if only because of the quality of the portrait of the donkey was well beyond that which could, or would, be done by a child. Nevertheless, I let the matter drop as far as he was concerned.

About two weeks later I was again in the area of Lydbrook. The contact I had previously bought from, with was expecting a house clearance about now, and he had invited me to revisit.

As I drove along the road from Ross to Lydbrook I recalled the riddle. I was still pondering the 'mark 3' clue and what it might mean. It was a vague question forming in my mind about whether this referred to miles. If so, then whatever the hint pointed to would be found 3 miles from Lydbrook on the way to Ross. Since, according to my car milometer, it was quite that near that point I pulled over and parked on the verge.

The Trespasser

Reggie and I got out of the car to take a leisurely walk by the river.

As we sauntered along, my eyes roaming far beyond my body, I nearly tripped over a small standing stone on the grass verge. On it was the declaration that Ross on Wye lay three miles further along this verge. What really amazed me, though, was that right next to this handy pointer, nearly overgrown with intrusive ivy of some sort, was a low standing drinking fountain obviously once fed by a hidden spring but now barren and dry.

My excitement was so exuberant that Reggie was quite alarmed at my sudden outburst and swerved away from me in shock. "That's it. That's the clue. From Lydbrook to Ross, at the three-mile marker, there is water. This is the place, Reggie."

I recalled the next part of the clue in the puzzle. 'Above it is mine.' My glance looked up the hill on the other side of the road which was spotted only sparsely with trees allowing a fairly clear view. I was seeking something which might conform to this puzzle.

I was very shocked to see a man walking, almost bent double, across the hillside. His gaze was firmly fixed on the ground in and around his trajectory. I was even more stunned to identify, on squinting to better my focus, that the man in question was none other than Robin.

I called up to him and because this whole area was not plagued by noise pollution, he heard me and instantly stood erect looking round for the source of his name. I waved. He saw me. He just stood still looking down at me, making no effort to descend across the space between us.

"Robin. Here," I called again. "Come down." He continued to stare but made no attempt to move.

Now, as I have explained, I am not the most agile or athletic creature, but even so, I began to spy the terrain between me and him for a path I might use. A hedge, unfortunately, stood guard all along the pathway and there was no way I could navigate past it. I was impotent to bridge the distance between us. It was then that he finally spoke.

"Beattie," he called to me. "Wait there. I'll come down." At this, he turned to face the opposite direction from where he stood and began to walk, at a brisk pace, back the way he had obviously come.

Reggie and I stood still watching his progress until he disappeared from view over the crest of the hill. We waited. Finally, I spotted him trudging in a decided manner along the road from Lydbrook towards my location. Again, I waited but this time entertaining myself by devising what I would say to him. He reached easy hearing distance and I began…

"Robin. What on earth are you doing here?" Of course, I knew the answer. He was looking for my treasure.

"Ah, Beattie. How nice to see you again. Yes. Well. Since I was in the area, I thought it might be nice to see if I could solve the clue you showed me, so that I could present whatever it refers to, to you." "A likely story" I thought ungraciously. By now, he and I were standing together, with Reggie standing on guard at my heels and looking earnestly up into my face as if waiting for the command to attack.

"And have you found it?"

"No. But I'm very close I'm sure of it. I just can't fathom the last bit about whatever it is being mine."

"So, what were you doing when I spotted you?" The accusation in my voice was only thinly disguised.

"The final clue must be somewhere on that hill." He pointed to the area described. "I was just scouring every inch of the field and surrounds, using a methodical search pattern, to see if anything leapt out. That's when you saw me."

"I see." I felt as much defiled as if a burglar had entered my house. The engraved stone was my find, not his, and it was my prerogative to solve the puzzle, not his.

I shan't bore you with the details but summarize it as follows.

By, grudging, mutual consent we continued his search pattern together. Finally, it was Reggie who once again came to the rescue. My faithful companion located an opening into the hill which was almost totally overgrown by a dominatingly large thorn bush. Only a dog could have found it.

Robin entered the opening on all fours and after much huffing and puffing, having reversed back out of the hole, emerged dragging a box.

He carried this to my Cortina and placed it on a splayed newspaper in my car-boot.

I could tell he was beside himself with frustration at my refusal to open the box there and then which, in itself, brought me more than a little pleasure. With a promise from him that he would visit my home tomorrow to see what was in the box, we parted company.

It was all I could do to contain my sarcasm and not respond with "I can hardly wait."

Dearest Cousin,

I ended my last epistle prior to opening the box because, frankly, my right index finger felt as if it was developing callouses from its protracted work on the keyboard. I can at least boast that now my left-hand index finger is also occupied when a capital letter is required. Can I now boast to being a two-fingered typist? Probably not an attribute I can attach to my c.v. then?

Besides, I hoped this short delay between scripts has whetted your appetite with the same enthusiasm which had apparently afflicted Robin.

During the next enclosure I shall explain how, having found the treasure, I then proceeded to lose it again.

Yours in appreciation of your patience,

Beattie

(Encl.)

The Intruder

Having finally returned home very late that evening, fed myself on the great British standby of toast, and my outstandingly clever companion on the inevitable tin of dog food, which is 'pumped through with goodness', we are assured. I read for a little while.

However, I found that my eyes kept closing such that the adventure unfolding in the book, bore no relation to that written by the author. It was this realization which persuaded me I kept nodding off. Lights out. Head down. Time for sleep.

Some time later I was awoken by a muffled thud. I am a very light sleeper; this being a status I had developed from living alone for so many years. They say that a blind person often has acute hearing; a deaf person frequently develops exceptional eyesight, etc. Well, a person who lives alone develops a heightened sense of foreboding.

Reggie too was on high alert judging by his aggressive stance in front of the closed bedroom door – nose to the floor, bottom left unheeded in the air. Dogs really do raise their hackles. The hairs all down his back, from his neck to his tail, stood proud. Under calmer circumstances it might have amused me how like a dinosaur his tiny frame now mimicked. But these were not calm circumstances. We were both on the very edge of fear.

Quietly, and without putting a light on, I shoved the bedclothes back, swung my legs out of the bed and allowed my feet to slot into the appropriately placed slippers. On reflection, I find that perhaps one of the biggest differences between men and women is their propriety in such moments. Strangely, my first thought was that under my long nightgown I wore no knickers! This omission I corrected before deciding what the next action was to be.

A weapon. I needed a weapon. I looked quickly round the room, viewing, then rejecting, all the items at my disposal. I finally settled on a rather heavy, silver handled, hairbrush which I had inherited from my late, maiden aunt.

Even in such a tense moment I couldn't help but imagine what the intruder would say, for I was sure it was such, when he saw what I held. To myself I mused that he might mistakenly believe I was about to brush his hair! Part it, maybe – brush it, no!

On slowly opening the bedroom door any idea I might have had about sneaking up on the intruder disappeared, as Reggie burst onto the landing barking and snarling. He hurtled down the stairs as if he were chasing a rabbit and was instantly gone, yapping the whole time. This prompted me, in fear for his brave but tiny frame, to put the light on and hurtle downstairs after him.

Reggie had made a beeline for the sitting-room which prompted my direction too. The door was slightly ajar and my hand entered the room first as I felt for the light switch. This appendage was quickly followed by the rest of me as the illusion about the safety of light emboldened my courage. It has long been a mystery to me why heroines in films blunder about in the dark when they have a lightbulb available to them.

There was nobody but Reggie there. He was over by the open window and repeatedly jumping on his hind legs trying to reach the sill to follow the escaping intruder. His height, or lack of it, foiled him but he kept trying, bless him.

I rushed over to the settee, certain that there was no-one hiding behind it, but needing the reassurance that I was right. Next, I quickly walked through the downstairs rooms, turning the light on before entering every room, until the ground floor was lit up like Blackpool illuminations and I was certain that I was alone.

Returning to the sitting-room I closed the window, which had been shut when I went to bed, and began the process of calming Reggie.

It was only once he was silenced and the hair on his back lay flat again that I thought to investigate what might be missing or had been damaged. A single glance which assured me that the television, video and Sky box were still there. A little more investigation also showed that my ornaments, pictures and furniture were untouched. A trip into the kitchen ascertained that nothing was untoward in this room either.

I didn't bother to check the downstairs loo because if they'd taken anything from there, they were welcome to it - toilet rolls are cheap. The absurdity of this passing thought didn't impinge on me until days later.

I lastly inspected the offending window and ensured that the glass was intact and the handle which locked it was undamaged and back in its preferred slot of locked. I didn't bother to inspect upstairs since, due to my size, let alone my keen eyesight, no-one could have passed me on the stairs I reasoned.

My next action was a 'phone-call to 999 for the police. I keep the number of the local police station on a pad by the 'phone because of living alone. This, I felt, warranted the national telephone number though. Actually, having established that it was the police, rather than any other service that I required, I was put through to them. I began the conversation with the humble words. "This is not an emergency – but …" Having listened to my reason for calling, the policeman rebuked me with his opening statement. "That IS an emergency, madam. Someone will be with you shortly."

It relaxed me greatly knowing that help was on its way for my shattered nerves. By way of preparation for their arrival, I rushed upstairs and put my, very respectable, dressing-gown on. Then I put the kettle on to make tea – such is the British way!

Two very nice Constables arrived when the tea had reached its perfection of being stewed for just the right amount of time.

They asked all the usual questions like "was anything stolen?" "Had any doors or windows been left open?" "How had the intruder entered?" "Was I alright?" "Was there any damage?" I say the 'usual' questions purely from my knowledge of popular detective stories – I've never actually been broken into before. Nor do I verify the sequence of their questions, since by now I was more than a little unsettled, as the seriousness of the situation was hitting me.

Anyway, we enjoyed a 'cuppa' together and having assured me of a visit from forensics the next day, with a warning not to touch the window by which the intruders had gained entry, they departed. To be honest I didn't expect a forensics scientist to arrive since nobody had been murdered. I was not wrong in this assessment – but it made feel better at the time – so no harm done. Maybe the policeman who had set that expectation was also a fan of murder drama's?

Sleep was no longer an option for this night. I was wound up far too tight to relax. Reggie also was reluctant to use his bed and instead spent the night curled up on my lap. We watched overnight television programmes, which incidentally are rubbish or repeats, and waited for the light of dawn to arrive.

It's funny how when you're hungry every advertisement is centred around food; likewise, when you're feeling on edge it seems the channel planners have put every scary programme into their schedule for just such an occasion.

To my amazement I found that I *had* slept because when I, as I term it, opened my eyes from momentarily closing them to check my eyelids for holes, I unexpectedly saw that daylight had arrived and was in full bloom. I knew that the programme I'd been watching was boring but … I went about my usual morning rituals with the sole topic on my mind of who had been the intruder and why? Since nothing was missing had I interrupted him before he could take anything? Worse; had he not thought anything of mine worth taking? I was affronted. How unreasonable is that?

It was approaching lunchtime before I remembered that Robin had said he'd call on me today. My inclination was to put him off, on the excuse that I was waiting for a visit from forensics, but then the temptation to relate my adventures, to anyone willing to listen, won the day and I decided he was as good a candidate as any.

I sat in my armchair idly, half-heartedly flicking through a magazine. I loathe waiting for someone to come or waiting for it to be time to go out. One can't settle to anything, I find, and the whole day is dominated by what may be just a tiny fraction of that day.

Truly stunning me by his arrival a forensics apprentice did arrive. He must have been practicing his art in a non-critical situation. However, by 11 a.m., the young chappie had gone, having left an unsightly black dust mark on my window. He had informed me, as he finished his work and began packing up his bag, that there were no fingerprints discernible on the woodwork or glass. Never mind, laddie. Next time maybe?

Once he had left my thoughts turned to Robin and his impending visit. I was surprised that he hadn't called me at the crack of dawn, so eager had he been to discover the contents of the box we had discovered.

It was whilst this train of thought was passing through my mind that I, for the first time, looked for the article in question. It was nowhere to be seen. Surely, I'd put it on the table? The table was bare. I walked around the room searching for it but it wasn't evident. I then employed my memory into solving the mystery of where I might have put it. I was sure, the more I thought about it, that it should be sitting on the table – but it wasn't.

Surprisingly slowly, having searched the whole house, it dawned on me that my night visitor might have been Robin and that his curiosity had prompted him to take the unbelievable action of breaking into my home to retrieve it. Surely not? After all, who else knew of its existence? I know he's a bit of a crook, but burglary, that's too much… No, he wouldn't – would he? The box is supposed to contain some treasure … but even so … The more I tried to persuade myself that this action would have been too radical, even for him, the more I came to realize that he might just be crooked enough to try it.

I decided against informing the police of my suspicions, since that is all they were, just suspicions. However, having received no answer from my numerous 'phone-calls during the day I did decide to initially confirm my doubts or clear him from my unspoken accusations. If I didn't hear from him by tonight, I should visit him tomorrow at his workshop.

"Reggie. We may be going to see Robin tomorrow. Do you think he's got my box? Do you boy? Do you think he's got it?" Reggie's response was to slowly rise, stretch with his bottom shown to the air and his front paws bent to the ground, and saunter into the kitchen to have a drink of water from his bowl.

"I'll take that as a yes then," I called after him.

The Recovery

By morning I had still not heard from Robin despite the numerous pleas that he responds to the messages from me left on his answer machine.

Throughout my ablutions and breakfast my determination resolved to confirm or deny these suspicions about him, one way or the other. I set out in my Cortina, with Reggie onboard as usual, for the Gloucester docks.

Some of the warehouses round and about had been converted into individual units for storage or display by individuals with a need for such facilities. Robin, I knew, rented such an establishment to display his wares to the public and fellow dealers, whilst also using it as a storage area. I had gone there several times and knew exactly where it was.

As Reggie and I ascended to the first floor, the site of Robins' lockup, my mind was running in top gear about how I might broach the subject and then how I would know if he was telling the truth. Reggie leapt from one step to the other with an abandoned determination which aptly displayed my own feelings at the time.

The whole of the first floor had retained its original wood surround but had, by use of temporary stud walling, been separated into individual units of varying size and frontage.

In one corner of the almost open plan space was a small café, manned by a single, plump and aging, but jolly lady who, on seeing me emerge from the stairs greeted me with a warm welcome.

Whilst I didn't imagine her establishment was as popular as, say Costa Coffee, I was sure she maintained a steady flow of demand, dispensing supermarket coffee and newly cut sandwiches to the unit holders and their visitors. I'm not sure I would have relied on this business for income but she had the look of someone who did it as a reason to get out of bed in the morning rather than to make any discernible profit.

Reggie and I made our way with a determined walk, or trot in his case, towards Robin's area. This comprised a display 'room' at the front separated by a stud wall to create a little back office. I call it an office, but it more resembled an attic, of piled junk with a desk somewhere near the middle.

As I entered my eyes swivelled back and forth identifying his wares and mentally ticking off whether I wished to own them or not. Old habits die hard. Reggie trotted silently beside me conducting his own investigations by using his nose and extraordinary sniffing ability. Robin was not there. Since the door to his back office was open, I headed for it to peek round the corner and see if he was at his desk. He was.

It unreasonably gratified me to find him with one leg raised up and supported by the cluttered desk. On his leg was a sock loosely covering just his toes; no shoe. The ankle was firmly wrapped in a slightly bloodstained bandage.

"Hello," I called in none too friendly manner. To be honest, as I had walked up each step to his domain, my mind had set more on the realization that he was the intruder into my 'castle' and any sympathy for him had waned with the ascent.

He tried to get up, but the angle of his injured appendage betrayed him and he ceased the struggle almost as soon as he had begun. This movement, or attempt at movement had cast a visage of pain across his now pale face.

"Oh. Ah. Yes. Hello," he responded guiltily remaining seated but looking as if he wished a hole would at this moment swallow him.

My eyes fell to the contents of his desktop. Amid the numerous documents, which were obviously unfiled bills or receipts, there plain as day, sat my box. It lay open. In a cascade of disarray, various documents were spilling out of it as if either trying to escape or leap back in. I wasn't sure which from their picture of disarray. The paperwork obviously belonging to the box did not look the same as those others spread throughout his desk. They looked older and more voluminous than signs of everyday trading.

"I see you've opened my box," I uttered with all the accusation in my voice that I could muster. My head nodded towards it with my hands clasped together across my front, under my ample bosoms, in the posture of a dominating washerwoman. The only difference between me and a Les Dawson skit at that moment was that he was funnier.

"Ah. Yes. Well." He was spluttering and I could almost visibly see his mind working frantically trying to find a feasible excuse for him having this possession which he, blatantly, had no right to be holding.

Reggie, in almost unprecedented manner, began to growl in a low voice. He had entered the back office as soon as I had begun speaking and stood there by my feet like a miniature guard dog, for all the world as if he might pounce on Robin at any moment in attack.

"And what," I continued, "might I ask did you find in it?"

Robin looked totally dejected as his head lowered in capitulation. "Nothing. Nothing at all."

"No gold then?" I knew that this understanding of his motives would suffice to make him feel even more foolish than he did already.

"No." His confirmation was uttered so quietly that had I not been listening for it I might not have heard it.

"And what, may I ask, young man, do you think gave you the right to invade my home? How dare you? How very dare you?" The pitch and pace of my voice rose with each word.

From the guarded calm of my arrival at his workshop, I now found that my "dander" was up, such that, as each second passed, I could feel a raw anger rising from my very core and bubbling, like an exploding volcano to the surface. It was a rage that I was incapable of controlling. It was like an alter ego of the quiet and, (mostly), gentle me. Like the Hyde to my Jekyll. At that moment I could easily, had I not exercised extreme and deliberate control, have lashed out and slapped him across his crooked face.

"I'm sorry." He muttered this in the same sotto voice he'd just used. His appearance took on the vision of a naughty schoolboy having been caught by the teacher doing something for which he knew that punishment was imminent.

"Sorry? Sorry? Sorry doesn't even begin to excuse it. How dare you break into my house and scare me half to death. It's illegal what's more. The police will be informed I can assure you." My voice was rising to a booming crescendo. Afterwards

I wondered what the people outside this thin walled domain must have thought since they couldn't help but have overheard every word.

At this, it was as if his energy which had been drained, suddenly surged back into life. He moved as if to rise but his leg prevented it and he again slumped down in his seat. "Please. Please, not the police. I didn't mean it. I didn't mean any harm."

"How dare you take something that doesn't belong to you? How dare you invade my home and steal from me?"

"It was a moment of madness; just a feeling which overwhelmed me. I've never done anything like it before – and I never will again. I promise. Please don't report it to the police." His voice, his eyes and his body all pleaded with me in total supplication. I've never seen such utter desperation before and it acted like pouring a salve onto a wound. My raw anger began to subside.

"The fact remains," I began once again applying logic and a quieter voice to the situation rather than the uncontrollable rage of a moment ago. "The fact remains that you committed a crime and stole from me. I will not let you get away with it. The police will be told and that's an end to it."

It was as if he knew that he'd been caught red handed, which he had, and his defences crumbled before my eyes. "I'm so sorry," he submitted again. The emphasis on the 'so'. I didn't doubt it for one moment. His ankle obviously hurt like fury.

"What *was* in the box anyway?" The moment had passed for me and having vented my ire I was now the consummate professional of my chosen craft.

"Nothing of any interest. There's just a pile of paperwork most of which is in a foreign language. Look, it's all here." He was grasping at papers as if they were to be offered as sacrifice to a watching god.

I picked up a chunk of the bundle balanced on the tip of the box. Then I reached further down into the receptacle and found a really old looking script of some sort.

"Yes. That one looks old," he offered, "I thought it might be from the middle ages or something. I tried to read the one in English but it was so boring I gave up."

I began to gather the writings together. I missed one which must have also come from the box and he passed it to me mildly with a "…and this one."

"What have you done to your leg by the way?" Finally, my humanity was returning and I was once again taking up the natural composure of a compassionate woman.

"Oh," he said looking down at his raised foot and reaching one hand towards it along his leg in an act of comforting massage. "I left your window at such a pace when your dog suddenly appeared that I cut it on something. It bled like a pig for ages. This morning when I got up, I could hardly move it. I'm wondering if in my panic to get away I didn't realize I'd broken it or something. It certainly hurts like hell."

Although the words formed in my mind, I resisted the temptation to voice "it serves you right." Instead the more reasonable response of "You probably need to get it checked out by a doctor," came from my mouth. "Now." I searched the immediate area with my eyes. "Are there any more papers from my box?"

"No. That's the lot."

"And is there anything else of mine that you've stolen while I'm here?" Looking around the office I couldn't restrain this cutting remark from escaping.

"Absolutely not. No. Beattie, I am really so very sorry. I don't know what came over me. I just kept thinking about the treasure that might be in the box and … I couldn't think of anything else. I'm really, really sorry." He looked at me with his most appealing face.

"I'm sorry too, Robin. I reported the break-in to the police so I must tell them that I've found the culprit so they stop looking for him."

"No, Beattie. Please, no."

"It isn't reasonable to waste police time. Besides, I don't want some poor innocent being charged for your crime. I don't want that on my conscience. But I will tell them that you have co-operated when confronted – that should bode well for you when it comes to the charges."

Robin was wracked with pain and broken of spirit. With a mighty sweep I turned, the box containing its papers tucked under my arm, and left calling "Come on Reggie. Let's go home."

As I re-entered the open area containing the café seats, I couldn't help but notice that the lady behind the counter was staring at me. As I drew closer, she smiled at me with an expression on her face of silent relief that I was well. She had obviously heard the ruckus and would, no doubt, delight others for weeks to come by relating this episode of excitement in the otherwise demure surroundings.

Having returned home and informed the police by 'phone of the recently unfolding revelations, I settled down with Reggie to the normality of a peaceful day.

It was after a light, if slightly late, lunch that I ventured to explore the papers in the ill-fated box. Any residual excitement which might have been around me from my confrontation dissolved into the ether as I read the statements contained therein.

As I mentioned, I have something of a talent for languages and even the obvious age of the French transcripts did not phase me. I read them as if they were penned in my mother tongue. Needless to say, my French has vastly improved since the 'fromage' incident.

I was astounded by what they revealed. Each manuscript, was accompanied by a translation in French. The original document, often in an unidentified language, contained a French translation folded in with it.

When I at last came to the oldest text and read the French translation of it, time stopped still and all the earth seemed to dissolve into an unfocused plane.

During this reading frenzy, darkness had drawn in and unconsciously I must have reached up and turned on the light near my chair, for thus I found it, when I finally returned to earth late into the night.

As I crawled into bed, my mind was totally absorbed by the unprecedented events unfolding in the stories which I had just read. So much so, that to my dismay I realized that I had inadvertently locked Reggie in the sitting-room – a fact he was now noisily and indignantly informing me about.

I rushed downstairs to his rescue. Not waiting for an apology, as I opened the door, he leapt upstairs and into the bedroom with me following obediently behind apologizing the whole way.

"Oh, Reggie. I'm so sorry, darling. Mummy was lost in thought. There's a good boy. Good boy." With this profuse supplication I hugged him, having recovered him from his bedtime basket by sweeping him up into my arms. In the nature of the beast he readily forgave me and I was rewarded with a kiss from his rough little tongue on my chin and wiggle of his wiry little tail.

As I lay silently in the dark of my room, with a gentle snore emanating from my faithful companion, I began to think about what the documents in my possession might really be. I hardly dared to hope.

What I had just read, if the French translations had been accurate and the original documents genuine, would be absolutely fascinating to certain academics. At least one of them also provided illumination on certain mysteries which had confounded the world for centuries.

My Dearest Cousin,

Having read the translations of the documents I found; I began my own inadequate research into the topics mentioned therein. That is where my limitations showed themselves and where your superior knowledge comes into play.

What I have now in my possession is a single key document, which has been passed, hidden, through generations by a number of different people. None published the original key document.

As you will see in the extract below, I did try and make some enquiries as, what I shall call, the next step.

I realise that we are still talking hypothetically, since you are ignorant of the topic of the documents, but that will be rectified as I bring you up to date with events so far.

Whatever the truth behind these documents, they throw an entertaining light upon characters from the past. I am sure that your knowledge and connections can verify the veracity of the participants tales.

As you will see from the enclosed, I have carried out my own limited research. In fact, I have arranged for a visit to what I hope is an authority in the near future. I shall update you with any results as soon as I return.

Yours in deference to your advanced skills,
Beattie
(Encl.)

The Research

I began research on the web to find out if the earliest text, now in my possession, was known about by those who know about such things.

An idea, or is that a realization, began to form in my mind on exactly what I might have gotten hold of. A certain codex kept popping up in my research. Could it possibly be the hypothesized 'Document Q'? Was that too fanciful? Perhaps not!

Document Q, which is short for Quelle, from the German meaning 'source', was a conceptual written account of the words of Jesus, otherwise known as a logia. Many scholars have the idea that, perhaps, it was this hypothetical document from which two of the Christian New Testament Gospels were written. Those of Matthew and Luke, supposedly used Q in conjunction with the Gospel by Mark.

Now, as you know, Jackie, I am a little lukewarm on the topic of faiths and their sources. However, even with this attitude, I was intrigued to read of the exploits of characters from both the near and distant past. There is often drama included in their scripts which added depth and, critically, a sense of reality, to the documents' authority. Many of them came from far more dramatic climates; politically, socially and geographically, than that experienced by us today.

Back to this 'mythical' Document Q and my research on the topic.

I read that a stranger had, it is believed, borrowed the Greek text from the old Jerusalem trader, returning it sometime later. Could this stranger possibly have been Matthew or Luke, or one of their followers, on an errand from their apostle? The hairs on the back of my neck rose as I realized that I might be holding the very document which they had also inspected.

I was unreasonably gratified to discover that it was an Englishman, Herbert Marsh, in 1801, who first postulated the idea of a source document.

I read a lot on the subject of Q from a number of different web sites and, as with any hypothesis, there are arguments for and against its existence.

However, I could not dispute the fact that I had in my hand a document which reported on the sayings of a man called, by modern translation, Jesus; which was either a very good quality forgery or actually as old as it claimed to be; whose reported sayings almost exactly, but in some cases not precisely, quoted verses from the New Testament; and which had been in others' possession before me and was believed to be so volatile that they had decided not to declare its existence and publish it.

"Well, Reggie. What a 'to do'. What 'doings' indeed. What do you think boy? What shall I do next?" Reggie just raised his head languidly and looked at me. Deciding that my question did not require a response he laid it back down and closed his eyes again. I was obviously not going to receive any guidance from him.

As is the way of my nation I decided that a cup of tea was called for. I went to the kitchen having come out of the internet so the screen was back in its 'saver' mode. Ages before I had selected a screensaver of pictures from around Britain which circulated beautiful images ranging from the very tip of Scotland to the bottom reaches of our varied and beautiful landmass.

On returning from the kitchen, cup of tea in hand, my glance fell on the current picture. My memory stirred – well not so much 'stirred' as screamed at me. I knew that view. I had seen it before in real life. Where was it? Where? I know! It was a picture of the monastery on the top of the hill across from where I'd first come across the stone clue. It was in Lydbrook, or just outside it, in the Forest of Dean. Well I'll be. What a coincidence!

As I sat in my favourite armchair and sipped the piping hot liquid, the thought kept nagging at me that if I had been overheard enquiring as to my next step, then perhaps that monastery held the help I had been looking for. No, surely such things did not happen in this modern age? It was a pure coincidence – or not.

Either way, it set my curiosity afire and, having finished my beverage, I once again wriggled the mouse to stir my computer into life. Try as I might I could find no reference to the building I sought on the web so, in a moment of inspiration, I rang my contact in Lydbrook.

He immediately knew the place I was seeking and gave me the name. I didn't explain why I wanted it but did retain manners enough to enquire as to his and his wife's wellbeing. A more focused search on the web with this key word brought forth the results I desired. There was a telephone number listed – success. I poured another cup of tea while I thought about the question I wanted to pose and when I was ready, I dialled the number.

"Hello?" This rather terse and nondescript response took some of the wind out of my sails. However, having established that I was speaking to the right establishment and addressing one of the resident Fathers there, I then launched forth with my enquiry without giving away more than a casual interest in their establishment.

"… so, I was wondering if you are open to the public at all?" I didn't really know why I wanted to go there, but if the picture on my screensaver had happened to be more than a coincidence, I just had the feeling that if I got there, answers would be forthcoming.

"Indeed we are. We welcome all to our Sunday morning service and offer tea and biscuits to follow."

"Excellent. Thank you. Is that every Sunday?"

"Yes. We are a teaching establishment and so are always pleased to welcome both our usual non-residential congregation and passing Christians."

"Thank you so much for your assistance, Father. I shall certainly visit you the very next Sunday that I'm in the Forest. Thank you." I placed the 'phone back on the table and felt satisfied with my mornings work.

"That's good then, Reggie." He opened one eye, let it find and focus on me, and then closed it again by way of his usual understated response.

The Advisor

It had not been my intention to again visit that part of the country for some time to come but my curiosity won the day and I found myself packing a picnic lunch for the following Sunday.

Loading the plastic bag of goodies, Reggie and the box with its contents into my yellow Cortina, with the sun showing promise in the cloudless sky, my little party set off for the Forest of Dean.

I eventually found the monastery and was gratified to note that I was still slightly too early for the "open to the public" service. Thus encouraged, I poured a welcome coffee from my flask and tried to think through the actions I would take. I really had no clue why I was here I just felt that I was in the right place to solve the mystery of what the box contained. I would have to play it by ear and remain alert for any hints of what to say and do.

Filing into the attached church I joined the dozen or so other 'civilian' attendees. This congregation was soon swelled by the arrival of about twenty monk-looking-type men. Not all of these wore the tell-tale habits of the profession but they did all arrive together and they did all look serious, so I surmised they were something to do with the monastery.

The church looked much like any other such building and nothing leapt out at me as being noteworthy. Mind you, I am not what you might call a frequent flyer, that is, I rarely attend such services. I'm more a birth, marriage and death kind of gal.

I managed to muddle my way through the service thanks to copious sideways glances to my neighbour to see what page I should now be on. Why do they go to the trouble to print books detailing the order of service and then add bits in, and take bits out? Is it just to generate confusion for the uninitiated?

Once the monk types had processed out, the rest of us shuffled after them. I followed the crowd and found myself in an old fashioned and rather austere looking room. To one side two tables had been placed close together and a paper coverall hid any unsightly marks which might be lurking beneath. Gratefully I saw that a large, tin teapot was gracing the waiting array of cups with its precious liquid and a middle-aged monk was pouring the golden liquor into them. Having picked up a cup and doctored it with milk and sugar I turned to face the room having taken the requisite three steps away from the serving area.

The room was well lit thanks to large windows decorating the oversized bay-window area. It was furnished with comfortable looking armchairs and any barren walls disguised with a multitude of books, ancient and modern, (like the service agenda), seated in creaky looking wooden bookshelves.

In one corner, near but not in, the bay area sat a very elderly gentleman. He looked completely relaxed and the wrinkles on his face told of a countenance (wrinkles) which had known much laughter and happiness. He wore the habit of a monk but somehow it didn't cry out of depravation and abstention; it more hinted at learning and contentment. I decided that this old boy was 'my' type of person and I was drawn to sit in the chair next to him.

"Hello, my dear. I haven't seen you before have I? Forgive me if I'm wrong, but at my age, I forget."

"No. This is my first time."

"Ah, good. The old memory hasn't let me down then." He seemed delighted at this discovery and his face fell into a smiley posture. He continued in the age old traditional and non-committal question of "Have you come far?"

"Gloucester." I replied and smiled to myself as I remembered that, on attending my sisters' wedding years ago, my brother had rushed up to me and asked the very same question. My other brother who was within earshot rebuked him with "That's your sister you fool." We had never been a close family. It is many years now since I've seen any of them – except of course for the obligatory Christmas card.

Realizing that I was giving this poor old boy no opening with my monosyllabic answers I continued, "I saw this place from across the river and thought how nice it would be to attend a service here." I then realized that I was telling a lie to a monk and corrected myself somewhat, "I felt drawn here."

"Ah. You are not the first to feel that, I can assure you." He raised his cup from its saucer and took a sip of the tea. I did the same.

"There is a question on your lips, yes?" The prophetic nature of this exclamation from the monk pulled me up short and I sat up in sudden alertness.

"Why do you say that?"

He smiled, "Because everyone who comes here has questions. That's why they come." The smile broke into a chuckle.

"Yes. Yes, I do, as a matter of fact."

He put his cup back into its receptacle and looked at me earnestly waiting in silence for me to elucidate.

It is not often that I find myself speechless so we are already well into the territory of miracles. Fortified by this realization I gathered myself together, took a deep breath, and began.

"Father," it seemed right to first acknowledge his rank – if that's what they call it – and set the scene for the part he was to play. "The fact is that some information has come into my possession and I am wondering what I should do with it."

He placed his cup and saucer on the table within easy reach of the armchair and turned slightly, so that he could stare into my face more directly, but did not speak. These very actions mimed the words "go on."

"Well, you see, this information may be rubbish, or it could be the most startling revelation of … ever. I don't know which." I stopped not daring to put into words what I was coming to believe about the contents of the box.

"And what is the nature of this disclosure?"

"It may be …," I paused still unexpectedly afraid, "it may be that I have discovered an ancient text recording the actual words of Jesus."

There; it was out in the open. The moat had been crossed and I was entering the castle. I stared intently at the old man, whose face was passive and body unmoving, to assess his reaction.

"I see. And what makes you think that this is what you have found?" I told him an abridged version of the discovery, its theft and recovery, and the contents of the box. I then added how I had researched the matter on the web.

Throughout this tale he remained completely unmoving.

"Are you aware, my child," he added this to further support
the relationship we had temporarily formed of priest to advocate,
"that in the apocrypha, which is a collection of codex's rejected
by the early church, there is supposedly a Gospel of Thomas,
which apparently lists just this, the sayings of Christ?"

I admitted that I had come across this by title only, but hadn't
delved any further to read it. I then, apologetically, explained that
I had come across a Document Q which most scholars, at least
on the web, agreed likely to exist. I left the statement unfinished
in inference that what I held might be that very document.

The old monk made a bridge of his fingers by resting his
elbows on the arms of the chair and leaning his arms inwards. It
would be impossible to decide if this new posture he had adopted
represented thought or prayer. After a few moments in this silent
meditation he spoke again. "Do you happen to have this codex
with you?"

"Yes. I brought the whole thing, all the documents, in my
car."

"Good. Will you allow me to inspect them?"

"Oh, certainly. I'd be delighted, Father."

With this we both rose immediately and headed towards the
entrance with the destination of the car park in mind. He didn't
move quickly, for it was beyond the ability of his age, but I was
in no doubt that this man's brain moved much faster than his
body was able to. He was both astute and wise which reflected
in his sharp eyes.

When we reached my car, Reggie registered his delight at my
reappearance and began jumping and yapping in welcome. As I
opened the rear door to let him taste freedom the old man
immediately reached down and petted him with affection,
muttering doggie effusions. Reggie responded in kind and any
final misgivings I'd held about the veracity of this monk floated
away. If Reggie liked him, he must be OK.

I reached in and recovered the box. As I was about to open it
the old boy stopped me and bid me follow him back inside. I
recovered Reggie and safely installed him in the locked motor
again and we set off.

The room he took me to was empty except for hundreds or
even thousands of books and a desk. Leaving the door wide open

in an act of propriety we entered. I placed the box on the desk and he proceeded to investigate its contents having retrieved some spectacles from some hidden pocket within his garment. I stood silently and waited.

The text he paused on was the one written in Greek. This he seemed completely at home to read as written. Then, gently sorting through the bundles, he isolated and drew out the second part of this account – the one containing mostly single, or double, line entries. This, I knew from my own reading, was the record of the sayings.

Placing it carefully down on the desk he suddenly moved over to a bookcase and returned with a book. Fumbling through the book, he found the page he was looking for, and appeared to compare the record on the text from the box with the one in the book, glancing swiftly from one to the other. I remained both silent and still.

"Well. I have established one thing for sure. This is not a rendition of the Gospel of Thomas. This book contains detail of the papyrus and codex recovered at Nag Hammadi. What you have here is different." With this, he removed his reading glasses and looked directly at me.

"So, what shall I do with it? What do you advise?" I enquired.

"Will you leave that thought with me for a while? Here, you take the box home. I shall pray on the matter and get back in touch with you once my prayers have been answered. Will you trust me – and God – this far, child?"

I assured him that I was more than happy to do nothing more until I had heard from him again. He, somewhat belatedly, introduced himself as Father Ignatius, so that I'd know who he was when he called. Reciprocally, I wrote my name and telephone number on a paper he provided. Without more ado he saw me out to the front door with my box and contents intact and bid me farewell with a cheery "Goodbye for now."

I drove home content that the problem had been removed from my shoulders onto those of one far more qualified than mine to judge.

As good as my word I did nothing with the treasure; although I read and reread the exciting accounts supposedly written by people who, through the centuries, had faced my exact same dilemma. Make an announcement or keep secret?

Their accounts proved so historically accurate, as far as my limited knowledge could ascertain, to the time and place in which they were written, that with each reading, and after further research, the conviction that what I held was true, grew and grew.

The characters in the adventures took on such solidity for me that, in my mind, that I could visualize each one clearly. It was this which prompted me to draw pencil sketches of each of them. Of course, the real hero of the piece is my beloved Reggie. The pencil sketches I drew of him finding the stone and then the mine is placed in a single frame and now hangs, proudly, on my bedroom wall.

It was several days before the telephone rang and on answering it discovered that Father Ignatius was on the other end of the line.

"Good afternoon, Beattie. Father Ignatius here." he cordially greeted me.

"Ah; good afternoon, Father."

"About the matter on which we spoke recently; I have given much thought and prayer to the subject and would like to invite you to come and see me again that I might enlighten you as to your next course of action."

"I'd be delighted, Father. When would you like to see me?"

There was a slight pause before he responded. "I suggest that we make it midweek and in the morning. To be honest, my stamina is not what it used to be and during the afternoons my attention is not at its best. What day would suit you?"

"Well, I'm a bit tied up for the rest of this week, Father. Could we possibly make it next Tuesday morning? Does about 10.00 a.m. suit you?"

"That is ideal, thank you, Beattie. I shall look forward to it."

With this he replaced the receiver before I was able to respond. I detected that, in common with many gentlemen, his preferred method of communication was certainly not the telephone and once the information is passed, they replace the receiver as if they might catch something if they remain holding it for too long. Men are funny like that.

I arrived at the monastery, at the appropriate time, on the following Tuesday. Reggie, curled up in his usual spot in the car, immediately leapt to life as I pulled on the handbrake; his eager little face pressed to the window in an attempt to identify if this was his beloved park. His enthusiasm to escape did not diminish in spite of his not knowing where we were and so, donning his lead, I walked him on the grass leading down the driveway. Depositing him back into the vehicle with encouragement that he was a good dog and was not to bark, and with assurances that mummy would return soon, I headed for the main entrance of the monastery.

I rang the brass, round doorbell and took one step backwards so as not to appear threatening to whoever might open the large, wooden, double door. A crack appeared and to my great surprise it was a woman's face which peered out at me.

"Good morning" I began. "I have an appointment with Father Ignatius."

The door opened further and an austerely-clothed lady, of at least sixty years I assessed, invited me to enter. She showed me into the room where I had partaken of tea and biscuits on that earlier Sunday. With assurances that she would alert the Father to my arrival, she closed the door and disappeared.

I was too wound up to sit, so instead I wandered idly along the bookshelves reading the titles therein.

It's a strange habit, of particularly women, that when observing books on a shelf one is drawn to reach out and touch them. It's as if we feel that by this contact some of the magic of the contents may be transferred to us. So it was that my finger ran idly from book to book, as I crooked my neck at an angle to read the binding titles. Many of these tomes were obviously ancient being bound in strong but weathered leather. Some titles captured my imagination and I lingered on them trying to discern what wisdom they might hold.

After some time of this imaginary pondering, the door opened and Father Ignatius entered slowly. I noted that he had only opened the large door sufficiently for his slender frame to gain access and he had silently then closed the portal behind him. It was as if he didn't want to disturb the room by his presence. It was an unconscious act of humility.

"Hello, Beattie. It was very kind of you to come to see me. Thank you."

"Hello" I responded a little taken aback by this reversal of thanks. After all, it was I who was grateful to him for seeing me, not the other way round.

He pointed towards one of armchairs, in the large bay window area, with an open hand as encouragement for me to sit. I obeyed without speaking whilst ensuring that my skirt was pulled demurely around my legs. He sat in an adjacent armchair and silently just looked at me.

Feeling a little uncomfortable at the silence and feeling the urgent need to fill it I ventured "It's a beautiful day." With this statement I turned to look out at the garden.

"Yes. Indeed it is. I was in the vegetable garden tending my peas when you arrived. I apologize for the delay in my arrival but before greeting you I needed to wash my hands."

"You didn't keep me, Father. I was engrossed in your book collection actually."

His tired eyes looked towards the collection. "Yes. We have a fine collection here. Our brethren are very lucky. For myself, I unfortunately require the use of a magnifying glass to read in comfort now, but at least I am blessed with the gift of sight. One of our brethren has been blind for many years so we take it in turns to read to him in the evenings."

Silence fell between us again.

"So, Father. Do you have some advice for me in regard to these documents which have come into my possession?"

"Obviously I did not have time to thoroughly inspect them. However, I was very impressed with the Greek text which you, so kindly, allowed me to glance at. Being, as you are aware, very familiar with words of Our Lord, I found myself able to recall some of the sayings recounted in the Greek record as being the same, or similar, to the ones in the Holy book."

I was not inclined to comment and so just looked eagerly at him willing him to continue.

"You are, I am sure, aware that during the first century after the death of Our Lord, the early church spread His teachings by word of mouth. Only the Apostles were granted the inspiration to commit to writing these accounts. Their words were inspired by God Himself and hence we have the Bible as we see it today. It is a sacred and holy collection which is, as I'm sure you know, referred to as 'The Word'."

I felt my heart sink as I realized where this monk was heading with this preamble. He continued in the face of my continued silence.

"There are Apocrypha, which purport to be other texts of the time, but these have been rejected by the church – and rightly so. There have also been other codices discovered in more recent times which have, again, been rejected by the church. You must realize that the church is guided by the Most Holy Spirit of God and therefore whatever decision it makes is obeying His will."

At this point my spirit was crestfallen. I knew what this monk was recommending. That the documents I held were of no value and that they must be disregarded or worse, destroyed.

"Therefore," he continued "I suggest that you not only ignore their content but, further, since they might cause disharmony, they should be destroyed without further question."

"But I've read the accounts of those in past centuries who've come to own the Greek record and they seem so sure that this is a true account. The people in them are so real," I spluttered in defence.

"There are many good adventure writers who also create lifelike characters in their books. Perhaps this is what you have here – a work of fiction?" He countered my resistance.

"The paper, it is so different in age, some of it is so old, it must be genuine." I made my final plea to the old man to convince him that this was no modern work of fiction.

"Perhaps. I didn't inspect it all. What I am sure of, is that the church cannot be wrong, and the church does not accept any writing but that contained in the Bible. As such, what you have, whatever its source, is not only unsound, but potentially dangerous, and I urge you to destroy the entire collection."

My spirit deflated; my heart felt heavy; I took my leave with unenthusiastic thanks and returned to Reggie's uplifting company. We drove home in silence.

That evening, I withdrew my sketches from the box and looked again at the portraits of the characters I had felt so sure were real. I felt as if I knew each one of them and had been privileged to glimpse into their lives.

It was the Italian recluse who first came into my troubled sleep that night. He had, at first, had much the same attitude towards the Greek script as Father Ignatius; and yet, in the end, had decided to preserve the potentially sacred writing.

A parade of the other writers from history then marched through my dream, in a vision that preserved their memory, as I had visualized them in my drawings. They all silently pleaded with me. It was as if their spirits rose from the grave in distress at the thought of the treasure, they had so carefully guarded, from being destroyed.

I woke suddenly with an unusual perspiration on my forehead and threw my bedclothes off me in a sleepy attempt to cool my now fevered body.

The next day I did none of my usual chores but instead devoted the whole day to rereading the adventures I now knew so well. The sketchy pictures of the men and women I had hewn from the tales silently staring at me across the dining table where I sat.

As I rose to make my umpteenth cup of tea an idea flashed into my mind of how to resolve the dilemma of what to do with this treasure box. It was actually something Father Ignatius had said which might solve the dilemma. He had referred in his mild, but determined, reprimand to modern fiction writers.

"What do you think, Reggie?" I enquired of my trusted companion. "What if I write an apparently fictional novel to reveal the story of my find? What do you think of that idea, Reggie?"

His response was unusual. From being curled up in his basket, more asleep than awake, he rose, stretched and sauntered over to me. He stood on his hind legs and with the gentle, light touch of a butterfly, laid his head onto my lap.

If I could talk "dog", I would interpret this action as him saying "Whatever you think, mummy. I will love you whatever you do."

My Dear Cousin,

I enclose a copy of the letter penned by someone who lived in the Forest of Dean.

His tale is short on requiring verification but, nevertheless, I should be grateful if you would verify that his story holds generally true to what you know about that time and place.

I wait with interest for your reaction.

Beattie

(Encl.)

The Forester

19th Century

How bist ol' butt? I honour you with our traditional Forest greeting but on reflection, in case you don't understand the phrase, my words translate in common English to 'How be you, old friend'.

My brother and I are both from the Royal Forest of Dean.

The year is 1851. I only happen to know this because there has been much talk of Prince Albert sponsoring a great Exhibition at somewhere called the 'Crystal Palace' in this very year. This solitary piece of information stuck in my mind because the name forged a vision of the setting in my imagination. Can there really be a palace made from crystal? How grand it must look as the sun hits its towers?

This important definition, of 'Forester' or 'Commoner', gives us a certain status, in that within the confines of the Royal Forest of Dean, having reached the age of 21, we are permitted to the title of our own mine. At least the rule is that if we work a mine for a year and a day we may register and be declared a Free Miner.

Since these mines are worked by a single family, or at the most two families, this grants us ownership of an asset whose location is guarded with the security of a Kings' treasure. We also have the 'Commoners' right to graze our sheep freely, with no financial penalty for doing so; this being another cherished asset of the status. Both of these privileges are of great importance to we Foresters. We enforce them rigorously, with violence if necessary, to prevent outsiders from claiming rights erroneously.

On a cold, Winter's day, such as the current Season affords, it is delightful to look across a patch of green and see the multicoloured sheep (colours denoting ownership) calmly searching out any residual grassland peacefully together. The Winter rainbow, I call it.

Having recently given birth to my young brother, Sam, our parents had moved to Gloucester. Our mother died soon after and the sole care for my brother fell to me since our father felt unable to deal with him.

My brother is a very special person. After our father's death I took the decision to return to the Forest in order to safeguard Sam. Did I mention that Sam is special?

But I race ahead. Allow me to back-track a little to explain. My father worked all daylight hours, and then some, at a timber mill in Gloucester. From the earliest years I knew that Sam was different from other children. He did not, for instance, babble in baby language the way others did.

Nor, once his eyes focused, did he allow them to descend upon me; he, rather, looked away from me when I was holding him as if struggling to get away from me. Being just four years his elder I remember feeling hurt at such behaviour.

He was my charge and I lavished all the care on him that my young years allowed and yet he refused to acknowledge me. When he had survived the confinement, unlike my other expected siblings, I well remember my joy at the thought of having someone to play with and confide in. This expectation was to be confounded.

The first time I realized the depth of my responsibility to Sam was, as I returned from some errand to our rented lodgings, I found Sam outside being chided viciously by the other children in our street. I must have been about seven at the time and Sam just three.

"Mad boy. Mad boy." The lads, some seven or eight of them, were pushing Sam around in a circle they had formed as a makeshift arena. As they pushed him from one to the other, they shouted this unkind slogan into his face.

As I ran towards them along the muddy path, he suddenly lost his footing and fell. To my absolute horror they continued the chant and changed their pushing to replace it with kicking. Poor Sam was beside himself with terror. His eyes, unfocused as always, stood out on stalks in uncomprehending fear. I screamed at them.

"Stop. What are you doing? Stop." My feet have never moved so fast as I tried to propel myself towards my brother. "Stop it now. Go away. Leave him alone." My arms flailed in the same action I use to frighten rooks away from the crops.

"Mad boy. Mad boy." The chanting continued and the kicks kept coming. Sam was now curled into a tiny ball in a futile effort to protect himself.

Finally, I reached the crowd and began pushing the antagonists away from Sam. "Stop it. Stop it. Leave him alone."

The children laughed and looked ready to continue despite my best efforts. Thankfully, at that moment, a neighbour appeared and angrily stepped in to save us.

"What are you kids doing?" She was an enormous woman, who had rushed out of her home wielding a wooden washing spoon. She had quickly assessed the situation and chased the boys off with threats enough to frighten the dead. I, meanwhile, was bending over Sam trying to assess the damage.

"It's alright, Sam. They've gone now. Come on, stand up." Sam did not move although his eyes were open and staring at the ground. "Come on, Sam. You're safe now. Come indoors with me."

The woman from hell, who had proved on this occasion to be our saviour, had returned to us having discharged her duty. "Is he alright?" she enquired matter-of-factly.

"Yes, I think so. He's just frightened I think."

"Right. Well you see to him. I have washing to get on with." With this she departed back through her door. Never had I felt such a need for an adult and never had it impinged on me so forcibly that Sam and I were alone. He was truly my sole responsibility.

It took me several minutes to get Sam to rise and when he did, he clung to me as if his very life depended on it. I half carried, half dragged him into the room, where I sat him at the table. As I went to move away from him to get water from the bucket to clean him, he grabbed onto me and refused to let go. His eyes still portrayed more than fear – in them I saw sheer terror. Never had I felt so protective towards him as in that moment.

Gradually, over the course of several hours, his fears began to subside and I felt his grasp on me lessen. When father returned, I told him what had occurred. He simply grunted and seemed quite disinterested.

"Will you talk to their parents?" I enquired wanting justice for this terrible act the boys had taken.

"Why? They are right, aren't they? He is mad."

The anger and frustration rose like bile in me. "He is not mad. He's not. He's …. special."

"Special?" Father laughed derisively. "Special? That's a good one. Ha, special my arse. He's mad, that's what he is." I glared angrily at him barely containing my rage and seeing a red mist before my eyes.

"Don't you look at me like that boy or you'll feel the back of my hand - and that moron too." This last was delivered with such a venomous look at Sam, who still sat by the table, that he visibly tried to shrink into nothingness.

"Now; where's my supper?"

So passed the incident; but it will always remain with me as one of the worst days in my life. I was only seven then and there were many more, even worse, days to come. My anger towards our Father in that very moment was so great that I could have stuck him with the knife if he had made just one more unkind remark. Lucky for him he was more interested in his supper. Equally luckily, he died within the year and I was saved the trouble.

When a mill worker came to the lodgings to inform me of our father's death, it was with relief that I received the news. This turned to near joy when he went on to tell me that the purse he held contained father's wages for the last two weeks. He had explained that the mill was short of money and so the workers were employed with the understanding that they should be paid later. Later was now, on his death.

Added to this I found, in his chest, another purse which also contained some small amount of money. I will say one thing for father he never drank and was a very 'careful' man. This is to his credit although the debit side of him far outweighed his virtue.

At the end of the street on which sat our lodgings I had noticed a family had moved into the address just the day previously. They had arrived with a small pony and cart. Sam and I had petted the pony and Sam particularly had seemed to connect with it in a way I had never seen him do with a person – even me. He named it Jasper.

I was wise enough to know that our survival in the city was uncertain at best, now that we had no bread earner in the family and so it was beholden upon me to find work. I did not know what the cost of our lodging was but I was shrewd enough, even at that young age, to know that the pittance in money we now held, would not suffice for more than a few days. So it was that a plan came into my mind. In the country one might survive on berries and harvested produce. I vaguely remembered happier times when we had lived in the Forest and determined that this should be our destination.

I made it my business to meet the newly arrived family and with what little money I had, bargained for the pony and rough cart. It took everything we had, since I had to throw in such meagre furnishings as belonged to us as well, but I procured the transport.

The one item which I couldn't sell was the rolled picture belonging to Sam. He had been given this by someone – I can't remember who now – and had treated it as his personal possession, of greatest value, ever since. A toy to cuddle was far beyond our means but staring into this picture brought him joy. When father had been in a bad mood, which was most of the time, Sam would unroll the picture and stare at the happy looking family therein. I must confess that it brought me comfort too, as I imagined being part of such an idyllic and loving party. Anyway, nothing on earth would have forced the picture from Sam and it was a small enough possession that I didn't begrudge him.

Food for both us and the pony, Jasper, was of the highest priority. So, the very next morning, as dawn broke, we set out for the countryside. Jasper was able to dine on the succulent grass at the verge, while Sam and I searched the hedgerows for fruit. Filthy, but satisfied, we continued our journey. The Forest is a short distance from Gloucester and soon the trees began to envelop us in their sheltering boughs. As each step was taken deeper into the Forest of trees, I felt my heart lighten and my hope increase.

In spite of many stops to gather fruit, which also allowed Jasper to graze, we eventually broke out of the tree line and saw, in the valley below us, the settlement we came to know was Lydbrook. It is set right by the River Wye and is named after the brook of 'Lyd' which flows into the much larger waterway of the Wye.

I procured work on a local farm and we were housed initially in one of their outbuildings. This improved eventually to a shelter that Sam and I built using the copiously available fallen logs. After a few years, despite the minimal pay I received for my labours, I had saved enough for us to afford a simple but adequate Foresters cottage where we live to this day.

It was during these early struggles that I came to realize that Sam had an extraordinary talent. Whilst he could not, and never did, communicate with people effectively, he seemed to have the most amazing and uncanny ability to talk to animals. I would often find him, on returning from work, sitting absolutely still on some fallen log or other, apparently staring into the undergrowth mindlessly. I came to understand that this was in no way mindless.

"What are you doing, Sam?" I enquired one evening on finding him thus and being very tired after a particularly long day at the farm.

"Ssshhhh" His finger moved to his mouth in signal of silence.

I sat beside him sluggishly and looked across into his face to trace where his concentration seemed to be centred. It is a peculiarity I have never understood that when communing with the animals he was able to hold his gaze. Slowly his arm reached out and he pointed at a growth of bush near where we sat.

"Squirrel," he announced in a whisper. "There. Look." I followed his gaze and was unreasonably delighted to spot the small creature chewing on something held delicately in its front paws. The squirrel stared back at me as if he was observing me, not the other way around.

"That's amazing. How can we be so close and not startle him?" I whispered feeling my tiredness dropping away.

"He's my friend. I've called him Gregory." Sam's eyes never left the small creature.

The three of us sat for some time like this until I detected a heavy step behind us. Turning I saw Jasper, who was still a useful member of our family, sauntering up towards us.

"Shhh, Jasper. Don't frighten Gregory" whispered Sam without turning his head towards the pony. "Come and stand near us but don't startle our squirrel friend." To my disbelief Jasper raised his head from grazing, in which he had lazily been occupied, and moved slowly towards where we sat.

Gregory was less sure of Jasper than he had been of Sam or even me. With quick movements he scurried up the nearby tree and sat looking down at us somewhat accusingly.

"Now you've scared him, Jasper. Go and eat your grass further away, there's a good boy." With this instruction, for all the world as if he understood it, the pony turned and walked off.

We left the log shortly after that, and it was only as we made our way towards home, that I realized that Sam had conducted this whole talk without stuttering or mumbling once. He had been in total control of the animals and his own body. I had never noticed that aptitude in him before. For me, any residual tiredness I had felt had dissipated and I felt surprisingly refreshed.

Over the years we have made many animal friends thanks to Sam. We've rescued more than a few too. Our house always seemed to contain some unpaid lodger or other who was recuperating from injury, delivering babies or just visiting socially. One of Sam's special friends is a deer whom he calls Jeffrey. One day I was very alarmed, on entering our small home, to be faced with Jeffrey standing in our room staring back at me.

"What? What's he doing here?" I, not unreasonably, demanded.

"The hunters are in the Forest. Jeffrey asked me to shelter him until they have gone." For all the world Sam seemed to think nothing strange in this arrangement.

"He can't stay here, Sam. He's a deer for goodness sake. Deer don't live in houses."

"He's not staying. He's just sheltering until nightfall then he'll be on his way." I couldn't think of one response to this extraordinary piece of information so I just gave up trying. Instead I merely poured water into the bowl to wash in silence and resignation.

The whole time, as I prepared our evening meal of roots, I kept staring back at the deer, Jeffrey. Each time my glance fell on him he would raise his head and look back at me. He was totally unafraid. I was stunned. As I dished up the stew into our bowls Sam seemed to come to a decision.

"Come on now Jeffrey. Time you went home. We're going to eat now. The hunters have gone." So saying Sam opened the door and Jeffrey sauntered out. "Come and see me any time," he called gently after the departing animal. Jeffrey did indeed visit many times although he never again ventured into our humble home.

Since I was now approaching my twenties, being I believed in my late betweens, and had managed to save a little money from my farm work, it occurred to me that it would be wise to invest in a few sheep. Their wool I could sell at market. The ongoing cost associated with such animals would be minimal as I could declare that I was twenty-one, thus ensuring free grazing rights. Who could disprove it? No one, or very few, held records of birth days; if anyone ever cared to check. The key thing was to mark the animals with a distinctive, durable paint to identify them as belonging to us. The farmer offered to help me with this requirement.

So it was that Sam and I set out one day for the local stock market. In spite of Sam now being in the between age, his mentality was still one of a young child. Thus it was, that whenever we walked on a road, I held his hand to prevent him wandering off. Thinking back, it must have presented a strange sight. We reached our destination without incident.

As we sauntered between the makeshift pens, erected by the local farmers to display their livestock, I let go of Sam's hand and, in short order, realized he was no longer following me. I retraced my steps with some agitation, neck craning to try and see over the marketers and cattle all of whom were taller than me. I was nearly on top of him before I realized it was he, for he was squatted down talking to a ewe face to face through the fencing.

"We must bring her home", he pleaded as I touched him on the shoulder to indicate my presence. "Please may we?"

I looked with a critical eye at the beast whilst recalling all I knew about sheep in an attempt to assess her as an investment. "She seems sturdy enough. Why do you want this one particularly?

"She is so very sad. She's told me. Look at her eyes. Can you see the sadness?"

Now, to me, all sheep look sad. I had not, you understand, made it a habit to stare into their eyes, but they just seemed like a forlorn animal in general. However, in deference to my brother, I joined him squatting against the open fencing and stared deeply into the ewes' eyes. Her response to this closeness was to slowly move her gaze from Sam to myself. Indeed, something of her soul touched my soul and I was moved to rescue her.

"I do not promise anything, for the price of this beast will determine if we can have her, but I shall enquire of the farmer", I promised. So saying I rose from my squatting position and looked around for the ewes' owner whilst mentally tallying, for the umpteenth time, the sum of money in my purse.

"Good day to you young sir," came a voice from just behind me. It was the farmer who must have been observing us closely.

"Good day," I responded cordially. "Can you tell me how much you are asking for this sheep?"

"Well now. This one's a good lamber. She's just given birth to that little one over there in fact. No trouble." Thus saying, he pointed to the cutest baby sheep, who whilst happily dancing in the small space still maintained an astute closeness to its mother.

The farmer gave me a price, which with all the talent I could muster, I negotiated down. Part of the deal was that the lamb be included in the package. At first, he had been reluctant to agree but the market was soon due to close for the day, which I pointed out to him, and he was finally persuaded to allow me to take both beasts off his hands. I tried to procure a ram as well but that was too much for my meagre purse and we only bought the ewe and lamb.

On the happy journey home, Sam named the ewe, Peggy. The lamb, after consultation with its mother, we called Jenny. The ewe we secured by means of a small rope with no tether to the lamb who obediently followed its mother.

Peggy and Jenny have both proven to be good working animals. Each season the battle commenced as we tried, with borrowed shearers, to divest them of their wool. Sam proved invaluable in this exercise as he gently held them and spoke to them explaining that, despite the unnatural positions we placed them into, we were not going to harm them.

The farmer, for whom I had now worked a long time, was kind enough to allow me to forgo the mating fee from his ram and work it off instead by labour. Thus, our family gradually enlarged. The identifying colour of our livestock is, I must admit, a little alarming since it comprises a bright pink 'splodge' on their rear left flanks – but this doesn't diminish our pride in their ownership. The wool we proudly trekked to market and rarely tarried more than a couple of hours before the sacks were paid for at the asking price.

The one and only luxury item that we ever possessed was Sam's rolled up picture of the idyllic family in a room such as we had never seen in real life. The books in the picture fascinated us both. In the winter, when the nights draw in, we would unfold the picture and place it between us. From this position I would make up stories for Sam on the possible adventures that the books contained. Over the years, we have in this manner, travelled to the high seas full of pirates; to the great cities full of fine ladies and gentlemen; to foreign countries full of wonders and adventures; and to the world of pure imagination where trees grow rich with foodstuffs and sweet things.

No one but Sam and myself with the occasional, not so wild creature, had ever laid eyes upon Sam's treasured possession. Each time we finished viewing it, he carefully rolled it up again and placed it lovingly in the box he had crafted for it from a fallen log. This box was then placed under his cot until it was again called for. That is, until an accident opened its wonders to a stranger.

Sam and I were deeply involved in a fantasy book from the background of the picture one Winters night when a sudden knock on our door made us both jump and lurch back to the present with a shock. Even the rabbit, currently recovering from a misadventure, in a wooden cage near our fire, jumped then began thumping in agitation and warning.

Gingerly I rose and move towards the door. No one ever called on us and certainly not during the night-time. Whoever could it be? With every nerve jangling I slowly opened the door just a mite and peered out. I used my hidden foot as a doorstop to prevent whoever this intruder was from pushing the door open further.

The man who stood on our threshold was of senior years I would determine. He was clothed in a capacious cloak whose collar was pulled up to protect his neck from the chill night air and a hat with a floppy brim which was pulled down to protect his ears from the same chill. In fact, there was little of his face which was visible. This had the effect of making him seem even more sinister than my nervous state judged. My foot remained firmly planted as I enquired of him his business.

"Please accept my profound apologies for disturbing you, young sir. But my horse has become lame as I journey and I need some shelter for the night. Can you advise me?" With this he looked earnestly at me and stood back slightly awaiting a reply.

Had he used any other excuse for his intrusion then Sam would have in no way responded and indeed remained hidden in the room. However, the words about a lame horse were too much for his animal loving spirit and he suddenly appeared beside me trying to peer out through the narrow gap.

"Your horse is lame you say?" I felt the need for evidence of this statement.

"Indeed. Look." So saying, the man who still held firm grip on the reins, stood back and walked the horse just two or three paces along the front of our cottage. The poor animal had a pronounced limp in its left hind quarters. Having achieved this substantiation, he looked again at the gap in our doorway containing our two peering faces and continued.

"I am very fond of my steed and unwilling to cause it further discomfort. In the morning I can seek a blacksmith to replace the shoe, if that is indeed the problem, or at least advise me on her recovery but for tonight …" He left the sentence unfinished.

The next decision was removed from my domain as Sam grabbed the door, kicked my foot out of the way, and opened it fully. Thus positioned, he was able to exit our home and slowly approach the horses head. He spoke some gentle words to it, stroked it, and only then moved towards its rear to inspect the injured foot.

Without words he took the reins from the stranger and quietly, reassuringly speaking the whole time to the animal, led it to where Jasper grazed. He spoke to them both, as if affecting an introduction then, having removed the stranger's horse accoutrements, and placed them safely on a nearby stump, he returned to our startled presence.

This of course left me with no option but to invite the stranger into the sanctity of our home. This I did. Having stepped over the threshold, and following a quick glance around our one room, he divested himself of his cloak and hat. That was when I was again startled by this stranger. As his hat was removed it surprised me to find that either side of his head ringlets fell onto his face. This was a fashion I had never before observed. Sam also, judging by his reaction, was surprised.

The man, seeing our bewilderment, laughed. It was a kindly laugh and went a long way to allay our fears and suspicion.

"You find my appearance strange, yes?" He chuckled. "Never fear my friends, for these are a worn related to my faith; for I am a Jew. They are called payot and the hair is worn like this following the Law outlined in the Hebrew text of Leviticus."

Sam looked at me for confirmation that he might feel reassured. I nodded to him and further supported this state by offering to heat some of our stew for the man. He accepted gratefully and I set too warming the meal and breaking off a portion of bread. At this intimacy, that of feeding the stranger, I decided that an introduction was in order, and so gave him our names. Meanwhile Sam sat in his chair and invited the man to seat himself in mine by means of a hand gesture. It was too much to expect that Sam would speak in the presence of the stranger but his sign language was more than adequate to fulfil most needs. There the two sat whilst the man carefully took in his surroundings with Sam scrutinizing the stranger.

"You have a cosy home here," he declared having finished his inspection.

"Thank you. We try to make it comfortable. Tell me, why are you travelling this way?" It was time, I decided, for the stranger to throw illumination upon his identity and motives.

"Forgive me. I should have told you." The man shuffled in his chair as if making himself more comfortable. "My name is Abraham Mashat. I am a broker in fine stones. I was recently informed about a rare stone being landed from foreign parts by a ship entering Scarborough port. It is a very long journey across the land but, unfortunately, sea passage is not an option for me. I feel very unwell on even the gentlest flowing river – besides, I confess, I am afraid of the water.

So it was that I set out from Gloucester on my faithful, if a little aging, horse to that far off destination. It was earlier this evening that I noticed that the usually comfortable seat of my saddle was imbalanced. I dismounted to find that my horse had gone lame. I walked her slowly for some miles before spotting your light. The rest you know."

My curiosity was aroused. "You say you are making this great journey for a single stone?" The whole concept of desiring something so material that you would allow it to disrupt your whole life was foreign to me.

"Ah, ha, my young friend! It is no ordinary gem. I have been informed that it is landed from a ship from far off Africa. I believe, from its description, that it may be a diamond of substantial acclaim. Acquaintances in my trade are also travelling to the site to place offers for the stone. Hence my frustration at this forced delay."

The stew was now thoroughly heated and I placed it in a bowl on the homemade table near Abraham. He eagerly devoured it with his spoon alternating with a mouthful of bread until not a scrap of either was left. There was no conversation since the man's mouth was never empty enough to facilitate any. As he placed the spoon back in the bowl from the table where he had put it so that he might soak up any remnants of stew with the last piece of bread, he pushed the bowl away and sat back in the chair resplendent in his satisfaction.

"That, my young friend, was surely the finest feast I have tasted in days. I am eternally grateful to you." It was at this moment that he seemed to look at Sam's picture for the first time. It had been visible all the time of course because we had not rolled it up once the knock came at the door but now, he really looked at it. He leant forward for the purpose.

"That is a superb picture." He turned to Sam, "Is it yours?" Sam, naturally, looked skyward. It was beholden upon me to answer.

"It is my brother's fondest possession. He loves it."

"I can, indeed, see why. What a masterpiece. May I?" This question was directed at Sam and indicated Abraham's desire to pick the picture up. Sam, of course, did not seem to have heard and even less, reply.

"Of course." I affirmed that he may handle it. "But please be careful. Don't let stains from your fingers smudge it." Abraham wiped both his hands on his waistcoat before leaning forward to raise the picture.

"Magnificent." His approval warmed me. "How did … Sam, did you say? How did Sam come by this?"

"We don't really remember. Someone gave it to him when we were both very small."

"And you don't remember who?"

"No."

"Well, whoever it was must have really loved you, for it is a portrait worthy of any gallery."

"What is this?" He leaned right forward so that his eyes were but inches from the picture. "There is something written on this scroll on the desk in the foreground". He squinted to better focus his vision. "My goodness! It is written in Hebrew. I can't quite make out the lettering though."

"Hebrew? That is the language of your people isn't it?" Exactly where this piece of trivia had come from, I do not know.

"Indeed, it is, my young friend. Do you happen to possess a glass cup or bowl perchance? That might just magnify it enough more me to see."

"No, I am sorry. We own no glass."

"Ah, wait. I am a dull wit. I shall use the spyglass which I use to inspect gems." With this he patted his waistcoat seeking, presumably, the tell-tale bulge. Finding none such, he rose and went to his cloak. He repeated the patting procedure until his face lit up in exaltation. Reaching into an inside pocket of his garment he extracted a small, black, tube. He then returned to the painting and looking through the tube slowly identified the words written there.

"There is some sort of symbol at the beginning of each line. It is best described as a flattened circle. No. No. It is like a slightly opened mouth! No, wait. It is a child's drawing of a fish, minus its tail." It would be hard to determine who was the more intrigued in that room at that moment.

He continued, slowly and deliberately, calling out one word at a time. Then, as a finale, he read the whole inscription together.

(Tailless fish) Walk beside the river leading from the white settlement of Streonshal.

(Tailless fish) Forty-two steps from the man who smiles find the truth he guards behind the fall.

Silence descended upon the assembled company. No words seemed suitable for the occasion. Was this the clue to some treasure? Or was it merely a prank? Who might have gone to such trouble to write such a mysterious passage? Why should it be written in the ancient language of Hebrew? Was it a Jew who had placed the clues there? Abraham looked at me. I looked at Sam then Abraham. Sam stared at the ceiling as if he might find the answer there.

"Well, my young friends. It seems we have solved one mystery and found another, even greater."

"Where was that place mentioned again?"

Abraham, using his spy glass again, read out the name. "… a white settlement of Streonshal."

"I have never heard of such a place. Have you?" I enquired of Abraham.

"It means nothing to me, no."

Resigning ourselves to never knowing the answer to the mysterious clues we retired for the night. As I lay on my cot, with the soft sound of Sam purring and the wind rustling the leaves on the trees outside, I tried again to make any sense of the message. None came to mind – but sleep did.

The next morning, I allocated the task of leading Abraham to the blacksmith in the nearby village to Sam whilst I attended to work on the farm. When I returned that evening, I was delighted and not a little surprised to find that Abraham had prepared supper.

The sweet aroma of stewing root vegetables delighted my nostrils on opening the door. Immediately my body leapt into a state of hunger, saliva forming in my mouth, and a gentle rumbling issuing from my stomach. Almost as I opened the door, Abraham began dishing portions into our bowls. I quickly washed up and we sat. Thus far, not a word had passed between us but a muttered "Abraham?" from me as a declaration of surprise at him still being there.

We all attacked the meal as like a starving man and were several spoons into our meal before Abraham spoke.

"I am afraid I must crave your indulgence and rely upon your kindness for a little while longer, if I may," he ventured. "Sam took me to the blacksmith, who examined my horse, and was of the opinion that it was a sprain of some sort. Obviously, in my haste to travel I had allowed us to journey into dusk and it seems my horse may have stepped awkwardly. The blacksmith assures me that with a couple of days rest, her leg will repair naturally." He took another spoonful of stew. "However, that behoves me to ask if I may remain here whilst this mending takes place." He looked up at me for an answer.

I looked across at Sam and recognized in his eyes the same pleading he had used for many injured animals before. He was silently begging that I may permit him to care for the animal.

"Of course. You may stay as long as you need to."

"Thank you, my young friend. Your kindness shall not go unseen nor unrewarded by God."

"I do have some good news for you," he declared triumphantly after spooning one more mouthful. "Sam and I have discovered the location of that place Streonshal." He looked across at Sam with a sparkle in his eyes and a smile on his lips. "We were speaking to the blacksmith whilst he tended my horse, or more truly, *I* was speaking to him …" he smiled across at Sam. "In idleness I enquired if he had heard of the name. He had." A look of triumph graced his visage.

My hunger was surpassed by my curiosity. I put my spoon down and looked enquiringly into his eyes.

"You will never guess where it is. It is very near to my destination – no more than 20 miles or so apparently. I am travelling to Scarborough which is a mere stones' throw from Whitby." With vigour he tore at another piece of bread and sat there staring at me whilst he chewed it. For all the world it was if the bread was his just reward.

"Whitby. Near the port you are seeking?"

"The same. The very same. What is more, I have distant relatives in Whitby that it would bring me great pleasure to visit."

Hunger again took dominion over my curiosity and I resumed the welcome meal. Since we were all in the same state no further conversation ensued until all three bowls were empty and every last crumb of bread consumed.

"If you will permit me – and indeed trust me – it will be my pleasure to follow the clues now that I know the starting point and am in the town anyway. I shall be pleased to repay your kindness by discovering, and if relevant, recovering, whatever I find there. Then, on passing this way on my journey home, I can stop here and deliver my findings to you. Will you permit me to return your kindness in this manner?"

"That would be most welcome. Thank you. We accept." It had not escaped my intelligence that the prospect of our visiting so far a destination was nil.

"If I may make so bold, it is the way of business that one shakes hands on the settlement of a contract. Will you take my hand to seal the bargain?" So saying he held out his right hand, which I took. We shook on the deal and the matter was settled.

It was rare indeed that this matter again crossed my mind. Truly, I only thought of it when Sam and I were engaged in the world of imaginings of an evening and I again saw the writing on the scroll. Abraham had, true to his word, left us a couple of days after that evening, but during his stay had more than proven himself, by preparing supper each night, collecting and chopping wood for our open fire and constructing a third chair so one of us did not have need to squat on a cot whilst eating. I wondered if he might also construct a third cot but he did not. If he visited again, (dare I hope the 'if' be replaced by 'when'?), he would have to bed on the floor as before.

It must have been several months until Abraham again called. The winter was passing and the signs in nature indicated that Spring was stirring nature into activity after its long sleep.

It was late one afternoon, whilst Sam sat on his usual log staring into a bush, no doubt at some passing animal or other, and I busied myself collecting twigs to fuel the beginnings of our fire, that my attention was drawn to the sound of hooves on the nearby roadway. The animal was in no hurry and the slow plodding of the approaching sound caused no alarm. On raising my head in enquiry, I was gratified to find a shape, cloak and hat not dissimilar to Abrahams making its way ponderously towards our house. Luckily, I had been released early in the day from the farm because it had been a particularly early start to the working day, and my kindly employer had allowed me home before dark.

It was, indeed, Abraham. My heart leapt with a quite unexpected joy.

"Hail, my young friend," he greeted as he approached. "How has the world treated you since last we met?"

"Abraham. How pleased I am to see you. Sam, Sam, come here. It is our good friend Abraham."

Sam immediately stood and walked quickly towards Abraham's horse. This he greeted with friendly excitement. Abraham, he did not acknowledge. I had no fears that Abraham would be offended by this, since this gentleman had always calmly accepted that my brother was 'special'.

"Come. Come. I have not yet begun to prepare the meal and shall just add another root so that you may eat with us."

"Oh, I have so much to tell you. I have longed to be here again to regale you with my adventures." So saying, Abraham dismounted and placed his arm around my shoulders like a favourite uncle and we proceeded into the house.

My first act was to ply our friend with a warmed broth to stave off the worst of his hunger. Whilst he sat and drank this gratefully, on his new chair, he and I chatted as if we were indeed related.

It is not relevant to my tale to detail this chat, punctuated by much laughter, but I shall proceed immediately to the pertinent points in his adventures. Sadly, he had not managed to procure the stone he had so avidly desired and which had inspired his long journey. Another trader had outbid him. However, he was not disheartened since he had found and bought some other precious stones which he was sure he could make a handsome profit on.

He had, as promised, when time and opportunity allowed, pursued the clues from the scroll on our behalf.

"It was amazing how accurate the clues had been in reality. I am sure though that, without actually looking to follow the directions, there is no way anyone would have found what I uncovered. Do you remember the bit in the clue about the smiling man? Well it was this bit which surprised me the most. There, absolutely naturally, when one knew what to look for, was a smiling face formed by the stone."

"But you found it?" My excitement was barely contained.

"Indeed, I did. In a cave, which itself was hidden by Mother Nature herself, I found a box. It sits even now in the sack on my horse." So saying, he rose and went to the door to retrieve it. I followed him outside.

"What is in the box?"

"I have no idea. It is not mine to explore. It is you to whom it belongs and I treat myself as merely the messenger."

"You mean you did not open it?" My curiosity could not have been appeased with such discipline. What strength of character Abraham must own?

"Certainly not! Our bargain, and we shook on it, was that I should bring you whatever I found - if anything. It is not in our contract that I should have any rights to view my findings."

We both walked quickly to where Sam had led Abraham's horse. Jasper and Abraham's mount were engaged in some sort of animal greeting with lots of nuzzling passing between them. The reins and saddle sat astride the stump. The sack was on the ground near them. Abraham bent and picked it up and we both turned back towards the house. Sam remained with the horses, gently talking too and stroking them alternately.

The sack was placed heavily onto the table and in my eagerness, I opened it and retrieved the box. On opening it, my heart sank. The only thing contained within were papers. I extracted them in hope that at the bottom may lie some jewellery, or a gem of value, or even some coins – but I was to be sadly disappointed. Dismay upon dismay, upon closer inspection I found that what was written on the pages was not even legible. It was written in some foreign language and meant nothing to me.

"Is this Hebrew?" I asked Abraham hopefully.

"No. It seems to me that at least some of it may be in French, or something similar." He picked up a page and looked closely at it. "Look, here is a word, 'maintenant'. I recognize that as French because it has always struck me as odd to use so many letters for such a small word as 'now'.

"Are you sure you cannot read it?"

"I am so sorry, my friend. My reading skills only extend as far as English and Mosaic Hebrew. I know just the odd word in other languages due to my profession, but nothing more."

"What about this one?" Having rummaged through the pages I had found one document which seemed to resemble the writing on the scroll. This I passed to Abraham.

"Yes. Yes. This is a form of ancient Hebrew. I can't quite make out what the subject is though. It seems to be a series of quotations. There are also some longer paragraphs. It would take me some time to translate it fully and I cannot guarantee that it will illuminate the subject matter more. Would you like me to take these pages home with me and translate them for you? If they do prove interesting or important, I can always return one day."

"No. I cannot ask you to spend your valuable time in that task. They probably have no significance anyway. Thank you for honouring your contract but I believe I will keep these papers together."

To be truthful with you, my spirits were so low at this time, that my whole outlook was tending towards the negative. I had dearly hoped that there might be some treasure contained in the box which would lighten my brother's and my own lot in life. Papers held no allure to me, especially as I could not read – in any language.

Abraham also seemed dulled by disappointment and we gathered up the papers, returned them to the box, and placed it under Sam's cot. Abraham spent the night in the shelter of our home and early the next morning set out for his own home town.

We never saw Abraham again although we still sometimes talk of him fondly. He is the perfect example of an honourable man and we are pleased to have known him.

Life returned to normal and for the next few years I have nothing to report. Rescued animals came and went. I became increasingly proficient at farm husbandry. Jasper, sadly, died and was replaced with a new foal, whom Sam named 'Jaydon'. Where he got this name from, I never truly understood, but the animal seemed to respond to it well enough. Our scattered flock of bright pink marked sheep increased and the income from their wool ensured we never went hungry.

I was delighted to be introduced to our new school mistress. She and I immediately felt a common bond. It was a meeting of the spirit as well as the mind and we married just one year after her arrival at the little, local school. This set the tongues to wagging but, in our bliss, we did not mind nor heed them. Sam adored her too and she adopted him as if he was her own born. We lived happily as a family and I blessed the day fate had stepped in to allow us to walk on the same path.

It was she who, having been raised in the sort of family to own a good education, finally discovered and then translated the papers. Her French she assured me honed exponentially, (a new word she taught me), as she translated and read the inscriptions for our attentive ears. It is she who has been kind and long suffering enough to transcribe this poor account as I dictate it to her night after night.

Nobody could have been more startled than she and I as each new writer's tale unfolded. It was only as time passed that we came to realize the true import of the documents. I had longed for treasure to be in the box so long ago but could never have envisaged, in my wildest imaginings, just how valuable the treasure truly was.

The very words of Jesus, the Christ, Himself had been given to me for safekeeping; for there was no doubt in my mind that this was what we were privileged to hold before us. My humility was profound and the responsibility daunting. It was Sam, in his simple specialness, who provided the solution of what must be done with them.

"I do not think that God would have given them to us if He wanted them to be announced," he suddenly pronounced from his place by the fire. For one of the very few times in his life he looked at me squarely and held his gaze on me in total control and concentration. "If He wanted them declared He would have given them to a man of the church. I believe we should keep them safe and pass them on to the next people to live."

Bethany, my wife, and I looked at each other in stunned silence. Sam continued to hold his gaze on me.

"I think he is right. What was it that one author wrote … 'care taker' … you are the care taker. We should take care of them. We should hide them again and do nothing more with them," declared Bethany with final conviction.

Bethany was wise. I was in no doubt that she was right. Just to be sure I asked "But should we not take them to the local parish priest?"

"No. I cannot tell you why I feel this would be wrong, but I feel it within my very core." She looked at me earnestly. Sam also continued to stare – never once allowing his gaze to ascend. The unusualness of this was so profound that I knew something strange was happening.

"Agreed. We shall place the box safely and allow it to continue on its journey through time." My mind was made up and I was at peace with the decision.

The hiding place I chose was a small mine which had obviously not been worked for many years; whether the Forester had not had male children who could inherit it, or whether the mine had been worked out, was unclear. Whatever the cause of its disuse it would serve my purpose admirably. It was dry and high in a rough hill. It had a small entrance with no visible supports so it was not obvious as to what it was. Of greater importance, was that it would be easily identified by one seeking it, but only with certain pertinent information at their fingertips. The mine was, you see, marked by both a mileage stone indicating that Ross-on-Wye was just 3 miles further along the road, and as a comfort to a traveller, where a small water fountain had been placed. Both of these signs would suit my clue ideally.

Bethany and I set too creating a clue as to the box's new hiding place. Said box was to contain my account here included.

(I drew a tailless fish) From the Lyd to Ross mark 3 with water. Above it is mine.

(I drew another tailless fish) Therein find treasure of value above gold.

We both decided that we would not hide the names of the places as our predecessor had done, so that they might find the location without help from others as I had had to do. I had been blessed to find Abraham but it would be too much to expect that such virtue might come forth for the next caretaker.

The challenge was where one might hide the clue itself? I looked to Sam for this element of the undertaking. He had taken up a hobby of carving pictures into stones with a small hammer and chisel and, if I say so myself, most of them were a delight. Naturally, his creations contained portraits of his beloved animals and I saw no disadvantage to this special stone also containing this theme. I found a suitable rock with a flat surface on one side and of the right proportions and passed this to Sam. He was delighted with the raw material.

Far from launching himself into the task Sam sat and pondered the words we had written on the paper for several days without lifting his chisel.

Finally, I was encouraged to inquire if the task I had set him was too much for his imagination.

"Indeed, no, brother. I just want to make sure that I choose the right friends to portray to indicate the gravity and importance of the treasure. A squirrel, whilst being a delight in himself, in no way stresses the value of what is contained in the box. Likewise, a deer, whilst royal and alert is too easily alarmed to express the solidity of the texts Bethany read to us. A sheep, whilst calm and passive in nature is too closely associated with stupidity to allude to the wisdom it must point to."

Thus, pacified that Sam was indeed giving the matter the gravest thought I was content to leave him with the puzzle. It was two days later that I spotted him, sitting on his favourite log, and heard the unmistakable tap, tap, tap, of his delicate workings. I did not wish to interrupt so was content to await his result whenever he would present it to us. This he did nearly a week later and it was clearly his best work yet.

Proudly, one evening he entered the home where Bethany was preparing supper and I was sharpening a cutting tool at the table. He carried the stone in his hands as if it were made of crystal and the beam on his face indicated his pleasure at presenting the result of his thoughtful labours. He laid the stone on the table face upwards so that we might inspect his creation.

There on the stone was carved the most exquisite picture of a donkey. He stared out of the relief into the eyes of those viewing him. We were to discover that those piercing but gentle, large eyes seemed to follow one wherever in the room one looked from. The cross, famously appearing on all such breeds, was clearly visible on the donkey's back. Set in the background of the carving was the outline of a rock-face with a single, dark opening in it. The darkness was achieved by being carved deeper than the surrounding picture.

Most importantly, the clue we had composed, Sam had painstakingly carved into the rock-face. It was in such fine detail as to be clear but not overwhelming. It was a work of beauty and cunning. The eye of the beholder was constantly drawn back to the gentle face of the donkey but the clue was there for the seeking.

"Sam," I exclaimed with astonishment poorly hidden, "Sam, this is your most amazing work yet. The detail! The depth! The symbolism! Bethany, come and look at this."

Bethany was as stunned and excited as me. "I almost wish that we could keep this. How kindly your donkey looks. See, his eyes reach out from the stonework and touch my heart. Sam, you are truly gifted."

"Where did you find a donkey to model from?" I enquired.

"There is one in the field along the way. His name is Jacob. I explained that I wanted to create a picture of him and he stood still long enough for me to make a sketch of him. I used the sketch to carve this." The pride in Sam's voice portrayed his pleasure.

"Look how clearly the words of the clue stand out and yet how they may seem to be just flaws in the rock to the casual observer." This statement from Bethany summed up the cleverness of design.

Sam volunteered "I chose a donkey because of Jesus entering Jerusalem on one."

"I am so proud of you." My love and pride at that moment knew no bounds and, much to Sam's alarm, I could not resist rising quickly to hug him. He was tense and his eyes looked upwards to the ceiling.

I remembered at that moment how 'special' he was. Then I corrected myself as I placed the emphasis on the word 'special' with a greater understanding of how 'special' just meant gifted in ways other than the more normal social interaction.

The stone we placed face down by the side of the road, by the small drinking fountain, which lay 3 miles from Lydbrook and 4 miles from Ross-on-Wye.

As I laid it carefully, I wandered who would chance to find it. Then, again I corrected myself, as I remembered that it would not be discovered by chance. No, indeed! Its uncovering would be by Design.

My Dearest Beattie,

I read this tale with some degree of fascination. It does indeed ring true, to both the period and the environment, I am reliably informed by one of our English history lecturers for the periods.

I wait in anticipation for the next documented translation.

I also cannot help but wonder if you have progressed beyond a two-finger typist yet?

Kindest possible regards,

Jackie

Dear Jackie,

Thank you for your comments and verification. Please find enclosed, without introduction from me, the story of the travelling Parisian.

I eagerly wait for your response on the likelihood of this document being genuine.

Most gratefully,
Beattie

The Parisian

16ᵗʰ Century

I live in a time when it seems the whole world is changing.

Whilst I remain anonymous, in the tradition of my predecessors, I feel that it is important that my successors know a little of my situation and the climate around which the find was made.

I live and work in Paris as a lecturer at the University of Paris. My specialist knowledge revolves around the subject of Roman and Greek architecture; a topic most popular during this the period of what is being called the Renaissance. The year is 1561 AD. I am fortunate to be married to Nicole who remains a lady of some title and means, and to whom I have been wed now for fifteen, nearly sixteen, years. Fate has not blessed us with children so, since both she and I have no siblings, nor did our parents, our lines are sadly to end with our demise. It is this fact which is to play a dominant role in the story I am fated and compelled to unfold.

In order to fully understand my actions a little socio-political history of the time will be of benefit. This may be prompted by my propensity for academia, but I ask that you indulge me anyway.

Paris seems to be in the same unsettled stage common to childbirth; as disruption and pain are common to new life entering the world, so too is the temperature and temperament of this great city. Even in my short thirty-four years I have witnessed such magnitude of change that many 'Papers' have been spawned on the topic by my esteemed colleagues at the University.

In the last half century Christianity has reached a state of division with two streams of belief parting company acrimoniously. Whilst the central figure of Jesus is common to all elements of Christianity that is the only true point of union it seems. We are traditionally a devoted Roman Catholic country; nowhere more so than in Paris itself. Some forty or more years ago a German, by the name of Martin Luther, protested against the Catholic teachings and set up an alternative, so called 'Protestant', doctrine which claimed to more closely follow the teachings within the Bible.

My father remembers all too well the chaos and ill-will between neighbours, or even members of the same family, that this radical opinion caused. It was a natural progression that these 'Protestants', be they followers of Luther, Calvin or any of the other so called 'Reformation' doctrines, were declared to be heretics by Catholicism.

Vicious wars have been fought in defense or defiance of this 'Reformation', but thankfully an unsettled peace has now descended upon the country – though how long this calm may reign is undetermined. My personal assessment is that we are, in fact, in a lull before the storm.

The Reformists are no longer deemed actually unlawful in this country although their ideas are not to be encouraged within suitable conversation. As near as I can gather, they seem to believe that every word of the Bible is the Word of God and do not allow any allegorical essence therein. Another of their primary ideas seems to be the individual responsibility for actions, rather than adherence to Catholic doctrine, as the means to salvation.

This may be a drastic oversimplification of their beliefs - but then I am no expert –neither in their beliefs nor those of my Catholic brethren. I believe that God exists and that Jesus was His Son – and there my belief both begins and ends.

Another horror which has been released upon the world is that caused by the scientist, Copernicus, who claimed some twenty years ago, to have evidenced that the planets revolved around the sun rather than, as we had hitherto thought, everything revolving around us. This flew in the face of previous scientists who had assured us that the religious doctrine of the Earth being the center of the universe was scientifically sound. Add this to the already unsettled religious disagreements and religion, as a concept, is thrown into frenzy trying to answer how this could be explained if God created our planet and, indeed, the universe.

Confusion reigned supreme and a scientific revolution went into battle, not only within its own ranks, but with the science of religion. The ordinary folk, like myself, are left in a complete quandary on both the topics of the emerging sciences and the turbulent religious beliefs. With no clear outlines on what is fact and what is fiction it is easier to not believe anything – hence my attitude.

It is against this unsettled and even religiously venomous backdrop that I came into possession of the texts around which my story revolves.

My wife had inherited from her parents, now both sadly deceased, a minor title and a small but wealthy estate on the outskirts of Paris. Luckily this area of land became more in demand over the years and so, finally selling the farming interests and manor house of which it comprised, we were able to procure a large apartment near the center of the city, which we still own. For myself, I was raised to own a good education and the opportunity of continuing in my father's business. However, the art of high finance eluded me and it was quickly decided that I should pursue my own destiny - with my Father's blessing. He meanwhile installed a manager upon his retirement who, to this day, allocates donations to me from the established Trust Fund associated with the profits and investments of the craft.

Nicole had naturally, upon selling her land-associated possessions, not abandoned the finer examples of furniture or decorations from the property which now adorn our luxurious apartment. She had also retained the jewels passed down to her from the generations of women in her ancestry. One of these items has been a quite magnificent ruby broach which is recovered from the bank and worn only for the most prestigious of occasions. Our greatest regret was that no other woman from our family would ever be adorned in such grandeur nor hang the strings of fine pearls around their neck. Such was our belief at the time but I am glad to say that this too, like the city of our birth, was to change.

One day Nicole entered my inner sanctum, which I call my study, in a state of high excitement. This was a most unusual demeanor for my spouse and immediately diverted me from the letter I was in the process of composing.

"I have made a discovery of import," she declared rushing over towards my oversize desk. "Look what I found hidden in my broach." She thrust forward a tiny scrap of paper. The broach in question was in her other hand and defined itself by the unique ruby. This had been withdrawn from the bank only yesterday in readiness for the wedding, tonight, of the daughter of a friend of ours who was of the landed gentry. It would be a grand affair and one in which an auction was to be held in aid of the less fortunate. This would cost me a princely sum; however, it would serve as my annual gift to those less fortunate. Everyone of substance in Paris would attend and it was the ideal excuse for the ladies in our company to display their finery.

"Look. See what I found hidden between the ruby and the gold filigree." I took the slip from her. From the creases on it, the fine grade paper had been folded into eight equal segments though it now lay opened.

"How did you find it," I enquired. "Surely you would have discovered it before?" I enquired before determining what lay on the page.

"I have never really studied the broach before. I have been reading a book about early jewelry and its noted creators. Because of this I was, for the first time, really studying the pattern of the filigree to see if I could determine if it matched that used by past masters. Then I suddenly spotted the tiniest scrap of white where gold should have been. Using tweezers, and believing the same to be just something caught up in error, I gently pulled the scrap. No one was more surprised than I when it transpired to be a folded piece, obviously deliberately hidden."

Taking the magnifying glass from the center draw of my desk I inspected the paper in detail.

(What looked like a tailless fish) Find the guardian of the Saviour drawn from the water.

(Another sketch of a tailless fish) Take three paces south and in a metal tomb lies the caretakers charge.

I confess that I found this intriguing as I reread the message. Questions flooded into my mind about the meaning of the words and more importantly, and possibly more revealingly, who might have hidden such a cryptic clue and why. What a very strange place to conceal it as well?

As is the talent of the brain possible solutions rose in answer. It was likely to have been one of Nicole's ancestors who had hidden the note. Nobody else would have had access to the jewellery nor the desire to hide anything in it. The writing was small and cultured so this supported the premise that a lady was the author.

"Did your Mother ever mention the fact that the jewel held a secret? Or even that there was a secret she guarded?"

"Never. This is a complete mystery. I am sure if Mamma knew of the paper, she would have mentioned it."

I then remembered that her Father, many years ago, had mentioned over dinner one evening that one of his ancestors had begun the family fortune by inventing and selling safe areas on trading ships.

"… in a metal tomb … That would indicate that your ancestor used a safe of some sort in which to place whatever this clue pertains too."

"Yes. Oh, yes. That's it," she squealed with childlike delight and clasped her hands together.

"Again, the fact that it is referred to as a 'tomb' indicates that it must be buried."

"Oh, you are so clever. Yes. That is exactly the inference. What do you think it means by the 'caretakers charge'?" Rarely had I seen such exuberance displayed by my wife. Her normal mood, even when entertaining and thereby laughing hospitably, always held a reserve of buried sadness. I always thought that this indicated the depth of despair which she felt for being childless. This unfettered excitement was most endearing and it was my earnest desire to foster it.

"Well whatever the caretakers charge is, it must be important. It's an odd phrase 'caretakers charge'."

It is a peculiarity of human nature that strong emotion is oft transmitted from the source to those around. The high degree of Nicole's interest and excitement quickly infected me. I found myself completely enraptured by the intrigue presented by this innocuous slip. Only once before had I experienced such exuberance. That was when, accompanying one of my colleagues, he and I had uncovered the most perfect mosaic from the base of a Roman villa in England. As each meticulously placed piece of stone was brushed clean of the debris of the years, my heart had become lighter and more focused on the task. The whole had engulfed me such that the sky could have turned green and I should not have noticed. This slip held me in the same rapture.

(A sketchy tailless fish) Find the guardian of the Saviour drawn from the water.

This was the real test of the piece. Once we had solved this riddle the physical instructions contained in the second line were simple. Unfortunately, nothing came to mind. Search the recesses of my mind as I would, no resolution about this strange incantation revealed itself. The path was cold. Luckily, I have a talent for not letting a seemingly dead end stop my progress. Such is the very nature of my chosen profession which oft times is based on sheer tenacity of purpose.

"I shall see if the library at the University reveals any clues tomorrow. It seems that this line may be referring to a fort or garrison building guarding something. The real task is to interpret what or whom 'the Saviour drawn from the water' is."

"Will you? Oh, thank you. I really want to find out what this clue is about and why one of my ancestors felt it necessary to so hide it, that it remained undisturbed over, what may have been, so many generations." With this Nicole recovered the broach from my desk where it lay and turned to leave my study with the comment that she must begin to dress for the evening.

True to my promise, the next day having finished my lectures, I repaired to the library. I spent several hours reading the titles of the many bound volumes held therein, to see if any of them hinted at a possible resolution. I extracted five or six books and glanced through their index but, frankly, nothing held any portend of success. The problem was that I had no point of reference from which to decide upon even which country, let alone topic, was worthy of exploration.

Before leaving the well-stocked library, I decided on a whim, to enquire of the librarian who was sitting by the administration desk. It was a forlorn hope I knew but most of these fellows were widely read and as such in possession of a broad base of knowledge.

"Excuse me," I ventured. He looked up from the tome he was studying.

"Oui, Monsieur. How may I help?"

"I don't suppose in your research that you have come across the expression 'Saviour drawn from water', have you?" The man donned a faraway look in his eyes as if he was spiritually wandering along the darker recesses of his mind. I remained silent, as did he.

"The phrase does ring a bell, I must admit, but where from I cannot think at the moment. It seems to me that it is a long time ago I read of it or heard it. But I cannot quite put my finger on the incident at the moment. May I ask you to return tomorrow, Monsieur, and in the meantime, I shall try and recall the context in which it came to me?"

I thanked the man whilst, almost subliminally, noting that he was obviously drawn from one of our foreign students judging by the twang in his accent. With that I returned home determined to again visit the library on the following day. In spite of Nicole's disappointment, she maintained a calm expectancy. She was not a lady of impatient nature thankfully; and since friends, unusually, called upon us unannounced that evening there was no opportunity to discuss the matter again.

The next day, having discharged my duties, I stepped out for the library. The same man was by the desk. Without further ado I approached him.

"Bonsoir, Monsieur," I began.

He immediately and with some excitement laid down the book he had been studying and returned the greeting.

"I must thank you, Monsieur," he exclaimed, "for had you not enquired of that phrase yesterday I should not have spent such a pleasant evening sauntering along the lanes of happy memories." I was stunned. How could these two instances converge?

"Pardon me?"

"As you may have guessed, from my imperfect Parisian, I am not from your fine country. Indeed, no. I fare from Scotland; a kingdom north of the lands belonging to the English King."

"Really?" I tried to sound interested but whether I succeeded or not is unknown. My mind was focused on a solution to the riddle not on his heritage.

"As I mentioned yesterday the phrase rang a bell in my mind but I could not place it."

"Yes. That's right. I remember."

"So last evening, whilst I supped, it suddenly came back to me where I had heard that expression. It was from my Mother; God rest her soul."

"Really?"

"Oui; indeed. My mother originally hailed from a group of islands off the northern-most coast of Scotland named the Shetland Islands. That is where the term you enquire about comes from. One of the islands, my mother knew the names of them all, is called 'Mousa'. This in turn translates to 'Saviour drawn from the water'." He stopped speaking and looked at me triumphantly.

"An island, called Mousa, you say? How do you spell that?" He spelt it out for me and then continued.

"Ah oui. A most bleak place to be sure but that is certainly what the phrase is referring to."

"You have been most helpful, merci beaucoup, Monsieur." I passed the man a few coins in gratitude. I was about to take my leave when another thought occurred to me.

"Is there a fort, or castle, or a guard-post of some sort on this island?"

"No, Monsieur. There is not." I was disappointed until he continued. "Mind you, I believe there is a broch there."

"A broch? And what may a broch be?"

"Well, my Mother told me that brochs exist on many an island. There are apparently over a hundred of them. They are tall, round structures of man-made origin, though made by men of a far-gone era. No one really knows why they were built but there they stand to this day according to my Mother. If my memory serves me well, she did mention that there is one on Mousa."

I concluded our meeting having the impression that I had pressed all the information I needed from this fine fellow.

"Again, merci beaucoup, Monsieur. You have this day brought a deserved accolade to our University by possessing such obtuse but invaluable knowledge. A fine job indeed." With this praise ringing in his ears I took my leave and hurried home to update Nicole with my findings.

It was a simple matter for a man of means, such as myself, to acquire a ship and crew to carry me to our destination. So it was that Nicole and I set out for the island of Mousa, off the coast of Scotland, during my extended sabbatical gratifyingly approved by the University.

I shall not tarry on the details of the how Nicole and I made the discovery. Suffice to say, that we followed the clues. Having explored the terrain of Mousa we found its mysterious broch. Which, incidentally, It is purported was built around 100 years B.C. during the Iron Age. Having stepped out the requisite number of steps South, we dug down to form a shallow grave. At this location we came across a leather pouch. In it were a number of documents.

It was after this point that things really took a turn in our lives.

Having brought the precious package on board ship we instructed our captain to sail to England. We required him to head for the port of Scarborough, this being a busy, international port, from where we might continue our journey if we so desired. So it was, that here we alighted and decommissioned the vessel.

We knew of this town specifically due to its annual trading festival being of common knowledge in Europe. Scarborough had held this six-week event since 1253, if memory serves me, which information we had learned from Parisian traders attending the event.

It is also a factor in our decision that my beloved wife's family originally came from Scarborough. It therefore seemed more like a coming home, than a stop on our adventures.

It was here that we purchased a suitable house, overlooking the sea, and spent our remaining days. I was only to return to our beloved Paris apartment once more. Sadly, Nicole would not accompany me as she had succumbed to the fever and died.

Soon my study in the Scarborough home was ready for occupancy. I again unfolded the collection of documents held in the recovered box and reread them; culminating with the texts recorded by the Jew from Jerusalem so very long ago.

Our cursory inspection of them whilst aboard ship had not left the same deep impression now experienced in the quiet surrounds of my study. Many times during this second reading I stopped and, looking out onto our beautifully manicured gardens, reflected on the implications of the words therein. It was during these times that I first truly realized the importance of this treasure.

As I continued this task, slowly and deliberately, it occurred to me that only the educated or religious could even begin to read them.

Whilst the first document had been written in an old form of Greek, (which even I had to use a lexicon for), the whole was only accessible to those, such as myself, who boasted a sound knowledge of Latin. No more so than because some of the words and phrases used were no longer in common use in the language.

So it was that I determined to devote my otherwise idle days into the task of writing all the accounts in French.

I planned to retain the package intact but include this modern translation into the anthology. I deduced that by the time I had finished this exercise, the collection would have become too vast to be held within the original leather pouch. So it was that I decided that a new container must be acquired to house both the original texts and my French translations.

As you will have discerned, I am not a flamboyant man by nature. This is a malady I put down to a complete lack of effort required by me, to this point, in having to achieve anything. Everything I own has been handed to me with no effort on my part.

Whilst this may sound idyllic to those who strive for even the basics of life, allow me to assure you that it has a side effect of suppressing desire and even hope. Ambition is unknown to me. I have never needed any.

It was onto this blank slate of passion that the words, as I wrote each one, forged a deep groove. As the Jews' records were painfully translated, the messages therein wrote into my heart, inspired me and caused a change in my very nature. For the first time I began to care why I lived and what I was to do with my life.

Nicole, too, was undergoing a breath of passion in her life. She had quickly allowed herself to become immersed in the social gatherings afforded by and for the ladies of Scarborough. On one such occasion she had attended an assembly where speakers delivered entreaties on behalf of the poor. As she and I sat by the fire late that evening she regaled me with some of the ideas and experiences of which these wordsmiths had spoken.

"Some people cannot even afford to house themselves and many die during the winter months unattended by any." A pause. "Women give up their babies, or even knowingly leave them to die outside, because they cannot produce the natural milk to feed them."

"Perhaps they should have been wiser not to allow themselves to become with child?" I uttered in a more gentle manner than the written word portrays.

"It is not, I understand, always the woman's choice or desire to conceive. Sometimes it is unfortunate circumstance, or even poverty itself, which causes the conception. Mr Hilliard, one of the speakers, said that many women have to turn to selling their bodies to men in order to feed themselves and perhaps the children they already have. How must it feel to be a surviving sibling knowing that one's younger brother or sister died so that you may live? It must be a terrible burden upon them."

"Perhaps they do not know or do not care? The will to survive is strong. They may just feel that they are the lucky ones and that their younger siblings were merely the object of misfortune?"

"But how must the mother feel? How could anyone, who has carried a child for nine months, then give up their baby without being wracked by guilt? How could she?" My wife's distress was evident as she struggled to understand this apparently callous behaviour. She naturally felt deeply on this subject seeded from her own heartfelt desire for motherhood.

"I do not know, my dear. We cannot possibly understand another's thinking without having been in their position."

"But – (pause) - we must do something. I cannot stand by and let this happen. It is completely unacceptable to ignore this travesty." She paused again and I, upon looking at her, could almost physically discern the rapid activity within her thought processes as she struggled to find a solution. None came to vocalization; instead her eyes fell upon the fire until finally a look of futility masked her face.

"I will give the matter some thought," I promised.

That ended the conversation that evening and try as I might to lighten the mood before it was time to retire the pall of the situation remained present in the room.

The next morning over breakfast the topic continued as if there had been no interruption.

"There was one woman there yesterday whose husband and two sons had been drowned in a storm whilst they were fishing at sea. The look in her eyes of hopelessness and sorrow burned into my heart. In one day, her sole means of keeping house and indeed buying food had gone; this on top of the sorrow of losing her whole family in one misfortune."

My first thought was for the peace of my own wife and so I responded a little impatiently. "I am not sure that you should be attending such meetings, my dear. They obviously upset you greatly. It is the task of the church to deal with such issues not the ladies of Scarborough."

"It was the church who organized the meeting. They used it as a forum to elicit donations."

"Well I think it was careless and underhand of them to do so. If the church needs money it should approach the men-folk not burden the wives with such matters. I disapprove strongly."

"Why? Why should women not be informed of such travesty existing? Women are the ones who care the deepest on such issues and as such it is women who will beseech their husbands to increase their donations. I think the church was absolutely right to approach us."

"My sweet child; women are the gentle sex. They are to be protected by men from even an awareness of such travails. I have always undertaken to keep anything upsetting far away from your gentle countenance and I am disturbed that the church has seen fit to over-rule me in this matter."

"By what right do you keep me in ignorance?" Her eyes sparkled with indignation which beauty had the undesired effect of making me even more protective of her.

"There is nothing to be done, that is why. The world is a cruel place for some and that is an end to it. Why should you be troubled by things you cannot change? We men are aware of the injustices in nature and see no reason to burden your sweet selves with such matters."

Silence fell over the repast. I continued my meal whilst she, by way of protest I am sure, noisily placed her utensil on the plate and sat unmoving staring at the table. As I rose mumbling about returning to my study she did not move. As I walked to where she sat to deliver the customary kiss before departing, she did not move. I kissed her on the top of her head this being the only place open to me and took my leave. She did not move.

I continued my work on the translation, but with only part of my mind on the subject matter. The emphasis of my thoughts surrounded the contretemps of the morning. I hated arguing with my wife, preferring peace to any other state, even if it meant agreeing to something where I felt I was in the right and her opinion was flawed. I had never seen such charged emotion emitted from Nicole and it made me realize just how placidly she normally accepted things. In some strange way I found this unexpected passion in her, endearing.

Eventually I determined to resolve the matter in the time-honoured fashion which had served me well all my life – with money. I should make an outstandingly generous donation to the church for the welfare of the poor. At dinner tonight I would announce this to Nicole and she was bound to forgive me and feel satisfaction that she had done something directly to solve the injustice she had discovered. This would pacify her conscience and peace would once again reign in our household.

She sat opposite me as usual that evening over the main meal of the day and had continued her countenance of not meeting my eyes directly. I put my plan into action.

"I have been thinking about what you said earlier and have decided that you are right." That was sure to act as a healing balm over the troubling wound. "And so," I continued, "I have decided to donate a substantial sum to the church as alms to the poor." The emphasis placed on the word 'substantial' indicated the unusual nature of the intended donation.

Slowly she looked up at me and responded in a manner I was not expecting. "That is very kind of you, dear. However, I wish to do more. I too have given the matter further thought and I have decided that it is beholden upon me to take direct action to alleviate the burden of these women so cruelly and unjustly afflicted."

My surprise was so sudden that I dropped my knife with a loud clatter onto the plate. "What do you mean? In what way?"

"I intend to open a home for these unfortunates which will provide a bed and a meal each day for those inmates. It will particularly cater for mothers of children and the home will contain a nursery area for the weaning of babies. I will not tolerate any more babies left to die on the streets."

"What?" Never before had I heard of such a thing. My mind was a flurry of imaginings trying to picture how such a scheme might work. Words failed me since so much of my mental capacity was taken up with these thoughts.

She hurried on adding descriptive detail to her plan. "I have spoken with the Priest on this idea and he informs me that there is a warehouse near the docks which will suit the purpose. He can procure it for the church for a very reasonable sum and is happy to do so as long as we meet the bulk of the cost of purchase." During this her tone had tempered and become less dominant with a hint of pleading entering her voice as if she was beseeching my approval.

It is true that one may be struck dumb with shock. So I was at that moment. I felt my mouth open as my jaw dropped but words were not an option. I was truly struck dumb. Even my mind was afflicted as I tried to translate her words unsure that I had heard correctly. This while, she was silent and just looking at me expectantly with a pleading sparkle in her eyes.

"But," I ventured, "but what will these women do? Who will feed them? Is that burden to fall upon us as well?"

"No. I believe that they can carry out tasks during the day to aid both the fishermen and traders in their industries. The warehouse can be a place where, if a fisherman's net needs repair, he may bring it and the women will mend it for him; or if a trader needs goods unpacking our women can do this work. There are many menial tasks, which do not require the strength of men-folk, which can be delegated to our women, in such a busy port. In this way they may earn a small living – at least enough to provide food."

"And how, exactly, do you mean to provide food for those with new-born babies who cannot work yet?" I did not mean this unkindly, but as the solid thought of a man's mind.

"I believe that, administered by the church, all money earned by any resident be put into a common kitty so that all women will be fed from the one community chest. That way, those who are able to work will earn food money for those unable to do so at the time." In spite of her apparent clarity of scheme I knew that she was only now deciding the fine detail for the plan.

"Do you really believe that there will be enough work for them? What if they turn to…" I hesitated "…selling themselves? How will you prevent that?"

"Lady Greasley, for one, has agreed that the fishing fleet her husband owns will employ the services of my women."

Shock again took hold of my very being and my innards shook. "You have spoken of this … idea … to Lady Greasley? Without asking me first? You have no right?" I blurted out indignantly.

Her anger rose instantly like a volcano which could no longer contain its explosion of fire. "I have no right? I have no right? I have every right. I am not your servant; I am your wife." Her chin stuck forward in defiance and her hands splayed on the table either side of her plate taking up the countenance of a tiger about to pounce. "I am a free Frenchwoman. I do not have to ask your permission for my actions. How dare you assume that you may dictate 'my rights'?"

"But … Lady Greasley of all people. Whatever must her husband think of me?"

"Her husband, Lord Greasley, will do whatever his wife wishes. He does not own her any more than you own me."

Silence fell like a tangible pall over us as a battle of staring passed between us. Mine founded from a shattering of my comfortable senior status; hers based on a newly formed passion of conviction. I was dumbfounded. Appalled. Confused.

Slowly her hands moved from the table and again settled on her lap as her anger subsided as quickly as it had arisen. "My husband," she began in a calm, even gentle, voice, "you know I would do nothing to bring dishonour to your family or mine. I do this because I know it is the right thing to do. It is within our means to bring an end to unnecessary infantile death, at least in our little corner of the world. It is beholden upon us, as Christians, to bring aid and comfort where we may. I must do this, you do see that, do you not?"

The gentleness in her voice disarmed me faster than any anger on her part could have done. I listened, which I might not have been willing to do if she had still been raising her voice. It made me reflect on her words. Even so, silence was my only offering at this time since I did not know what to say. We remained thus for some time. Eventually, as my thoughts gathered, I dared to speak.

"I believe the Lord said 'There will be poor always'." I countered a little petulantly.

"He also said that we were to 'to visit orphans and widows in their affliction'. She continued; I believe that Isaiah, the prophet, also said 'Learn to do good; seek justice, correct oppression; bring justice to the fatherless, plead the widow's cause'." She sat and earnestly looked at me. Since I knew she was not an avid Bible reader either it was evident to me that she had prepared this statement in advance.

"You know that I am not a pious man but you also know that I do hold as precious the words of Our Lord. Perhaps you are right. Perhaps this is something we can do – indeed should do? Let us finish our meal and repair to the fire to discuss the practicality some more." That evening we concluded our initial discussions and I authorized the attendance of the Priest to discuss the price of the warehouse.

In two short months plans were in place to house the homeless mothers and their children. There was no comfort in the building, but flat stones were placed at intervals on the upper wooden floor, to allow small fires to heat parts of the expansive room. At least the unfortunates would be free from precipitation and protected from the vicious wind. An inspection area on the ground floor was allocated for the new-born babies and their mothers and a weekly visit, paid for by me, was arranged with a local doctor.

Strangely, it was finding women to house in our warehouse that proved the greater challenge. At first, they were suspicious of our offering and reluctant to take it up. The truth is that those in the greatest need rarely attend church so even the Priest was unable to help in this matter. It was not an option to go out in the evenings and identify those living on the streets and so it was finally decided that word of mouth, from the servants of concerned ladies, be used. This proved a fruitful approach and soon our warehouse was populated.

Lady Greasley and others were as good as their word and able to furnish some of the residents with small but welcome incomes. True, there were times of the year when I needed to open my own purse, but the annual Traders Festival always brought in greater profits than expenditure and allowed some degree of buffer against the leaner months.

Having completed this task and established it under the sole management of our local Priest, matters returned to the more normal. I continued my slow and painstaking translation work and Nicole contented herself with knitting and sewing garments for the residents of our warehouse – her emphasis always being on garments for the babies in the community. Peace once again settled on our household and I was content.

One evening in the late autumn however all was to change again. A knock at the door unexpectedly admitted the Priest in charge of the community, Father Francis. His cape swirled as he entered and showed signs of the heavy precipitation outside. He dispensed with the usual formalities but immediately apologized for disturbing us in such an unbidden manner. Nicole and I gathered with him by the roaring fire.

"I would not, as you know, presume to disturb you in such a crass manner unless I considered the matter most urgent," he apologized again. "The fact is that, under the terms of admittance to the home, it is written that children are only allowed entry if accompanied by their mothers, as you know." This was indeed a clause I had included so that children were cared for by their own relatives and need not be supervised.

"Yes. That is correct." I responded, nodding. Nicole did not move a muscle.

"Well, a short time ago a lad, of maybe six or at the most seven years knocked on the door and asked for entry." I waited.

The Priest continued. "As a rule, I should merely have driven him off but this lad was holding in his arms a new-born and my heart melted."

"Where did he come by the baby?" enquired Nicole instantly.

"As near as I can gather, his mother had delivered the baby girl just a few hours earlier. She had unfortunately died immediately afterwards, leaving the boy with his new sister and with nowhere to turn. The lad, his name is James I have established, knew of our home and had dared, driven by desperation, to approach us."

"Has the lad no other family?" I asked. "What about the father?"

"The boy informed me that his father had died some years before. His mother had earned a living from washing and sewing for some households but now that she was gone James had no idea what to do. He says there are no other members to his family." Father Francis stopped and looked from me, to Nicole, and back again to me.

"Where do they live? Do they rent or have they property?" This seemed a reasonable question to me, although had I thought deeper, I should have realized that none in their position would own property.

"James declares that they live in a rented room but they are already behind on the dues and had been planning on leaving as soon as the confinement was ended."

"So has the baby had any food yet?" asked Nicole stirring in agitation.

"I know it is against our agreement but I took pity on the pathetic pair standing sodden in the rain and admitted them long enough to allow a nursing mother to feed the baby."

"So what do you want us to do?" I asked since I, as yet, did not comprehend what the Priest's purpose was in visiting us.

"Sir; Madam; I beg you to allow me to admit this foundling boy and his sister to the safety and comfort of our sanctuary. The night is raw and I fear that if she has no shelter the baby will be dead by the morn."

Nicole looked at me, anxiety written across her face. I knew instantly what her instinctive answer would have been and admired her for not over-ruling my preferences in front of company.

"Who will care for the pair if we do allow this?" I asked.

"Sir, the mother who fed the baby has already expressed her willingness to do so. It was her, along with another three women, who begged me to approach you on this matter urgently. They are most anxious that the boy and the baby not be expelled into the night air."

"There is a problem with this. If we allow this lad and his baby sister to remain, what message will that portray in the town? Shall we not end up with every orphan in the neighbourhood clambering at our door? The warehouse is designed for those who may earn an honest living for themselves given the opportunity." My logic was inescapable.

"Where are the children now?" enquired Nicole with concern. She seemed oblivious to my last entreaty.

"They are with the mothers warming themselves by the fire, ma'am."

Nicole looked at me pleadingly. The angle of her head moved slightly to the side to enhance her request. I was left in no doubt which way her mind was resolved although, out of respect for me, her mouth remained silent.

"They may certainly stay for tonight, Father. I would not turn a dog out on such an evening. As for tomorrow, we shall review the matter again and decide what to do in the longer term."

"Thank you; thank you indeed, sir. My Christian solicitude is rewarded as you will be by the Almighty, I am sure. The mothers too will be most gratified by your generosity." With this the gentleman bowed and swiftly took his leave, again stepping out into the cruel autumn weather.

The next morning, I sent word that I should visit the Priest at ten of the clock, at his residence and requested that the children in question be in attendance for that meeting. As the time to leave approached I gathered my cloak and hat from the stand in the hall and turned to exit.

"Wait for me." This cry came from Nicole as she quickly descended the stairs pulling on her bonnet.

"Are you coming with me then?" I enquired.

"I wish to hear in what manner this matter is to be resolved."

"Now you know, my dear, don't you, that they cannot stay at the warehouse. In truth I am hoping that the Priest has found some alternative arrangements for them."

Nicole looked at me earnestly. Her mouth did not speak but I knew from that single glance that she had some "alternative arrangements" of her own in mind. I dreaded what these might be.

The day had turned pleasant with the sun shining brightly as if it was newly washed from the rain the night before. This gave one the illusion that the world was not such a tragic place after all. By the time we arrived at the Priests residence both Nicole and I were in a less serious mood. Indeed, Nicole seemed almost playfully youthful, like a child on the eve of the annual fair. This demeanour of hers transmitted to me and I, for unknown reasons, felt lighter of heart.

We were immediately admitted to the Priests residence by his housekeeper and shown into his study where he sat behind his desk. The two orphans huddled beside his unlit fire. On entry the Priest, of course, instantly rose, in deference to my wife, only returning to his seat once she and I were seated.

"Sir; Madam; may I introduce you to James and his sister." He pointed, quite unnecessarily, to where the boy sat on the floor cuddling his new baby.

My wife was the first to react. "How do you do, James, and what is your sister's name?"

The boy looked terrified. "Ma'am; I do not know. We never named her – not yet." He looked down at her lovingly. She remained awake but silent. Blue, sightless eyes staring upwards into the face of her brother.

"I understand your mother has sadly died?" Nicole held a kindly smile and a sympathetic tone.

The boy's eyes filled with tears as he croaked out "Yes, ma'am. Yesterday."

"May I hold your sister, James?" With this Nicole rose and stepped slowly towards James as one might approach a deer to not startle it. He showed no agitation at this request as if he sensed that his salvation lay in the hands of this fine lady. With care, and I detected pride, he gently held the baby up at arms lengths. Nicole bent and reached for the tiny child. Having safely grasped it, she drew it up to her breast and stood tall again. She then proceeded to become lost in her own world, dominated by the small creature, as she made nursery noises to it and rocked it gently up and down. The Priest and I just stared at the sight. It was clear that Nicole was a natural mother and had instantly fallen into the silent communion that binds a parent to its baby.

"Yes. Well," I cleared my throat which had contracted at such a beautiful sight, "we must decide what must be done with these children."

"Indeed." I was disappointed at the Priest's monosyllabic response. I had truly hoped that he possessed a solution. He obviously did not.

"Do you have anyone willing to take them in, within your parish?"

"No, sir. I do not. Most of my congregation are struggling with their own progeny and in no way able to cater for another. The women at the sanctuary are not against the boy working for them in return for nurturing but the baby is completely impractical."

"So what do you propose we do with it?" Again, I tried to make the Priest responsible.

We looked at each other. We both knew that deserting it onto the street was tantamount to the death sentence, and neither were willing to become the executioner. Then we both, at the same time, looked across to where Nicole nestled the babe. She appeared lost to us with her whole being centred around the mite, as she rocked it up and down whilst pacing one way then the other in gentle steps. As if sensing the silence which had fallen on the room, she looked up, first at the Priest and then to me.

She addressed the Priest. "I have an idea but must speak privately to my husband before voicing it."

"Certainly, madam." The Priest immediately rose and signalling James to follow him went to leave the room. James was a little more reluctant to be parted from his charge but having again assessed that his sister was safe with this stranger, followed. They exited the room with the Priest quietly closing the door behind them.

Before she spoke, I knew what Nicole's entreaty was to be.

"She is adorable, is she not?" My wife looked at me and her words directed my sight to the baby in her arms. As I looked for the first time at the infants face my countenance involuntarily melted and my hand reached out, unbidden, to touch its perfect face. I did not understand until that very moment how great the instinct to protect the young is in the human. Even the harshest nature of a solitary and disciplined man such as myself dissolved as I stared into that angelic face. The pure miracle of a new life impinged upon my soul and it was all I could do not to grab the baby and cuddle it to my chest.

At last, sense took hold and I forced my eyes away from the precious bundle. "Now, Nicole, do not get any ideas. We cannot adopt the baby."

"Why not?"

"Well, because … because …" I could not think of one good reason.

My mind became a whirl of visions. A child would change the whole way we lived our lives. There would be no more solitude and quiet. Our days would be dictated by the small creature. It would emit crying and temper and demands … she would encourage love and laughter and tears of joy. No. It would disrupt our whole life. She would bring utter fulfilment to Nicole. No, the idea was ridiculous. Why? At last I found a reason …

"James. How would James feel to lose his baby sister?" A terrible thought hit me. "You are not, I hope, proposing that we also take James into our family? Are you?"

"I had not thought of that, I admit, - but, why not? It would give you a son. You must admit you have always wanted a boy. I think that's a splendid idea of yours." She ended with a smile on her face.

I could not gather my thoughts fast enough to realize that she was suggesting that adopting James had been my idea. Surely, I had not suggested that? Maybe I had? No, I'm sure I hadn't had any such thought. But, was it such a remote idea? He seemed like a harmless child and he certainly showed a maturity beyond his years in approaching the warehouse. It was we Catholics who say "give us a child until it is seven and it will always be a Catholic". The boy was only just turning seven but more likely to be just six so I still had time to mould him to my ideals. He is young enough. With new clothes and a bath, he is a good-looking young lad too. Was it true that I was instantly and unexpectedly to become a father?

Nicole's attention had returned to the bundle in her arms. The baby made a contented gurgling sound as if she had been privy to the conversation and approved. Nicole spoke gently to her. "Are you coming to live with us, then? Yes. We have a lovely new home for you. Yes we have. And your big brother is coming too. Isn't that nice? Yes, it is." The infant gurgled happily.

Both children became ours.

The baby we named Michelle. James and Michelle brought utter disruption - and pure delight - into our lives. At times the children tested our patience but they also forged Nicole and I into a new form of partnership. We worked together in bringing them up in the values we held dear, and delighted in watching their individual personalities develop. They formed an added bond between us as we, with mutual respect, made decisions for them and about them. We had never worked together on anything before – and we like it. One of the greatest mysteries of parenthood is that, as we form the child, the child forms the parents. Nicole and I changed our opinion of what is important in life and we both mellowed greatly in our outlooks.

There was only one major decision left to be made by me. I had chosen the right wife. I had chosen the right children. Now I must decide what to do with the very important writings which had been put into my care.

My French translation had, finally, amid numerous disruptions, been completed and the package was complete. I had written my own account thus far, which I humbly submit here for your approval. The final decision was now ready to be made. What must I do with this invaluable insight?

Europe, I am sad to say, is still in total disarray with the various religious factions. In fact, if anything, the situation seems to be getting worse. Therefore, in spite of these revelations being of a religious nature, I feel insecure in favouring any faction with their contents.

I was right, so long ago, to assume that the package would increase in volume sufficiently to have outgrown its original pouch or even the little safe box. I was not of a mind, however, to remove the pouch from the collection since it was such an integral part of the collections' history.

I therefore only placed the texts and translations, Greek/Latin and French, of the original author, the Jewish trader, into the pouch. The later 'caretakers' accounts, for so I thought of we who are joined in harmony of responsibility through the centuries, lay loose in the little safe box.

I purchased a highly ornate wooden box from the Annual Traders Festival sufficiently large so as to contain twice the number of documents and comfortably house those already in existence, both in the pouch and outside it.

I have a premonition that more will be written in the future – perhaps much more. The inside of the box, I was delighted to discover, was lined with some sort of metal such that it would offer a modicum of protection from decay.

The little safe box, in which I had discovered the collection, I removed from the package. It remains to this day as the 'Family Box', into which all precious documents and records relating to our family are stored. This may be found in our bank along with

Nicole's jewellery which shall now be passed to our beloved son and daughter respectively.

In an effort to find inspiration for where I might conceal the treasure, for such was my decision, I enquired of many traders, from across the world, on the state of things. This, depressingly, repeatedly revealed that it was not just Europe which was in chaos, but that it was a common feature of humanity. If turmoil was not being caused by religion then it was affected by political issues, or economic climates, or plagues which were wiping out whole peoples. This was not a time to travel afar. It was against this backdrop that I formed the idea the bundle must be secreted as close to my present location as possible but equally not housed in any building or monument which might be destroyed. My mind was blank. I was without inspiration as to a trusted location.

As it had been Nicole and her jewellery which had set this saga into motion, so it was Nicole and her jewellery which concluded it. Her birthday approached and since most of her adornments had been inherited, I decided that something new would delight her. Thus, my mind was set upon purchasing for my dear wife a new and extravagant piece of jewellery. Putting this plan into action, some weeks before her celebration day, I took myself to a merchant who dealt in such items and of whom I had heard favourable reports.

"Good morning, sir." The merchant greeted me, bowing his head slightly, as I entered his storeroom. He was an elderly gentleman, instinctively I felt of Jewish descent, who wore nothing to denote any semblance of wealth or prosperity.

"Good morning," I replied. My eyes rose from his countenance and viewed, through the dimly lit housing, to spy any display of his wares. There were none. A table, two simple chairs and a single lamp were the only things visible. There was a door at the back of the area which obviously led to some inner sanctum carved out of the hill against which this room leaned. I continued, having lost some confidence in his ability to satisfy my needs, "I understand that you trade in fine jewellery. It is this that I am after. Have I the right merchant?"

"Indeed you have, sir. May I enquire the purpose or design of the vestment of which you seek?" Again, he gave me that little bob of the head indicating subservience. To be truthful, I found it a little irritating rather than satisfying.

"It is a piece of fine jewellery that I seek for my wife."

"And what, may I humbly enquire, is the preferred stone of your good lady?" The bob again but this time accompanied by a gentle rubbing of the hands.

"I really do not know. She has many fashioned pieces." For the first time I realized that I did not actually have knowledge of what she wore. She always looked delightfully decorated but as to the detail, I was in ignorance.

"I see, sir." These words were the opposite of the truth for nothing I had conveyed could have given this merchant any glimmer of understanding of the detail of my needs. He was persistent I will grant him that as he tried to glean more information. "And may I ask if the lady is of similar age to yourself?"

I confess I was taken aback by this impertinence. "I beg your pardon?" I barked in indignation. The merchant was quick to explain.

"Sir, please do not take offence at my enquiry. It is merely that a younger lady of quality would be attracted to the more garish and highly coloured gems, whereas a lady of more mature years leans, from preference, to a more sedate hue."

"Ah. I see." This, as a factor in my wife's choice of jewels, had never occurred to me. "Well then, my good lady is similar in age to myself and I should determine that the more refined costume is her preference."

"Thank you, sir. If I may be so bold, may I also enquire as to her general stature?" Even before I could open my mouth in protest at such impertinence he continued quickly. "The only reason I ask, sir, with the greatest humility and respect, is that a lady of, shall we say, fuller proportions, finds the more substantial vestments pleasing, whereas a lady who is fine of figure and small of stature often prefers more delicate adornments."

"I see. Very well then, my wife is small of waist, delicate of feature, gentle of nature, and dainty of step. Does that answer your question?" In truth, pride crept into my soul as I described her. These attributes of her unchanging beauty had not been the focus of my thought for many years and I enjoyed noticing them again as if for the first time.

"Indeed, you have answered fully my professional enquiries, sir." The annoying bob of the head again. "May I ask just one more impertinent question, which in truth holds great pertinence? Sir, do you happen to know your wife's favourite colour?"

"I do not believe she has one." I thought more while the old man waited in silence. "She wears garments of many colours. Her wardrobe is quite extensive I should say. For evening events she does possess a deep red gown. On thinking, I believe it is with this fine garment that I would wish her to wear my purchase. Yes. The stone and setting must agreeably sit with deep red."

"Sir. You have come to the right merchant. I have exactly the right stone and setting for your good lady." So saying the old man lit a second lamp which had been hidden beneath the table and disappeared with it behind the door at the back, shutting it behind him so that, try as I might, I could not see into the enclosure. Shortly he returned.

"Here, sir. The lady you have described could not help but be delighted with these." In his outstretched hand he held two of the most beautiful, delicately set, earrings I had ever seen. The stone which fell from each gold setting was as black as the night in winter. Rather incongruously, he then took one of the earrings and held it up to simulate it dangling from an ear. His head slightly to the side, displayed in splendour, the stones long drop.

"These will be a peacock's fan to the lady's fine long neck. Accentuating her beauty and by their simple design not detract from the delicacy of her face." He grinned. The picture, with him holding the earring to the side of his face, with his wizened look grinning, was quite grotesque.

"May I see them outside in the light?"

"Certainly, certainly, sir." The old man leapt into action and squeezed past me to the outer door clutching the earrings in his hand again. We both exited the building and he held up both articles to the bright sky like twin moons. They shone in dark perfection.

"May I?" I reached out my hand to grasp the pair of droplets. He acquiesced happily. I held them up myself and stared into each one looking for faults. There were none.

"And may I add, sir, that in my humble opinion, no greater compliment to deep red is there than deeper black."

"What stone is this?"

"This is named 'jet', sir. It is a fine gem in great demand by the aristocracy, of which I discern you are a member. It has been used to decorate ladies of special beauty since the beginning of time and was, I understand, a particular favourite of the ladies of ancient Rome.

"From where is it mined?" My curiosity was unleashed and would only be sated by knowing more on this remarkable fashion.

"I believe that it has been found in local mines but that is just hearsay. The Roman conquerors ran several such mines in the area but these have long since been exhausted."

"Locally you say? So, they are inexpensive then?" I could actually see the old man's brain running at full velocity as he struggled to undo his previous statement.

"No, dear me, sir. No indeed. As I mentioned the Romans took most of the jet from this area. These fine stones came to me from the other side of the world. There price must, obviously, reflect the cost of travel."

"From where then?"

"I do not know their exact history or discovery. I am aware that they are formed over millennium from the remains of what is called the "monkey puzzle" tree. These, themselves, are rare indeed."

I confess that botany had never been a favourite subject of mine and my knowledge on such matters was very limited. I was, however, taken by the fervour of this old man, as well as the demure grandeur of the articles in question, so that, following much debate and bargaining, I procured the jet earrings.

Nicole was delighted with her gift which I presented on her birthday. She was the more thrilled that I had had the discernment to decide what would suit her, even more than the gems themselves. They reside with her other jewels now and are brought out at every opportunity being the most favoured of her collection.

It was the smallest of topics, related to this event, which was to prove the resolution for a suitable hiding place for the documents which now occupied my mind with some urgency. The old man had mentioned that the Romans had mined jet in the area but that the mines now stood empty. One of these locations must surely provide the security and protection that I was seeking?

I made it my business, by asking many, to get some idea of the location of these disused mines. I found a most suitable one on an exploration along the Esk valley, not far from the steep Whitby harbour entrance. This valley is formed by sloping sides climbing steadily from the river further along, but steep near its entry to the North Sea.

Since the building of the toll bridge over the river at this point, some two hundred years earlier, it is easy to cross the water to explore both sides of the valley. The small entrance to the mine is part way up one rocky formation, itself partly secluded by the rampant tree growth. It has long since been owned by ground vegetation so that unless one is looking for it deliberately the mine entrance would be passed by undisturbed.

On entering the small cavern, armed with a filled lamp, I was surprised to find that after the initial passage it opened up sufficiently for me to, almost, stand erect. There were small alcoves extending from the main passageway but none of these made promise of leading further than a few feet into the rock. I soon came to the end of the passage and on turning saw that light still filtered from the entrance. This was comforting. What I found most pleasing was that the cave was utterly dry. There were no signs of water erosion within, nor moisture dampening the floor. Indeed, the whole mine sloped gently towards the entrance thereby forming a natural watershed for rain at the cavern's outer limits. It was high enough from the river to not be endangered by flooding. An excellent spot I decided.

Fallen around on the floor of the cavern were stones which some poor miner years ago had dislodged from its mother and left abandoned. Some of these were sizeable and would easily form a rough wall were one desired to have such. I was so desirous. The plan developed in my mind that to hide my charge safely it would be a small matter to simulate a rock fall at the entrance to an alcove off the main passage. This would discourage the idle from investigating behind the apparently unstable entrance and yet allow one guided to the spot to recover the treasure without too much trouble.

On exiting the ancient abandoned mine I stood still and visually explored the neighbourhood. It was also important, having found the hiding place, to describe how to find the right cave again. Unfortunately, I spotted no significant geological features with which to guide those who would take up the quest. I did not question that there would be such a person in the future. I returned home in a state of being both pleased and troubled. Pleased to have found the perfect hiding place; and troubled as to how to highlight, to the initiated only, its location.

I began to research Whitby and uncover its comparatively unremarkable history. As soon as I read certain facts, however, I knew in my heart that they were significant. The original name for the settlement, back in the mid six hundred, was 'Streonshal' and this name was changed to 'Whitby', meaning 'White Settlement', from the old Norse language, some four hundred years later Whilst the abbey there present has some remarkable history, I felt that it would be wrong to refer to it in my clue since, due to the present turmoil in the world, it may no longer exist when my successor looks for the treasure. I therefore decided to revisit the site and find a mechanism to guide the seeker from the town along the Esk valley.

It was some weeks later that Nicole and I ventured out on this adventure. She knew of the writings of course and was one with me in setting the clue for some future generation to discover, and perhaps publish, this remarkable find. As we sauntered leisurely by the river on that sunny afternoon, she revealed a sound idea she had had for where the clue might be hidden.

"I have given this matter some thought," she declared as we spoke of the clue. "I believe that we should have a family portrait commissioned to declare to those who follow in our family how the Lord contrived to grant us descendants; the very act of which was in itself a miracle."

"That is a wonderful idea." I did not as yet comprehend how this related to our present topic of hiding a new clue.

She looked across to me and I could tell that she knew I was still ignorant of her subject.

"The link you are struggling to find, my dearest husband" she smiled "is that within the portrait we shall secret the clue. I envisage the painting being set in your study with a scroll placed upon your desk and visible. On the scroll will sit the clue." I was stunned into silence. The plan was exceptional.

"I love the idea." I enthused. "How very clever you are?"

"Not really. I confess that I saw a painting at the gallery in Paris once which has forever stayed in my mind's eye. It contained a scroll in the background upon which writing was barely visible and I was enchanted by the idea of translating it. Try as I might I could not quite make it out, other than to establish it was written in some ancient language. The memory of the intrigue it aroused in me has always remained with me however."

"But what if someone other than the guided person finds the clue and uncovers the treasure?"

"There, my dearest husband, we must rely on God. He has brought the text this far through time and I am certain that He will protect it on its forward journey. He will touch the heart of the man who is to take up the treasure and dull the enthusiasm of one whom is not destined for it."

"Indeed. You are right of course. Sometimes it is easy to forget that man is not invincible. It is God who truly writes destiny. We shall do our duty, playing our part in His plan, then hand the caretaker-ship back to Him." I felt an emotion rising in me with the force of a tidal wave. It was a deep and abiding love for my wise and wonderful wife. I, at that moment, felt truly blessed and uttered a silent but fervent prayer of thanks to God for the unexpected blessings he had bestowed upon me.

"There. Look." This sudden cry had come from Nicole like the unexpected blast from a gust of wind. She had stopped walking, as did I. I looked in the direction that her hand pointed. "It is the face of a man - in the rock - see?"

I looked and as I stared, saw. There were his eyebrows; his eyes; his nose; his smiling mouth. It was unmistakable, once pointed out, that the rock formation did indeed form the picture of a smiling man. It was so clear to my vision now, that I wondered why I had not spotted it before on my previous sojourns. The answer was obvious – because I hadn't been looking for it, I hadn't seen it.

"How far from the mine is this rock?" Nicole enquired.

I looked around and knew that we were near to our destination. I had imprinted the view upon my mind before leaving the cave so as to find it again when the time was right.

"Near. Very near." With this I quickened my step and moved forward searching the line of the hillside. I continued until I spotted the tell-tale sign of the opening and ran up to it to confirm its location. This done I turned back and saw Nicole standing by the rock portrait.

"Walk back to me and count your steps as you do so" she called. I obeyed.

As I approached her, I declared "Forty-two. It is exactly forty-two steps from here to the entrance."

"Really? Forty-two steps? Then this is another sign that we are in the right place. Forty-two is a repeating and mystical number in Biblical terms. This … "she pointed to the ground in determined fashion "… is indeed where we are to deposit the ancient texts."

It was not practical for Nicole to enter the mine; however, she squealed with delight and clapped her hands like an infant as I took her to the spot and pulled aside the vegetation to display its opening. Enthusiastically, I explained the layout therein and my plan to simulate a rock fall to conceal the alcove in which would lie the box.

I commissioned the portrait and during its production wrote this account, in French as you can see, of my small involvement in this ongoing work of God. As I wrote, I was reminded me more and more of just how blessed I had been and it humbled me to believe that I had been a small part of this saga yet to unfold.

The artist, a local man of some repute, was a little surprised when I informed him of the setting for the family portrait. I did not divulge the purpose for the blank scroll I insisted on him placing upon my desk. As an added security, to ensure that the whole clue had room to display, I also insisted that a book with blank spine be sited in a bookcase behind the scroll. This would allow me more room, if it were required, for the clue to be discretely displayed. I did inform him that I should be adding some script to the scroll and took his learned advice on the pigment to be used. He never knew my purpose for such a strange addition but acquiesced to my exacting design and scale.

Nicole and I worked together on devising the clue and we eventually came up with the one you, dear reader, have followed. It was she who painstakingly copied the print with the finest of brushes, constant referral to textbooks and the copious use of magnifier. We copied the design of the childlike drawing of a fish without a tail to the front of each clue.

(Tailless fish) Walk beside the river leading from the white settlement of Streonshal.

(Tailless fish) Forty-two steps from the man who smiles find the truth he guards behind the fall.

This, as you have discerned, is what is written in Hebrew on the scroll. It seemed right to return the clue to the natural language of the original author. Look behind the scroll to the book and there you shall find my name and those of my wife and children as a testament to the miracle we were blessed to receive. The portrait I shall personally hang in our Paris apartment from where it shall, undoubtedly, begin its journey onward.

I pray that, as these documents are uncovered, the world is, at last, at peace. It is tempting to separate politics, economics and knowledge of God, but the truth is that they are all inextricably linked in the Divine plan. It is the very imbalance of these elements which is causing such discord in my time. I hope that humanity has recognized and rectified this misunderstanding by your time.

My Dearest Cousin,

I hope that the tale of the Parisian who moved to Scarborough, having found the treasure in Scotland, held you as enthralled as it did me? I found little direct humour in his writing although his tale was well worth reading. I could not help but observe his insular nature being slowly changed by his discovery. Did you notice it too?

The next author to explain his involvement in the treasure moved me to fits of laughter. I can so relate to his lack of common sense. Even so, my patience towards him, endeared me to love this strange, but wonderful, man. I hope you also find his exploits endearing.

I have given up trying to type in communication with you. Instead, the daughter of a friend of mine has agreed, for a minor fee, to type to my dictation. She uses all ten fingers. I am so impressed. My index finger is greatly relieved.

Yours in expectation,

Beattie

(Encl.)

Dearest Beattie,

Thank you for allowing me the privilege of reading about the exploits of the Parisian. I did, indeed, find the slow but marked change in the character revealing.

I took to the library, on your behalf, to ascertain the likelihood and veracity of this 16th century man. On all points, particularly with regard to the names of places and the Roman 'jet' exports, I found substantiation of the reality. Everything he illuminated about the time and geography is exactly how he expressed it according to our greatest historians.

I therefore conclude that this tale was genuinely written either at the stated time, or by one with exceptional knowledge of the period.

I am waiting with eagerness for the next tale.

Yours devotedly,

Jackie

The Alchemist

14th Century

It all started when I accidentally blew up the house. It was my sister's house. She was not pleased.

To be fair it was not totally my fault. I was distracted during a critical experiment – and – BOOM!

As an alchemist it was quite natural for me to be using black powder during an experiment. Was it my fault that someone cried out "Strangers approach", thus causing me to glance out of the window? I think not - it being a most natural reaction to such an unusual announcement.

When I turned back, however, no one was more surprised than me to find a bubbling cauldron, where previously calm powder had lain. I ran out of the door knowing that the experiment was past saving. Luckily, I was alone in the house.

BOOM! The house flew into hundreds of wood and wattle fragments. Only the floor and the sturdy structure beams were left unscathed. The roof was nowhere to be seen. I sat in the road and stared in disbelief at the remains of my sister's home.

The strangers had also been greatly alarmed. The two gentlemen, one a priest no less, had been riding past. At the explosion their horses, naturally enough, were greatly startled and had reared up, unseating their riders. The beasts had then taken off in the direction of the woods leaving the gentlemen sitting unceremoniously in the road. None of us spoke. We all three just stared at the very few remains of the house.

Fellow villagers were running towards us because, of course, everyone naturally runs towards an explosion! I must make a note of that illogical response. It must be a peculiarity of human nature. Personally, I feel that I would run away from such a commotion having more in common with the horses.

Realizing that my sister would, no doubt, also be running towards the loud boom, I stood and grabbed a sack from our sawing bench – which had strangely remained intact – and quickly began bundling anything which still resembled what it had been into the sack. It was my mistaken idea, that if I presented my sister with a sack full of her precious, if singed, possessions this would somehow lessen her agitation. I was wrong.

I prefer not to recall what passed between us. Suffice to say that my ears stung; my arm was black and blue for a week afterwards; and it was made clear to me that I was no longer welcome under her roof. Even though she did not now have one. Rather than be grateful for the collection I had made of her things, she declined to accept the sack, and suggested a use for it, the subject of which was not in its design.

And so it was that I found myself venturing out of the village with the offending sack carried behind me. I remained in Sweden the country of my birth. This was a good place to live since Magnus Eriksson had recently united both Norway and Sweden by his ruler-ship of both. In addition, many of our great cities had signed to become members of the Hanseatic League; this being a dominant trade alliance between ourselves and the southern countries on the other side of the Baltic Sea. It was this alliance which afforded me the opportunities important to my tale later.

For now, my priority was to earn a living. I pondered on this subject throughout my journey to Malmhaug, it being the second largest city in our land. I was attracted here because the name literally means 'gravel pile' or 'ore hill'. One thing an alchemist needs is a good supply of ores, so where better to settle? Besides, the dominant quayside here affords a struggling artisan an easy means of earning an income with all the sailors visiting here.

I earned my living as an entertainer. My ability to create different coloured smoke and flames never ceased to amuse, I am glad to say, so food and lodging were easily covered from my street art.

Mind you, the challenge was not without its setbacks. On first arriving at the port city I made the mistake of asking where I might procure the tools of my trade.

"Excuse me, sir. Might one enquire where I may procure ore?" I asked this of a passing trader who looked wealthy enough to know where to buy or sell any commodity. I surmised he was

British by his air of superiority and so addressed him, in what I hoped was, his native language. It is a fairly universally understood tongue and used commonly in trading, so I felt safe to apply it.

"Pardon me?" He looked quizzical. "You want ore?" He was obviously not Swedish, and I surmised that I had rightly applied the common trade language of English. Since I only hold a passing skill in English, it did not seem odd that he had reacted with a request for me to repeat my enquiry – which this time I did in a much louder voice, the better to aid his understanding.

He looked me up and down as if inspecting me before responding. "Well, indeed. I would not know, sir." I could not but detect a slight ire in his voice. "But I do hear tell that the Plough Arms has a back room where you may find what you are looking for."

"Thank you, sir. May I wish you a good day." Having thus responded I turned and began walking away. Turning back, I was a little perturbed to find that the trader was still watching me. He, in response to my turning, raised his arm and pointed to the direction in which I was walking, whilst nodding his head in affirmation. I was clearly going in the right direction.

There were not so many inns that the Plough Arms proved difficult to find, particularly as I now knew in which area it lay. I opened the door and entered. Not being one who frequented ale establishments I must confess to a little uneasiness on spying its occupants, which appeared to contain more than a few pirates. As I entered it seemed that every face turned to inspect me and an un-natural quiet overtook the room. I proceeded unabashed towards what appeared to be the bar area.

"Good day," I ventured to the very large man standing behind the serving area. "I have been informed that I might purchase ore here."

The man, who must have had a lot of experience dealing with strangers from foreign lands, smiled. "I might be able to help. How much are you thinking of spending?"

I had not anticipated this question and made a quick calculation how much, or how little to be more factual, I had available to invest. I informed him of a sum which should at least buy me two or three of the cheaper ore types from which I could concoct an entertainment.

"That much?" He laughed at which prompt my fellow occupants of the establishment returned to their beverage and conversations.

He then shouted towards a room behind the bar into which I could not see. "Kirstin. Come here."

Whilst awaiting the arrival of this lady I dared to look around the now noisy public area. It surprised me somewhat to see that two ladies, (I use the term loosely), sat upon the knees of gentlemen, (again a loose definition). This was not behaviour I had witnessed in our village. It must be a city thing I mentally concluded.

Kirstin appeared from behind the previously barely ajar door. She was certainly pretty but wore a little too much rouge for my parochial upbringing. "You want me?" She enquired of the bar keep, all the while staring at me.

"This gentleman has requested you." He responded.

"Well, that is not strictly true," I ventured. "Are you the one who sells ore?"

"Sells ore? That's a strange saying. Where are you from?" I was completely flummoxed by this question and was still trying to formulate an answer when she continued. "Never mind. Come on."

Relieved that she had bypassed that question, she indicated for me to follow her into the back room. This I did with some relief. My relief did not last long. I was expecting to discover racks of jars and boxes containing samples of metals and potions. Instead I found a room sectioned off by loose slung blankets suspended from a network of rope. She moved one "doorway" aside and there lay a bed. Not a rack of metals in sight. The light dawned on me in a flash of its own alchemy.

"No. No. Madam, you misunderstand." My horror was reflected by the involuntary movement of my body away from the bed.

"I am very excellent, sir. Well worth a good fare. Come." With this the lady lay prone on the bed displaying her lack of undergarments to full advantage. I was horrified. Fear gripped me and I ran from the room, out of the inn and only stopped some mile away from the Plough Arms.

Once I had regained a modicum of my composure, I realized how the mistake had occurred and spent some time thinking how to rephrase my desire. (I shudder even to use that word). It came to me that if I termed it in the form of requiring *iron* ore and precious *metals* then no hint of a misunderstanding was possible. I was immediately directed, by a port official, to the correct warehouse destination.

Duly armed with a mixture of metal ores, (I have never since left the word 'ore' unqualified), I found a spot on the quayside. Utilizing an old crate as a table, which henceforth became part of my entertainment kit, I began shouting for the crowds to draw near.

By alchemic action I would manipulate baryta so that, having exposed it to bright sunlight for some time it maintained a glow in a rather fetching pale green shade. This particularly delighted the ladies who would marvel at the properties of the pebble. Some even offered me items of their own jewelry and asked me to make them glow too. Of course, I never accepted the challenge. In my repertoire were many elements which I shall not identify for fear of giving away the secrets of my trade. Suffice to say that before long I had procured a heating method, containers which withstood heat, and tongues. These allowed me to perform startling flames, flashes and bangs in colours of red, orange, lilac and green; all of which delighted and amazed my growing audience. I became particularly favoured by children whose eyes would stand out in wonder at the magic of my exuberant performance.

However, my real passion was working with black powder. Many knew that when cannon were fired, such a volume of smoke appeared around the weapons, that they could not be used again because there was no vision to aim them. If I could but solve this problem then surely my fame and fortune would be assured. Mind you, I was very cautious when using this volatile black compound having experienced firsthand its destructive potential.

I did have one small accident. I was using a particularly volatile compound, intending to create a bright and startling climax to my performance, before making a final plea for funds from my watching audience. Unfortunately, what I had not taken account of, were the surrounding activities. I let my mixture ignite and create an ear-shattering explosion. There happened to be a troop of mounted soldiers passing. The chaos which followed was astounding – even to me.

Every horse, some frightened by the explosion, others by the fear from their fellow animals, reared and in one swoop nearly a third of the troop was unseated.

Some twenty men disappeared over the quayside followed quickly by a succession of splashes. One poor man landed in a large, open vat of black oil. He rose slowly like something from the deep sea indistinguishable as human.

One horse bolted and jumped in a flying leap into the well of a small, moored boat. The boat tipped up decanting the frightened animal into the water where it discovered, perhaps for the first time, that it could swim. The unfortunate oarsman was not so lucky. He did not swim and had to be quickly rescued by a nearby port official who unwittingly banged him on the head with his outstretched rescuing timber. The unfortunate oarsman disappeared under the water again. He was, I am pleased to report, recovered safely in the end, and apart from a lump on his forehead, appeared none the worse for his experience. His boat, however, was all but destroyed.

Two of the frightened animals had run off in spite of the best attempts to stop them by their riders. I never saw them again but just remember the bouncing bodies hurtling off towards the main street. This scene was followed by the unmistakable sound of women screaming coming from the direction in which they had galloped.

Needless to say, I did not hang around any longer than the time it took for me to gather my takings, tools and metal filings. I dared not venture out to the quay again that day and remained in my lodgings.

Probably the most startling experience which occurred was when I had the brilliant idea of harnessing lightening, by means of a metal rod, with the intention of bottling it in a flask at the other end of the rod. During an almighty lightning storm, I stood with my contraption on the roof of my lodging, cork in hand, ready to seal the bottle and oblivious to the rain.

"What do you think you are doing?" screamed my landlady as she hurried towards her door from the market.

"I am set to capture lightening." It seemed the most natural response in the world to me at the time.

"You intend to do what?" Her amazement at my reply had caused her to stop her headlong rush and stand still in disbelief with her head raised in my direction. She likewise appeared suddenly oblivious to the downpour.

"I am going to capture lightening and seal it in this jar".

"Why?" This question stumped me for a time. Why indeed?

"Because, madam, I am an alchemist and the art of experimenting with nature is at the base of my profession".

"You, sir, are an idiot! And what's more, you are not doing it on my roof. What if you burn my home down? What am I to do then?"

Memories of my sister's house returned but were quickly quashed as I assured myself there were no powders on the roof with me. "It is perfectly safe."

At that very moment a bolt from the sky struck a tree in the field next to the house. The ensuing bang and light was worthy of any alchemy I had performed to date. Due to the unexpectedness of the event I lost my balance and fell backwards, tumbling towards the edge of the roof. Catching myself just in time I clawed my way back to my apparatus. With cork recovered, I grabbed at the metal rod to remove it from the jar, in readiness to replace the rod with the cork, whilst hoping that a residue of the lightening was in my receptacle.

BANG! The resultant shock threw me backwards without touching the comparative safety of the roof and I fell, with velocity, onto the ground below. My rod certainly had held a residue I noted. As I opened my eyes, I found I was staring up, through a hail of rain, into the angry eyes of my landlady, who was staring down at me, hands on hips in the universal attitude of impatience.

"Idiot!" With this admonishment she retired through the door of her home slamming the door shut. I just lay where I had landed trying to recover use of my body which was still shaking. Shortly afterwards the window to the room I occupied was opened and my sack, bag and box were sent hurtling to the ground where I lay. "And don't come back," she screamed as she closed the window. I never saw her, nor my room, again.

The fact of losing my lodgings, added to by my reluctance to meet any military man in the eye since that previous incident, made my mind up. I had outstayed my welcome in this city. Reluctantly I came to the decision, as I sat in the pouring rain, that it was time for me to move on.

Thus determined I picked up my meager belongings and headed towards the quayside. On arriving there, I begged a lift from one of the trading ships, to cross the Baltic with them. Thus I landed in the southern states, at the Queen of the Hanseatic League, Lübeck.

My first order of business on landing was to procure supper by means of my talent for entertainment. The performance was warmly welcomed by this new audience and enough money was donated to afford me shelter and food for the fast-approaching night.

As with anyone in new surroundings I decided to take stock of my possessions and ascertain exactly which metal ores, minerals and powders I still owned. So saying, having fed on a delightful rabbit stew and black bread, I sat on my temporary bed and emptied out the entire contents of my carriers. It was during this inspection that I found a little, highly decorated cube, which I was sure I had never seen before.

"Hello, little fellow," I said to it as I picked it up. "And where did you come from?" The cube remained silent. "My; you are a fine piece, are you not?" Still silence.

Turning it over in my hands and moving it closer to the bedside candle I was delighted to discover that it was not a cube, but a box. "Ha! Useful as well as beautiful!" My probing fingers gently lifted its lid. What I found in there was unexpected to say the least. Wrapped in a fine texture piece of linen … was a fingernail. Just the one. A single, long fingernail.

"What?" My astonishment knew no bounds. I fully opened the linen on my bed and laid it out so as to see if there was a monogram on the box which might present a clue. Indeed there was. There, lying in a discreet corner was the unmistakable crest of His Holiness, the Pope.

I was so shocked that before giving it any thought I had leapt to my feet. In my hurry, I knocked the candle on the small table next to me and it fell accusingly to the floor. I was plunged into darkness as it had, incredibly, landed on its head. "A curse! I am cursed to Hell's darkness!" I stood absolutely still terrified, and stared unseeingly, into the blackness, awaiting sight of a demon. None came.

As my nerves gradually returned and the knots in my stomach slowly unwound, I formed a plan. First, I must restore light to the room. That, in itself, was a challenge. Normally I would light my candle from the central fire in the kitchen before ascending the stairs. The kitchen fire was always alight as it provided not only heat but the method of warming food. However, the thought of trying to negotiate the darkness downstairs was far from practical in my present state of mind.

Therefore, my only recourse was to locate both my tinder box and flints which were somewhere in my room. With trembling fingers, I searched my bed top for the flints which memory, not being hindered by light or dark, recalled had appeared when I had emptied my belongings from their holders earlier. My hand patted the bed. After what seemed a long time the sense of touch yielded a reward. My fingers further explored the hard surface and confirmed that this was, indeed, a flint rock. The other was quickly recovered being like a twin located in near proximity to my first discovery.

Click. I clashed the two rocks together. Light. Gone. Sparks had illuminated the room but for such an instant that had I blinked I should have missed their welcoming light. Click. Light. Gone. I continued in this instant creation of light then dark until my mind was at piece that no demon stood watching me. Now to find the tinder box. I had one smaller one which I carried as failsafe to my exhibitions, in case the lamp I normally used went out, and one larger one from which the small one was replenished as needed. It would be easier to locate the larger one whose home was under the darkened window. Click. Click. Click. I made my way across the room.

Click. Ouch! Stubbed toe. Click. Click. Ah! At last the instant outline of the box appeared. Now, using my fingers once more, (God bless the Almighty for thinking of such ingenious appendages), I was able to create a small pile of tinder on the top of the box having closed the lid. Click. Click. Light! The tinder caught hold of the sparks from the flints, and limped into flame. In an instant of one movement I recovered my candle and lit it from the pathetic but efficient flame.

My immediate task, having once more bathed the room in shallow light, was to face any Demons who might have been drawn to the darkness and my evil act of, albeit unwittingly, having stolen from the Pope. I held the candle aloft and searched the room thoroughly. I even opened the small cupboard therein. Why a Demon or monster should go to the trouble to hide in a cupboard or under a bed I had no idea but fears from childhood of such an eventuality fell upon me. Empty. Good.

It was then that I realized that I was not breathing. I let out a mighty sigh – and blew my candle out by mistake. Luckily the tiny pyre was still burning on the lid of my tinder box and I was able to relight it immediately. Having done so, I then used my shoe to put out the tinder fire lest I set alight the whole house by mistake. I knew this to be a possibility because I understood and acknowledged my unfortunate nature.

As I turned back to the bed, I again felt terror grip me. The fingernail. The box must be a reliquary. "Oh, my God. What have I done?" I crossed myself instinctively.

The mind is a wonderful thing but it can also hold horrors from the past which it will allow one to relive without bidding. As a child my father had taken me to the city. There we visited the Cathedral. It was a high day in the Catholic calendar and the one day a year when the relics, protected within the Cathedral walls, were on display to the congregation. My father had promised me a view of the very finger of a Saint. (I do not remember which one because the name was foreign to me and I was very young at the time).

With the lust for gore, which thankfully dies in a man after youth, my father and I joined the silent queue of people also waiting to inspect the saint's finger. The line of people, who greatly outnumbered the population of our village, shuffled silently towards the Holy sight. Deep disappointment awaited me. The black, shriveled object on the red plush cushion was like no finger I had ever seen. True, there was a clearly discernible nail at the end of the object but that was all that identified it as a digit. Next to the black finger was a highly decorated box I remembered. On our way out of the Cathedral my father had explained that the Saint's finger was preserved in the box, which was placed in a vault beneath the building, for its protection. This box, he educated me, was called a reliquary – a holder for a relic of a Saint.

"I have a Saint's fingernail. Oh, my God. Forgive me." I fell to my knees. As I remained in this posture, I tried to imagine what penance would be demanded of me at Confession for such an almighty sin. Slowly, very slowly, fear subsided and sanity took over again.

"Where did it come from?" I looked up at the box nestling still on my bed. "How did you get in my sack?" Somehow, I felt that if ever an inanimate object were to speak, tonight would be the time. I was disappointed. It remained silent.

My wonderful mind, for such I think of anyone's mind, responded in attempt to answer my spoken question. It played, backwards, my life up to this point. As it reached the time of my inadvertently blowing up my sister's home the truth was revealed.

The two riders whom I had unseated must have been messengers from the Pope delivering the relic to some distant church. One *had* been a Priest after all. Yes. That must be the answer. My memory now moved forwards from that time but in slow motion. I saw in its eye the panic with which I had grasped the sack and the fervour with which I had placed anything which still resembled itself into the sack. "I must have grabbed the box. It must have fallen from the Priest when he fell off his horse." The facts were indisputable. That must be the sequence of this unfortunate event. "Oh, my!"

With fingers which could achieve no greater delicacy had they been wrapping a newborn I carefully bound the fingernail into its protective cloth again. I felt, inexplicably, easier of mind once the Pope's crest no longer stared at me accusingly. The whole I placed gently into the now empty box.

Picking the box up, which now contained such precious cargo, I gently turned it in my hands inspecting the outstandingly beautiful artwork covering its surface. I imagined that, perhaps, the Pope himself might have done the same. The thought that I was holding something which our Papal leader might have also held thrilled me beyond reason. I was truly beginning to relax again when fate stepped in and my world, once again, became a torment of terror.

As I held the box the bottom of it suddenly separated from its top part.

"Oh, my. Now I've broken it." My despair was tangible. Of all the things in my life which I have broken none could be more devastating than this. I almost dropped the box in horror but something made me hang on to it against my will. I shut my eyes to block out the terrible sight. "Please forgive me, Lord. I didn't mean to break it. Please forgive me. I humbly beseech you to not unleash your punishment. It was an accident. Truly it was." How many times had I uttered those words? How many accidents had I had? How many apologies had I offered? At the moment it seemed my life had lurched from one accident to another - but none more serious than this.

Gingerly, realizing that I had not been struck down by a bolt from God, I opened my eyes. "Oh, my!" I despaired at the damage I had wrought on this Holy object. "Oh, my. Oh, my."

As is its talent my mind again cut in with its rarely failing calm. "Perhaps I can mend it?" I turned the box, with the gentlest of touches, so that the broken bit faced me. It was then I saw that it was not so much damaged as revealing a secret part of its nature. "That is a drawer! No. It cannot be. Yes. It is. It is a drawer."

Gently, gently, my forefinger alone pulled at the sticking out bit. Slowly, slowly, more and more of the layer was revealed. "Come on my little treasure. Come to Pater." A slip of something became visible. "Hello. What are you?" I enquired of what was becoming evident as being a slip of some sort. Changing tactic from pulling the drawer out, I invoked the use of my thumb to assist the forefinger. The pair, between them, extricated the slip.

(A child's drawing of a fish, with no tail, appeared.) In the city of the second Rome two ideas join to become one.

(Another tailless fish) In the growth which conducts this union find the first.

Such were the words inscribed on the slip when I carefully opened it. I read it out aloud. What was the Pope talking about - for indeed it must be he who authored this? "The second Rome? Where is that? Two ideas join to become one? What two ideas? What growth?" As with any alchemist, my mind was full of more questions than answers. Such is our discipline. Likewise, common to our art, I was driven to find answers to these puzzles.

As you will have gleaned, I am nothing if not resourceful. One has to be when one is as prone to accidents as my nature seems to be. I had no means to solve even the first part of this riddle. Therefore, it was beholden upon me to find someone who could. In order to encourage this someone, I must be in a position to reward them for the information. This part of my plan clearly defined; I began work on it.

My dockside entertainment was very popular and the generosity of the wealthy townsfolk and passing traders matched their enthusiasm. I had now secured a room of sorts and was able to afford food for at least two weeks hence. A fortune indeed. My stocks of metals and powders now fully replenished I found a little money in excess of requirements. This I exchanged for a bottle of blue liquid which the foreign trader had assured me contained the secret of recovery from all and any ill-health.

Placing this bottle in pride of place on my box during demonstrations I always ended my entertainment with the promise that it was a prize freely given if someone could tell me where the second Rome sat. Several weeks passed with no answers forthcoming. Then one morning a sailor, (I knew him to be such from his dress), stepped forward and declared that he knew exactly where it was. Indeed, he continued, he was a native of that great city.

"Bamberg is the second Rome." He declared proudly. "Or rather Rome is the second Bamberg." This joke drew laughter from the watching crowd.

"Can you prove this to be the case?" I asked him.

"Indeed, aye. For Rome sits on seven hills as does Bamberg. My hometown was, for a time, the very center of the Holy Roman Empire, as decreed by the Pope himself. Bamberg is the second Rome and no doubt," he finished triumphantly.

"And where is this holy seat of virtue my friend."

"Well now, that's easy," he quickly responded. "For Bamberg lies directly – and I do mean directly – south of this place. It is as near due south as any compass heading I've followed. South. Aye, south."

"How far south?" I was determined to mine this man's knowledge.

"Oh, some distance I remember. For when I headed here, I caught a cart with a pilgrim and we journeyed for some month and a half I recall. Mind you, my travelling companion did insist on stopping at every church and shrine along the way." He laughed as did the crowd around us.

"Friend, you have served me well. I thank you for your information and wish you prolonged protection from the scurvy which I understand blights your trade. Here take the elixir with my blessing." So spoken I handed him the bottle of blue liquid. The crowd around applauded and both he and I took a bow in an act of showmanship.

So it was I found myself riding to Bamberg some weeks later on a horse purchased from a stable selling such beasts of burden. Safely attached to the extremely uncomfortable saddle were my possessions. I set camp initially on one of the hills looking down upon the city since all my money had gone in purchase of the horse.

She grazed lazily while I gathered sticks from the surrounds for a fire. Setting a ring of stones in safety for the expected blaze, I set a bed of tinder, then the sticks, then began clashing my flints together to encourage a flame. Success. It is inexplicable how comforting to man a controlled fire becomes. As the flames grew so too did my spirits. I feasted (again) on black bread and dried meat by which time darkness had descended. I slept that night lying on my stomach as the back side of me was too sore to support my weight.

The next day my steed and I entered the city. I found what I believed to be a central location and began my unique entertainment. This was warmly received and as the day progressed, I knew that a real bed was to be my reward that night. My horse, Ops, named after the Roman goddess of the earth, meanwhile would benefit from a feast of grass in one of the many meadows thereabout. I had named her Ops because it reminded me of an utterance I frequently found myself making of "Oops."

The riddle was never far from my mind.

(Tailless fish) In the city of the second Rome two ideas join to become one.

(Tailless fish) In the growth which conducts this union find the first.

What may the 'two ideas join to become one' mean? '...two ideas ...'? It was a quandary. I was not, thankfully, to wait long for an answer.

The very next day I again set stall in the center to earn my wage. However, I was disconcerted to find very few people passing. This surely was unusual. I enquired of one of the lone passing pedestrians.

"Excuse me, sir." He stopped. "There are so few people today. Can you enlighten me as to why?"

"Are you a stranger?" I thought his response a little impertinent but since I desired an answer, I decided to allow him a little invasion into my business.

"Yes, indeed I am. I arrived only yesterday to your fair city."

"Ah, then, you won't know." He stopped speaking. I willed him to continue by moving my head and shoulders toward him in silent request. Eventually, he summoned up the words. "It is the feast day, when we thank God for the good harvest. All our townsfolk will be in the meadow for the festival and celebration. All, that is, except those of us who must continue with labour." He added this last with an unmistakable attitude of resentment.

At his words the businessman in me rejoiced. Where a multitude gathered for festival and celebration, there an entertainer of some repute would surely earn a handsome reward.

I enquired for details. "And where, my friend, might this festival be taking place?"

"You cannot miss it for you will hear the minstrels from the edge of town. It is in that direction." He pointed with a mud-covered hand toward one of the hills. I thanked him for his patience and as he hurried on his way with bent head, I packed up my belongings with high spirits.

The worker had indeed been right about the ease with which I found the celebrations. The music drew me like a moth to the flame. What had surprised me was that as I drew, apparently, nearer to the music it had seemed to remain the same distance away. I quickened my pace at least as much as my baggage would allow. The mystery was soon solved as I caught up with the travelling minstrels. They were indeed, literally, travelling. They marched in rag tag order along the road leading away from the town. I joined the children who accompanied them but refrained from dancing and jigging as they did.

The whole procession stopped at a great field which seemed to be cultivating, rather than crops, people. Rarely had I spied such a gathering. Surely the entire population of the town must be in attendance?

There were scattered tables, adorned with food or trinkets, as well as great knots of folk standing around talking in happily animated tones. In places women had placed rugs on the grass and families gathered around these crude camps. The sun shone. The men-folk held jugs of what I imagined from their jovial demeanor to be ale. The women shepherded unruly and excited children. This was, indeed, a utopian setting for me to ply my trade. I set up my box and quickly shouted for those within earshot to witness the magic and spectacles I had to offer.

The day moved into the early evening and the takings in my money pouch had rarely been heavier. I was delighted. Gradually folk had begun to leave and the minstrels were preparing to march back to town having gathered followers like a rat catcher gathers rodents. I also was happily weary and began to pack my wares together whilst wishing that I had had the foresight to collect Ops on my way out of town.

"Hello." I turned to find a vision of beauty before me. It was a young woman who had so greeted me. Her voice was gentle and low toned; her dress of bright crimson and her bonnet of matching hue. I assessed her as being in early twenties.

"Hello." I could barely get this single acknowledgement of greeting out so astounded was I that such loveliness could exist outside of a sunset.

"I enjoyed your performance. Thank you." Never had praise been so warmly welcomed. My spirit soared.

"No, thank *you*." This I uttered with the greatest emphasis indicating that it was I who should be thanking her.

"I do not recognize you. Are you from town?"

"No, ma'am. I come most recently from Lübeck and prior to that from Malmhaug."

"Oh, how exciting!" Her delight at my last place of residence seemed to illicit genuine joy from her. "I have heard that the fashions there are glorious."

"I cannot in truth say that I noticed, ma'am." Fashion had always eluded me.

"My father and mother are talking to the Mayor but I find him to be a man of little interesting conversation. Will you walk with me across this field to the river, that we may enjoy the final overture of this magnificent day, and you can tell me more of your travels?"

I looked up and, as if for the first time, realized that within a short distance lay a river bank. Sofia, for so I was to discover was her name, and I walked happily side by side alongside the rushing river. I was careful at all times to ensure we could still be seen by her parents, for such was my propriety, as I regaled this delight with exaggerated tales of my exploits. She soaked in every word and I felt, perhaps for the first time, important. We passed many minutes in such ecstasy.

"What river is this?" I enquired. I wished to remember every detail of this short interlude in my life.

"This is the Regnitz but some distance further it meets with the even bigger River Main. It is beautiful is it not?"

"Indeed it is, ma'am." I looked around at the trees bending towards the water on the far bank as if reaching down to drink. The sun, which was now in decline, just glinting on the bowing leaves. A pair of birds flew low across the water in what seemed to be a race along a predetermined track.

"Sofia. Sofia?" A disembodied voice called in the raised tones of an anxious mother.

"Here! I am coming." Sofia responded. "Sir. I thank you for your company but must now return to my family. It was delightful to meet you." So saying she raised the front of her skirts slightly and took off at a ready pace.

I called after her "It was a true delight for me too, ma'am. I hope to perhaps meet you again one day?" No response. She was already out of earshot or had returned to the world from which she had momentarily stepped. She was gone.

I returned to town with a buoyancy in my step not experienced for many a month. I had a purse full of coins, a contented horse in the meadow, and above all else had conversed with a vision of beauty and youth, who had seemed genuinely interested in me. What greater joy could one hope to know?

It was during that very same sleep-time that a beautiful dream graced my contented slumber. Sofia floated through my imaginary world like a fairy from the unworldly realms of Utopia. In my dream her eyes sparkled as she looked on me in loving gentleness, whilst dancing barefoot in our green meadow. I relived the words she had used to describe herself and her surrounds. Had any voice, outside of Heaven itself, ever sounded so sweet? Surely angels wept at her sound as the beauty of it touched their souls?

When I awoke it was with a longing to return to the land of dreams to again so that I might experience her delightful company. Reluctantly I lay there, allowing my body to slowly return to consciousness. I could still hear her voice. One phrase interrupted the languidness of my recall and acted like a trumpet blast causing me to sit bolt upright in my bed.

"This is the Regnitz but some distance further it meets with the even bigger River Main."

(Tailless fish) In the city of the second Rome two ideas join to become one.

"Could the two ideas joining mean the meeting of the two rivers?" The idea seemed far-fetched and yet something inside me encouraged me to explore the idea further. Such a degree of curiosity had not gripped me since my first explorations into alchemy.

Determined to at least rule out this possibility, it was with impatient expectations that I undertook my entertainment duties. If the crowd expected a performance at a certain time then they must be rewarded at all costs. The show, for such it was, must be performed. As the time of mid meal arrived no one moved faster than I to return my wares to the lodging and set out for the field where yesterday's Festival had taken place.

I walked eagerly along the banks climbing over obstacles as they arose and even, on one occasion, allowing my feet to get wet in order to not lose sight of the rushing waters. Some two and a half or three kilometers later my journey was rewarded. I had met a confluence of the waterways. The remaining riddle became instantly solvable.

(Tailless fish) In the growth which conducts this union find the first.

There, right where the two rivers joined, stood an ancient tree. I ran in excited expectation the last few yards. Circling the tree and staring into its skyward branches I felt the first stirrings of disappointment. I circled it again. Nothing. It then occurred to me to look down rather than up, and circling once again, I stared at the area where the root system met its upstanding relative. A hole! There is a hole in the base of the trunk! In one movement my hand shot forward to explore the opening whilst my knees took the weight of my body.

Again, I praised God for His inventive fingers, as mine felt diligently around the inside of the opening. "What's this? Surely this feels alien to a tree?" My fingers plucked at the unexpected texture. Carefully and slowly I withdrew the unattached bundle. A leather pouch. "Oh, my. How odd?"

Eagerly I opened it. I cannot yet recall if it was disappointment or excitement which overwhelmed me when I discovered parchment and not gold. As a man of alchemy, discovery of something is the highest achievement of our trade. As a mere man, wealth is our more immediate goal. It is therefore with mixed feelings that I returned to my lodging.

During my post noon performance my mind was not settled upon the task in hand but rather on the pouch sitting on my bed. It was probably this lack of attention which caused me, in a moment of misfortune, to set light to the tunic of one of my audience. The Greek Fire I had used had leapt, as if by magic, from its container and landed on his garment. The ensuing screams and chaotic running from those around had brought to an untimely end my demonstrations. I am pleased to report that the only lasting damage done was to the gentleman's tunic.

Therefore, returning early from my entertainment, and having eaten heartily, thanks to the lady who owned my lodgings, I retired to my room to open the mysterious pages that someone had found necessary to secret in the tree.

No alchemy held such amazing properties as what I read that night. I could barely believe that what was claimed was the truth. As I read the accounts from each author my expectations rose as to the writing on the most tattered pieces which I had left to last. It was with trembling hands that the last of my candle illuminated the words claimed to be the actual words spoken by Our Lord. As I looked up for the first time that night with the aim of lighting a new candle, the last having given of its best, it was with genuine surprise that I realized that dawn was already upon us.

"Oh, my. Oh, my. Oh, my." I was so stunned that no words of value came into my bemused mind. There were no words existing which would express my delight, my horror, my fear, at the revelations which had unfolded before me. "Oh, my."

I put the documents down on the bed and for some time just stared at them. Could they possibly be true? Surely not. It must be some author who is exercising his sense of humour? And yet, I knew this was not the case. If it be fiction then it was produced from the mind of a man who believed it to be true. The others, those in history who had also discovered the accounts, they too must have believed. They said they had. I reread the final pages of the accounts and confirmed my assessment. "Indeed. They had believed. Oh, my."

I was not an overly religious man but I had at least been raised as a Roman Catholic. I knew of some of the sayings of Our Lord and not a few of the prayers thanks to this background. This upbringing had also left me with a modest ability to read Latin. I must confess though that I had not given the matter of faith much thought since leaving childhood and the family home. My mother had been devout but her faith had seemed, to my mind, of improvable consistency. I had long ago rejected the premise that God would be pleased by the repetitive recital of the accepted prayers and as such saw no value, to either He nor I, in attending church.

"Why me?" I beseeched Him. "Of all people, why me? Why, in your greatness, would you allow me, of all people, to come into possession of such valuable text?" God did not answer.

"Lord. If this be truly an account of your life on earth, then please send me a sign." Jesus did not answer.

I could not eat to break my fast for my mind was too much in turmoil.

Instead I went to the location of a trader I knew dealt in books and waited impatiently for him to appear. As soon as he arrived, I purchased a Bible and hurried back to my lodgings to compare the words therein with the words accredited to Our Lord in the ancient Jews texts.

As I discovered the small but significant differences my mind became more and more unsettled. Each revelation spurred me on to find another. By the end of the day I was as an exile from my comfortable prior conclusions. My life had been turned upside down and for, perhaps, the first time in my life I was truly to be defined as a Christian – a follower of the teachings of Jesus – because again, for the first time in my life, I understood His message. I had never done that before. I clearly saw that the traditions and rituals surrounding the message obscured the simplicity of the message. It was an eye-opening experience and one which changed me forever.

I now pause in my account to move a few years further on since nothing much had happened – other than my renewed understanding.

After nearly two years of 'walking out' with Sofia she and I were married. It was a glorious day and the fulfillment of my deepest desire. I felt that with her by my side I could conquer the world. Unfortunately, her father did not share this vision and his disapproval found voice at our wedding.

"Now that you are married to my daughter it is time you procured a proper job," he declared on our wedding day in his speech at our celebration. He was not a man who kept his beliefs secret. "As such I have arranged for you to go to my brother and apprentice with him." He paused as if expecting applause for this, as he conceived it, magnificent wedding gift. Actually, the assembled guests and onlookers were as stunned as I.

"Where is your brother? What apprenticeship do you propose?"

"My brother lives in Altdorf, which I understand to be in the canton of Uri, part of the newly established Swiss Confederation. You are lucky indeed to be joining him there for he boasts that his home town is the very center of activity."

"And what, may I respectfully ask, is the proposed apprenticeship position?"

"Sofia's uncle works in the law. You will learn the art of his trade so that when you return Sofia to her home town you may open a respectable office here."

Since the whole matter of this move and training is upsetting to me, I shall not go into detail on our journey nor my unhappy relationship with Sofia's uncle. Suffice to say that the "law" held no interest for me and I proved unsuited to it.

However, what this unpleasant phase in our new life did provide was a lucky accident by which my prospects altered considerably and to a favourable outcome.

One of my most arduous duties was to secure the safety of certain legal documents which were to be held. These I had to record on a list before placing the actual documents in boxes which lined the inner office of the law firm. The boxes were sometimes made of wood, but if the items to be enclosed were of particular value, a blacksmith was commissioned to fashion a metal box to contain them. A crude locking mechanism was then applied and the box placed in a slot on the shelving.

In a moment of inspiration an idea for a new kind of lock, which was considerably more secure, leapt into my mind. I spoke to the blacksmith about this and commissioned him to make one to my very exact specifications. I was so pleased with the result that I made it practice that whenever I commissioned a new metal container, I also required one of my new lock types to be sent with it.

The design of my lock was such that only a very specific key, manufactured at the same time as the device, would open it. These keys I hung diligently from a rack in the inner office, having first labeled each with the exact location of the box it belonged to. This system worked superbly and greatly impressed my employer. At first he was disconcerted that his blacksmith bill had risen. Being a man of opportunity, he made it known throughout the town that his safe keeping methods were vastly superior to that of his competitors, and from this recouped any losses in the form of higher charges and greater custom. In spite of this small profit I brought to him he remained unsatisfied with my services - never more so than when the dowager, Lady Fabienne, visited our offices.

The outer door to the office opened unexpectedly one day and in swept a fine lady like a galleon sailing into port. The black finery which adorned her aging person was as superior as her manner and deportment. Her sudden appearance had a surprising effect upon my employer. In a single bound he leapt to his feet from his overstuffed chair and whilst performing the very act of standing, actually managed to turn it into a low bow within the same movement. I had never seen him move quicker nor with more agility. I followed his lead and also stood, but declined to bow other than a quick nod of my head.

"I have come for the papers belonging to my late husband." This was obviously a lady who neither practiced small talk nor, I surmise, tolerated it, having dispensed with the usual cordial greetings.

"Yes, ma'am. Certainly." My employer bobbed up and down in a series of mini bows with each phrase; his face having now taken on a reddish hue not common to his normal demeanor. Whether this was from the unnatural exercise or from being so flustered I was not able to judge. I just stared on with a rising sense of amusement.

"Now please. I am in hurry to meet my niece for luncheon." With this the lady descended onto the guest chair placed before my employer's desk and began to remove one of her gloves.

"Quickly. Lady Fabienne's box, lad." Having risen from his supplicant position the lawyer had now turned to me. The agitation his body portrayed no doubt meaning to indicate to me the speed at which I should address this requirement. Panic is an emotion which is easily and quickly passed and I felt anxiety rise sharply in my own body. This is not a condition in which I perform well and the response was that, in turning towards the inner door, I forgot to move one of my feet. I fell unceremoniously to the floor.

"What are you doing, boy?" Lady Fabienne was staring down at me from her chair with gross disapproval evident on her face.

"I am sorry, ma'am," I muttered looking up. "I fell." The blindingly obvious explanation did not placate her.

"I can see that. Now stop messing about and fetch me my box."

I scrambled vertical again and ran through the door to the inner sanctum. In here I quickly located the box her ladyship wanted from my list, and ascertained its shelf and position. I reached it down and placed it on the small table in this back room. Next, I rushed over to the rack of keys and reached up to pull the corresponding opener from its place. My hand stopped in mid-air. No key hung on the nail where it should be. I checked the floor. No key. I looked at the labels on keys either side of the one I needed. They were correct. The only key missing was the one belonging to the box on my table. Anxiety mushroomed instantly into panic.

With the fever of a man afraid for his life I wrenched each key down from its hook and inspected the labels. Having formed a disorganized pile of metalwork on the desk, it was clear that no label showed for the requisite box. In desperation I began trying to open the box with each key one after the other. My employer appeared at the door.

"What on earth are you doing? Why is taking so long?"

"I cannot find the key." All the while my fevered fingers were trying and discarding each new key I grasped. The pile on the left of untried keys was getting smaller while the one on the right of discarded keys grew.

"You … cannot find … the key?" The reddish hue of his face was now a crimson mask. I felt sure he would soon explode. "Here!" With this he grabbed a key from my discard pile on the right and tried to force it into the lock.

We alternated like this until my left-hand pile was gone. I would try the next untried key whilst he, as soon as the lock was empty, tried to force one from the right-hand pile into the recalcitrant opening. As one we realized that the key by which to open this metal box was not amongst the pile. We stared at each other too horrified to form words.

"What are you gentlemen doing, pray?" The aggravated tone from the outer office did nothing to calm us.

As one, we both turned away from each other and began circling the room with our eyes fixed to the floor looking for the wayward opener. As we rejoined each other in the center of the room a look confirmed that neither had met with success.

"Quickly. See if there is anything in your desk which will prize the box open." I complied.

"Nothing."

"Climb out of the window and run for the blacksmith. I'll talk to her ladyship and try and postpone her." The absurdity of this suggestion eluded both of us at the time. "Make sure you gain him entry by the same window." My upright lawyer of an employer added as an afterthought.

Shortly I returned with an out of breath blacksmith. Allowing him to gain entry via a window some feet above the ground proved a challenge. Eventually, with him pulling himself up and me pushing his back side he slid in ungainly fashion into the inner room where I joined him in short order. From his apron pocket he produced some dangerous looking implements with which he attempted to prize open the box. Failing in this, he reached again into his apron pocket and revealed a hammer and chisel. He began pounding at the unrelenting lock. It bent, certainly. It screeched in agony, surely. It resisted opening, definitely.

As the pair of us stood watching the lock hoping it would take it upon itself to release its sure grasp, the level of light in the room suddenly dropped. I looked up to find an angry lady glowering at me, then the box, then the blacksmith, then me again.

"What on earth is going on in here?"

"We … that is I … cannot open the box, ma'am." No amount of panic experienced by my employer was exceeded by my own. "I seem to have misplaced the key - temporarily."

"Here. Stand aside." Not in my wildest imagination could I have envisaged what happened next. The lady withdrew a long pin from her immaculate hair and bent over the offending article. With gentle and dexterous fingers, she inserted the sharp end of the pin into the orifice and began jiggling inside the hole. The blacksmith took a step back; I took a step forward and closer; and my employer stood still, stunned, in the doorway.

"No. It will not yield." The lady stood upright again and returned the pin which vanished into the ties of her hair. "My. What a sound lock." Was it my imagination or did I detect amusement in her voice?

"Milady …" began my master. She held her hand up as signal to him to stop talking.

"I have a jewel box for which the key has long ago been lost. With my hair pin I am the only one now able to reopen it. However, this lock is exceptional."

We four stood in silence for a moment. Then Lady Fabienne took command as was her nature.

"I am already late to meet my niece so I must away. Find the key or use the further skills of your blacksmith," she looked at him at this point as if realizing how out of place he looked in these surroundings "and bring the papers to my home as soon as you are able." With this she, in one movement, swept up a fraction of her full gown and slid out of harbour.

The blacksmith, my employer and I returned to his smelting shop. This time my employer had allowed him to use the door for which both he and I were extremely grateful. After a full two hours of heating, cooling and attacking the offending lock, he was able to release the retaining end from the mechanism. Gratefully I carried the box back to our office with the lawyer acting like an unarmed guard and clearing pedestrians from our path. Very soon after this the papers were delivered to Lady Fabienne.

This incident, whilst very distressing at the time, served me well. The lady had been so impressed by the impenetrability of my device that she financed me to have many more made. These were sold in great numbers, first by me, then by my employer and then by the blacksmith. Their reputation as secure devices grew exponentially as did their desirability. I gained much wealth in the venture and continue to collect revenue to this day each time one finds a new home.

I did make one improvement on my original design. For every key made, a duplicate was manufactured at the same time. This was kept by the blacksmith – in a locked box.

As for the missing key? We never found it.

With this new found financial security came an understanding that I also had new responsibilities. For the first time in my life I had 'time' itself. Instead of the constant battle to procure enough income to live I found that spare hours lay within my grasp. These I filled with long walks alone into the countryside surrounding our idyllic city. During such sojourns my mind was as occupied as my legs. The topic of my ponderings always returned to one subject; the texts in my possession.

I, like most believers, had faith that that the Bible was a 'magically' protected collection of documents. I, in common with most, firmly supported the premise that God was the inspiration behind its creation. So how do I reconcile this with the new revelation in my possession? Why is there deviation, albeit miniscule, on the words spoken by Jesus recorded in the New Testament and those written by the ancient Jew? After much deliberation I decided that my answer was only to be found by inspiration and so I handed the problem over to God and asked Him to respond. God did not reply …. at first ….

I decided to talk the matter through with Sofia and so one evening, once the children were in bed, I informed her that I had something important to speak with her about. We sat comfortably in our respective chairs before the fire and she remained silent whilst I regaled her with the story of how I had uncovered the texts from the clue. I cited two examples of differences in phraseology between the Testament and the testament. She remained silent. I explained my quandary on why there were differences between the writings. I put the case soundly that I could not understand the deviations or why they should have occurred.

At first, during my diatribe, she had stared into my eyes as if reading my soul to determine the truth of what I was uttering. Apparently satisfied that I was indeed in earnest her gaze had moved to the fire instead. Thus we sat for some considerable time. She silent - me talking - an unusual state of affairs in our household.

Finally, after a brief period of silence, she looked up at me again. Never had her eyes looked more beautiful to me.

"I think that you are asking the wrong question," she declared. "You should not be asking why there are differences in the texts. Rather you should be asking God what He wants you to do with them."

This clarity of thought surprised and delighted me. I confess this line of process had not occurred to me.

She continued. "I am reminded of the story of Abraham. When God demanded a sacrifice of his son, Isaac, Abraham did not question God as to why this was necessary, he merely accepted that it was the Almighty's command. Without asking 'why' he acquiesced to the demand. Thankfully, that had a happy outcome. Likewise, Joshua did not ask God why he was to command the blowing of the horns whilst circling the walls of Jericho, he just accepted that this was God's command. This also had an unexpectedly happy outcome. All through history, both related in the Bible and out of it, there are examples of how God commands people to do things with no explanation of why they should do it."

"But" I began "He is not telling me to do anything. So how do I know what to do with these writings?"

"When you told me of your discovery, your question was centered on 'why'. Why are there apparent variations in the writing? Your nature as a scientist was dominant instead of your faith. Your mind is now more properly centered upon 'what'. What should you do with them? This is the right question. Now

I am sure He will instruct you because you are asking the right question. Ask Him what, not why." She sat back in her chair as if settled that she had finished her important role in this unfolding drama. Never before had I fully appreciated, not only the beauty, but the deep wisdom of this fine lady.

The next day I set out on one of my long walks. My mind was re-living the words of my dear wife and feeding upon their wisdom. It was in this frame of mind that I mentally approached God for an answer. Instead of worrying about why the slight variations existed I asked Him to show me what He wanted me to do with the mysterious texts. God answered me …

I was walking along the rough path which led up to a high spot in the area. As I made my way I saw, set back a little from the path, a shrine. This was not unusual since the countryside was dotted with many such shrines, each dedicated to some saint or other, most of whom I had never heard of before. Something made me stop and look at this one though. In the shrine, which was forged from granite, was carved a small statue of a gentle woman. She was robed in the dress I associate with Biblical women and was demurcly staring at the ground beneath and in front of her. I bent down and read the inscription.

'Sancta Sophia: The Holy Wisdom of God.'

It was at that moment that I knew what to do with the texts I had inherited. Nothing! Sofia had opened my mind to the possibility that my original question may never be answered. Unlike my experiments into the properties of powders and metal ores, I might never discover the reaction of these two powerful elements, in the form of writings, colliding. I rushed home to Sofia re-invigorated with the enthusiasm of certainty.

"Sofia. Sofia." I called out in loud voice upon entering our home.

"Whatever is the matter?" She enquired as she rushed from the rear room.

"I know what to do! I am to let *you* decide what to do with the texts." Sofia was silent for a moment as I stared at her like a child pleading with its mother for wisdom on some important issue. She dried her hands on her apron whilst remaining silent. I said nothing not wishing to disturb her thoughts.

"We shall hide them again but this time in a new location. If God decided to let you find them, then He must want them moved – otherwise you would not have found them. Likewise, if He wanted them made known, He would have told you so, and how to do it." She nodded her head as if agreeing with her own words. I just stared, amazed by the ordered thought pattern she was adopting; one worthy of any scientific mind I noted with pride in her bursting from my chest.

It was decided that the documents should be housed in a new location. The final detail of this spot was to be determined by a chance occurrence which happened later in the same week.

I was unexpectedly called one morning to the workplace of the blacksmith with whom I had forged such a lucrative enterprise. On entering his premises, I found a wealthy looking gentleman engrossed in conversation with him. They were both speaking loudly since my blacksmith was all the while tending his bellows to enhance the flame. This caused some mighty noise and normal level speech was impractical. So it was that I was able to enter the workplace unheard and listen to the conversation unbeknownst.

"Yes. It is a fairly new city called Aemsterdam. This name comes from Amstelredamme which in turn means the Dam on the Amstel."

"Amstel? What is Amstel? Is it a waterway?" enquired the blacksmith all the while tempering his bellows and carefully judging the pressure to apply from clues given by the fire he tended.

"The River Amstel runs through our city. We, in recent history, claimed no fame for anything. We were merely a farming community in the days of my father. Life in farming was a constant battle of reclaiming land from the waters. He told me that one year, when he was a young man, he had lost almost all his crop to the waters. That was a bad year. Anyway, then we built a bridge which also served as a dam for the river. Immediately our fortunes changed."

"Did someone pay to use your bridge then?"

"Everyone! Except of course the families from Aemsterdam itself. We were exempt from fees. A fine arrangement! Anyway, our notability as a population center became greatly enhanced once we had joined the Hanseatic League. When I was a lad, I could recognize almost every resident of Aemsterdam. Not so today. Today the whole city bustles with activity and strangers." At last he paused. This was a man who loved to speak I decided before having even been introduced to him. I made a mental note not to enquire of him too much or my day would be spent.

"Really?" This single word of acknowledgement from the blacksmith elicited another dialogue of considerable length.

"Yes. But that is not our only claim to fame now." The stranger stood taller on his frame as pride swelled him. "No indeed. Now our greatest claim to fame is our Holy status." He paused obviously expecting the blacksmith to enquire about this intriguing statement. He did not. His fire was ready and he was impatient, I knew, to go about his noisy business of hammering some metal into a desired shape.

Undaunted the stranger continued uninvited.

"Yes indeed. We are now an official pilgrimage site. Just last year, in 1345, a miracle took place in our very town in a home near the kalvermarkt, the cattle market. Here, a dying man was being given the Eucharist, the Holy bread and wine of our Lord's Last Supper, when he vomited and ejected the Host. Most distressing for all concerned I am sure. Anyway, the Host, that is the bread wafer as you know, was recovered and thrown onto the fire. It did not burn. It just sat there in the flame. One of the attendees seeing this decided that since this Host was blessed, and now holy, he would recover it from the fire. There being no tongues nearby he, in a moment of extreme bravery, put forth his hand to recover the wafer. He did so. The miracle is reported that neither his hand nor the host were any the worse for the flame. Neither suffered signs of burn."

The stranger stopped speaking and looked expectantly at the blacksmith. This latter tradesman just stared in disbelief at such a high tale. It must be remembered that the trade of blacksmith involved working with fire the day long. No man called to this trade was spared the iniquity of suffering from burns to various degrees. It was, as the saying goes, a hazard of the trade. He obviously therefore could not comprehend the thought that one might put one's hand into flame and not suffer the pain of having done so.

"No. It cannot be done," he finally exclaimed in disbelief looking at the fire he had just raised to high degree.

"That my friend is why it is a miracle! Witness statements were sent to the Pope in Rome and he declared it to be so. Our very own miracle! Our proud city is even now being placed on the pilgrims' route by His Holiness. The trade which this will sponsor means riches for all."

It was at this very point that I declared my own attendance. I stepped forward and spoke.

"You called for me." This I directed to my blacksmith.

The artisan seemed relieved to be released from the perpetual tirade of the stranger and was eager to introduce me to the stranger.

"Yes. Thank you for coming so promptly, sir. This gentleman is named Meneer Geralt Holtman. He is from the northern town of Aemsterdam in the Netherlands.

"Goedemorgen." The stranger extended his hand to me in universal greeting. Having introduced myself with similar greeting he placed a hand on my shoulder and we walked outside the shop.

"You have asked to see me, sir?" I enquired of him once the thunder of the blacksmith's anvil reduced in volume due to distance.

"Indeed I did, sir. Your reputation for superb lock design has already reached my country and I have a proposition for you." I confess that my curiosity was equally matched by my surprise and delight that my fame had spread to distant lands.

"Proceed, sir."

"I operate a small but successful fleet from the port of Aemsterdam. Oft times my carriers are requested to conduct important people or documents to our trade destinations. This is lucrative business which I am keen to cultivate. I do not need to point out to you, I am sure, that this trade greatly enhances the value of the cargo which I would be transporting anyway." He paused only for breath.

"There was an unfortunate incident aboard one of my vessels recently which has caused me to review the detail of how I conduct this business. As I am sure you are aware every port contains unemployed sailors begging passage. One such character, a vessel of mine employed for the return trip to Aemsterdam. As luck, or misfortune, would have it I was carrying a small but relevant quantity of gold at the time as a bonus cargo. This was kept hidden in the Captain's cabin. Not hidden well enough unfortunately. For as he docked the Captain discovered the gold had gone missing – as had the new hireling. The cost to me of this incident has been considerable both in money and reputation. My gracious! What a scandal the rascal set in motion." He went quiet reliving the upheaval for a moment. I opened my mouth to speak but was cut off from utterance.

"So now, in order to recover my reputation and dare I say allow expansion into secure passage of small items, I require to employ a skilled designer such as yourself to set a safe area aboard my ships for the secure containment of such articles." Finally he stopped and stared at me intently obviously anticipating a response.

"When you say a secure area, sir, how big an area are you anticipating? For I am no blacksmith you know."

"I do know, sir. I do not expect you to do the work yourself but rather direct tradesmen to work to your specifications. I am thinking that the area should be large enough to contain perhaps three boxes containing jewels or gold and a bundle of documents comprised of some fifty leaves. We are developing an exciting trade in diamonds too which require security in transport. You can see the need for such a facility?"

"Yes, I see." I thought for a moment in silence. He also remained silent, which I took to be an unexpected blessing. My mind was inventing a safe box, made of strong metal, which could in some way be fastened into the wooden structure of the vessel. Yes, I thought. This was practical.

After mentally designing the required structure I again spoke. "How many of these safe areas would you be requiring, sir?"

"Ah, ha! Therein lies my plan." He became animated beyond reason. His hand raised, in posture of a revelation, with his right index finger pointing to the sky. "I intend to fit only my own vessels with this gadget so that I might maintain a monopoly on the safe passage of items. But then, and this is the clever part, I *shall* sell these gadgets and their installation to traders plying uniquely the Southern Seas. There! What do you think of that plan, sir?" He looked at me in what I can only describe as triumph.

I was not immediately enamored with the idea but it grew sedately as a plan worthy of becoming involved in. After not two minutes of complete silence, with him all the while silently interrogating my visage, I affirmed my interest. The very next order of business for me was to ascertain my level of reward.

"For your unique skills being involved in this venture I offer you the generous partnership of four tenths of all takings on installed safe areas." He seemed to believe that this offer was of such generosity that nobody could refuse. He was right. My mind was now ablaze with visions of a glorious future. It was true that I had become a little bored with the lack of employment in which I found myself and the prospect of new activity tempted me sorely.

"Presumably I shall need to inspect your vessels to design a suitable area?" I was already in the depths of detail for this new adventure.

"Indeed, sir. I envisage your coming back with me and setting up home in Aemsterdam from where you can effectively run the operation."

Moving home again! I had not anticipated that. How would Sofia react? How would she feel about moving so far? What of the children? Would they take kindly to being uprooted and removed from their circle of friends? There was much to think on and talk about. Taking my leave of the gentleman, and having ascertained where he was staying, it was agreed that I be allowed two days to deliberate on this venture before confirming my decision.

Sofia, my dutiful as well as intelligent wife, saw the advantage of the move and agreed to it with surprisingly little argument. She was the one who persuaded our children that a far greater future lay ahead for them in such a thriving and developing town as Aemsterdam, to the one afforded in Altdorf. She allowed them some emotion on the matter but then required them to put those feelings aside and view the move as an investment in their future. They too, with a little more reluctance, agreed.

We moved.

Suffice to say that we secured a suitably lavish home and the project was a great success. I was required to travel afar in the beginning; but our growing reputation soon meant that clients came to our city, rather than us having to go to theirs.

One evening whilst sitting by the fire, Sofia in her armchair, I in mine, she raised the topic of the pouch of documents again. I had by this time all but forgotten them but she had not.

"I think the time has come for us to decide where to place the texts."

It took me just a moment to realize the topic of conversation. "If you think so." I had long since mentally removed the responsibility for these documents onto Sofia and away from myself.

"I have been thinking and, indeed, reading the texts. I found it difficult and slow to translate parts of them since the only Latin I know is that remembered from schooling or knew from the church. I bought a translation text some months ago and painstakingly read the works though. As I read them, I became more impressed by their content. We must secret them I am sure."

"Whatever you say, my dear. I am sure you know best on this matter." The words on the shrine so long ago came from the dark corners of my mind to play on the surface of my inner vision. 'Sancta Sophia: The Holy Wisdom of God.'

"We must devise a clue as the others have done and hide it apart from the treasure itself." She was deep into the plotting of the task now and did not require my comment, just my obedience.

"I have been giving thought to the clue and where it might be safe. Do you remember that wonderful broach you gave me soon after we moved here?" She waited for a response but knew that it would only be paying homage to the obvious. The broach she referred to had been my greatest gift to her thus far. It was of a magnificent red and the perfect example of a pure ruby. This grand stone was set in a broad and extravagant gold filigree of master craftsman status. It had cost me a fortune but none was worth more, nor more deserving, than my esteemed wife.

"I do."

"Well beneath the stone is a small space before the golden backing in which the gem sits. I found it a few weeks ago. When I first saw it, I thought that it would provide a wonderful hiding place for a scrap of paper. What do you think about putting the clue in there?" She looked at me enquiringly.

"If you think that is the right place, my dear. Would the paper be visible though?"

"No. That is the beauty of the location. I tested it by sliding in a scrap of very fine paper and you cannot see it at all, neither when the broach is mounted on a garment, nor when the jewel is laid down."

"Could you get the paper out again?"

"I employed some sharp tweezers and with care was able to extract the paper undamaged. It is the perfect situation for the clue. Nobody would ever throw away an article of such value and or of such beauty. The clue will be absolutely safe until the next caretaker is assigned."

"Caretaker!" I had not thought of myself as that. Caretaker to the texts! Excellent. Not only did this describe my function in this intrigue but it absolved me from having to take action as well. "Caretaker. I really like that."

She smiled at me benignly and went on to answer my, as yet, unspoken question. "I have not yet decided the best place to lay the documents to rest but I have a few ideas. I am awaiting inspiration on this. I will know when the right place is found. It is in my mind, however, that this city will prove impractical."

"How so?"

"The ground is too wet. Think of it. Peat is everywhere underfoot. So wherever in this area we place the pouch it will likely become sodden and risk being destroyed. No. It is in my mind that you travel away from here and place the package on dryer land." My mind returned to some of the places I had visited in the early days of the safe area business. As it happened none of these previous destinations was to be the resting place of the package for which I was caretaker.

Aberdeen, in the distant island country of Scotland, had become an important city through its trade in wool with both Germany and the Baltic. It was to this site that Sofia and I set sail the following winter season.

My safe area business had been beseeched to provide secure areas in their trading ships and I was the only one available to set up this particular trade route. Whilst it was most unusual for Sofia to travel with me, since women on board a ship were deemed to be ill luck, she had expressed an earnest desire to accompany me on this one occasion and my generous bonus payment to each of the sailors on board seemed to allay any fears they might have felt.

It was an uncomfortable journey with my wife and I allotted the smallest of spaces; that being the semi-private area of the second mates bunk room. ('Room' is perhaps a poor definition since it was actually a space in the hold where barrels were stacked such as to provide some element of privacy).

The journey took us on a North, North Westerly course as we passed by the bulk of Scotland off our port bow. Before landing at Aberdeen our vessel was commissioned to first land cargo at Wick which is situated almost on the northern-most part of the island. It was then destined to plough south again and port at Aberdeen itself where Sofia and I would alight.

During the voyage, having provisioned with pens, ink and paper, Sofia set me the task of recording the journal of my time as caretaker. This is the account you now read although I did add some pages for the final stages of the task as you will see below. I felt in strangely esteemed company to realize that this account was to be added to the others already in the leather pouch. Sofia read each page as I completed it and, on occasion, corrected or annotated my work; this you can see adorn my otherwise neat pages.

One day a storm blew up as we were on the final leg of the journey to Wick. It was ferocious and caused great concern aboard ship. Sailors began blaming Sofia's presence on the vessel for the severity of the tides. Whilst we knew this was ridiculous, she and I agreed that the less she was seen on deck the better, and so she remained in the hold for the duration, climbing atop only at night to breathe fresh air. This proved a most hazardous event since the waves reached higher than the ship and the vessel barely struggled to the top of the next mountain before crashing into some liquid valley again.

After three days of these atrocious conditions the Captain sought us out and declared that we had been blown badly off course. We were in fact beyond the island of Scotland being much further north than he wished. This meant that the drop into Wick would run some days late as we had to travel south again from where we now found ourselves. He also informed us that he believed the worst of the storm had now passed and that a more stable journey was ahead of us. All aboard were mighty relieved I must confess and the lateness of our arrival was unimportant compared to the conviction that it seemed we should arrive safely. Even so, prudence dominated and Sofia stayed in the pattern of only emerging at night to take the air when there were few, if any, sailors on deck.

On this unscheduled southern course, I noted that we passed some islands on our port side. Wondering what they were I enquired of one of the riggers as he descended from his task.

"They be the Shetland Islands, sire."

"Are they of Scotland?"

"Well now, that depends who you ask, sire. To some they be of the Kingdom of Norway and to others they belong to the Kingdom of Scotland." It was this revelation which gave me a clearer understanding of just how far off course we had been blown. Norway was a long way from Scotland I knew.

He continued obviously proud to display his knowledge on the matter. "Mind you, they be of no real importance. I landed there once and noted that many of the islands had these strange buildings on them, even when there were no people living there. They were very large and round and formed of local stone. A ships mate told me that they were of some bygone era but I could see no use for them. There was no door to enter by. So what use they be, no man knows."

"Thank you, my man." I parted from him at this point and descended into the hold to inform Sofia of this point of interest on an otherwise uninspiring view.

One can, I found, become passionate on a voyage for any break in the monotony of only seeing water in every direction.

She was as excited as me to see something other than waves and determined that she would ascend to the deck earlier that evening, whilst it was still light, so that she could also spy land. This she did.

A ship can only carry a limited amount of fresh water. It is this fact, more than any other, which dictates that a journey must be plotted from one watering hole to another rather than take a single journey. Our vessel was on its last barrel of this essential liquid and so it was decided by the Captain that landfall must be made before our first destination of Wick.

The place chosen was an island belonging to these disputed pinnacles in the waters. Sofia and I were unreasonably ecstatic. As she climbed the steep ladder from the hold that evening, we both felt a shift in course of our temporary home. Indeed, the turn was so severe that Sofia had to hold fast to the struts not to be thrown from them. It was most unusual for such a pronounced turning but I assume it was the wind and tide which caused the vessel such a rapid alteration. Whatever the physical cause it left me with the impression that the ship was as keen as us to make landfall. On ascending safely to the deck, we spied the island we were to weigh anchor near dead ahead of us.

A tar was nearby so I enquired of him. "What island is this?"

"This? This is the island of Mousa, sire."

"Mousa? That is a strange name. Do you know anything about it?"

"Well, only what my shipmate, Amos, tells me. We were talking of it just last night as it happens. He told us that it gets its name from the Bible. Mousa means 'A saviour drawn from the water'. Amos reckons that it comes from the name Moses and refers to his time of the parting of the Red Sea."

"Really? How interesting." Sofia had come forward to listen to the sailor. She had found herself unable to remain discrete any longer. "Did Amos tell you anything else about it?"

The sailor looked a little startled to hear my wife speak and it occurred to me that he may well not have even seen her for a time, let alone realized she had a voice. He touched his forelock in acknowledgement of her status and replied "Yes, ma'am. He did mention that it is noted for its Broch of Mousa. That's one of them useless round buildings that some chump took pains to build for no purpose."

"Really? Can we see it from here?" She stepped onto her tip toes and leaned forward over the rail. "Yes. Yes. I see it!" The excitement in her voice was reminiscent of the delight of a child opening a Christmas present on the morning. This level of emotion from a 'bad omen' was too much for our shy sailor friend and he withdrew mumbling something about having to get back to work.

She turned to me again. "I have a feeling about this place. I think this is our destination. An island in the middle of a barren sea is safe from pestilence, politics and fire. Our charge would be safe here. This may be the place." With this she again leant forward to watch the approaching island.

Thus she and I remained for quite some time, neither speaking, but enjoying the wind in our faces blowing our hair back in streamers behind us. Darkness drew down as we stood together silently and utterly contented. Then a miracle happened.

The sky lit up suddenly with such an array of patterns and colours that it stunned us both as our eyes widened to confirm that the image had indeed occurred. The sky had formed into multi-coloured waves of its own as if to match the undulations of the water. Such colours! Never had I seen the like.

"This is the place," Sofia declared with certainty turning to face me. "This is a sign from God that this island has His blessing. It is here that we shall secure the treasure in its passage through time." She turned to me. "You must go with the sailors who are filling the water barrels and take the time to bury the pouch in our safe box by the … what did the sailor call it? … the Broch.

Later this day I shall carry out her instructions. I shall place this, my testament, carefully into the pouch, which I in turn, shall place inside the metal box.

We will leave it unlocked, reasoning that no man in the future would have a key. I shall next take the row boat to land armed with the ships spade. With the help of a sailor, encouraged by a purse, we will carry the heavy box to the Broch. Taking a measured three steps, exactly due south of the unexpectedly large

Broch, we shall then form a hole into which I will lay the precious cargo. This hole will be covered. The surplus soil I shall scatter so as to not draw attention to the hiding place. Onto it I will place stones in the form of the 'mouth' or 'tailless fish' as described by the first guardian.

Here ends my tale since the last part I wrote knowing my plan for the immediate future. Since no more has been added, it is safe to assume that the plan worked. All that will then remain for me is to seek Sofia's guidance on the content of the clue.

Sofia revealed to me, some days later, the text on the slip of fine paper which she will insert into her beautiful broach.

(What looks like a tailless fish) Find the guardian of the Saviour drawn from the water.

(Another sketch of a tailless fish) Take three paces south and in a metal tomb lies the caretakers charge.

Sofia and I send our prayers through the untold time to the next caretaker chosen by God.

My Dearest Cousin,

I send you this piece, written by someone who describes himself as a warrior.

It is another expression of a man's nature changing as time progressed. In his creation, I perceive that, he describes changing from a youth longing for adventure, to a man seeking the more valuable treasures of life.

I cannot help but wonder if this metamorphosis occurs in us all over our lifetime? What is your opinion?

Kindness and solicitude,

Beattie

(Encl.)

Dear Beattie,

First, I must agree with you that tears ran down my face upon reading of the adventures – or is that misadventures – of the haphazard Alchemist, such was my laughter. A man I should dearly have loved to dine with; if only to hear more of his tales.

I checked with one of the resident chemists here at the University. He confirms that our fated Alchemist would, indeed, have used such materials during his 'entertainment'. Although he also pointed out that Health and Safety would have banned such public use of them today.

The collection of lightening in the corked bottle even had my friend, a most dour man by nature, actually giggling. He knew of exactly such an experiment in the distant past. It had also failed!

I eagerly plan to read your next inclusion and have cancelled my planned 'afternoon tea' with friends to facilitate this desire.

Yours, expectantly,
Jackie

The Warrior

12th Century

Mine was a life of violence; but then I was born into an unjust world and violence is its natural companion.

The injustice began at birth, when I was born as only the third boy child delivered to a noble Spanish family. In this position I was therefore granted the breeding and desires of the noble, without the means to live as such, since it was my eldest brother who was to inherit the title, the estate and the money. I hated this brother and he returned the sentiment.

It was part of my private tuition to learn sword skills. I was talented with the weapon and soon realized that this skill alone would determine my future – for I certainly had no other prospects in Aragon, the city of my birth. As soon as I was old enough, I sold myself into the role of mercenary. I became a *milites Christi* (knight of Christ) and with many set sail for the Holy Land with the objective of recovering the holy city of Jerusalem from the Muslim heathens who had claimed it.

As I recall my memories so I write this account.

Unlike some of our companions, my close friends and I did not see this as a battle to allow domination of Papal reign in the world, in the name of Christianity. Nor did we join as an act of penance which some of our fighters did. I had nothing over which to do penance. I was young, strong and perhaps not as dominated by the Pope as I should have been. Frankly, I cared little for him or his religion although it would have been instant death had I voiced this. Europe was alight with religious fervour. Our small band was only interested in gaining money and power. That is the truth behind our motivation. My brother ruled over the family Estate, granting me the smallest of allowances and I intended to return from this backwater richer and more powerful than he. My friends, mostly, found themselves in the same, or comparable, predicament and were on a similar quest. This particularly applied to my closest friends, Adolfo and Conrado.

We had first met at the port of Venice whilst awaiting transport to Constantinople; it being our first port of call. The docks were crowded and I waited by a chandler's pondering the future and what adventures it might hold. Two knights came staggering toward me obviously the worse for ale.

"Hail fellow!" Adolfo drunkenly greeted me.

"Good day, sir." I responded politely.

"Are you for the army?" He politely enquired. Although I remember thinking that the sword which graced my side might have given a clue to a man not drenched in liquor.

"Indeed. I hope to set sail for Constantinople." I decided not to make a similar enquiry of him not wishing to prolong this conversation.

"We too!" Alfonso then, somewhat alarmingly, slung his arm around my shoulder and gave me hug. I went rigid; physical contact, other than with a woman, not being a part of my nature, in spite of my tactile inheritance of Spanish blood.

"Look, Conrado, another fighter in the Papal War." At this he had turned to his companion.

"Indeed." It was a clipped reply from his companion but I suspect that was because he was fighting an urge to be sick judging by the unsettled look on his face. I was proved right as Conrado suddenly lurched towards the edge of the dock and spent the next few moments bringing back the drink he had just paid for and consumed. I looked away in disgust.

Alfonso completely ignored his suffering companion and instead returned his attention to me.

"Spanish?" He enquired.

"Aragon," was my monosyllabic response.

"We, my friend and I, are from Castille." For some reason he seemed to feel that I would be interested. I was not.

"Oh." The sooner I could remove myself from this unwanted attention the better. I made to move off but Alfonso was having none of it.

"And why do you go to do battle, my friend?" This escalation in my status from stranger to friend was an anathema to me. By what definition did he claim to be my friend? I must extricate myself quickly.

"I have my reasons, sir." I thought my reply would warn a sober man that my business would remain my business. Unfortunately, the drunkard is not so discerning.

"We go to seek our fortune." As he declared this, he stood taller on his feet, with hands on hips and struck up a pose which he obviously felt showed his determination.

"Excellent. May fortune ride with us all." Polite but noncommittal I thought.

"You are a sound fellow." His arm reached out for me again and I stepped away. By this time Conrado had returned from making his contribution to the pollution of the water hereabouts.

"That's better." Conrado declared. "That last draught must have been off." I decided to make no comment.

At that very moment a party of some five drunken Frenchmen arrived. It was clear they too were drunk since they walked in a line, arm over shoulder, in attempt to support each other. This posture meant that they took up most of the dock space where we stood.

"Move," one of them issued the command to us.

"We shall not. You go around us." Alfonso responded indignantly.

"Move, I say, you Italian scum," this from the spokesman again. They must have assessed our nationality in the same way I had determined theirs; from recognition of elements of their accent. However, they had been wrong.

"We are Spanish, not Italian." Conrado had come to life and challenged them indignantly.

"Italian; Spanish; what does it matter? You are all the same - all cowards." This was too much for Alfonso and Conrado and, indeed, me.

"Why you French harlot lover!" With this Alfonso withdrew, with some effort, his sword and challenged them in their own language. "En guarde."

Taking the lead from Alfonso, we all, they and us, withdrew our swords and took up postures to commence battle. I do not remember who struck the first parry but the ensuing battle was invigorating. Alfonso, Conrado and I stood back to back whilst the French circled us like a besieging army round a settlement. The three of us returned parry for parry and defended each other as if we had been brothers for all time. We were impenetrable as each thrust by the French was successfully blocked.

After a surprisingly short time the French began to withdraw. One after the other they stood back and ceased hostility; still maintaining the meaningless act of bravado of shouting insults about the Spanish and our dubious parentage. The battle was over and the French returned from the direction they had come no doubt to drink away their humiliation.

Alfonso, Conrado and I bent over to recover our breath having sheathed our weapons. We then laughed, more prompted by relief than humour. As we straightened our countenance, we realized we had forged the inexplicable friendship that only brothers in battle can attain. Our arms reached out for one another and we stood in a circle, each with his arms around the shoulders of his comrades. As we laughed together, we knew we were destined to be friends from that moment.

It was in this same port of Venice that fate stepped in to guide our steps. We all knew that we intended to sail to Constantinople to become members of the knights of God but none of us had any idea how to achieve this. We knew from the criers, that Antioch, in the Holy Land, had surrendered to our forces and that a large company of knights were now marching towards Jerusalem. It was these warriors that we intended to meet up with. The question of "how" was about to be answered.

Conrado was the first to notice two noblemen beside the main path leading from the town to the dock. They were instantly recognizable from both the fact that they were seated upon fine stallions and they wore peacock coloured vestments. Each of them had two soldiers, in matching uniforms to each other, who were also mounted. The plumes from their fine headgear waved in an indiscernible breeze. We were drawn into their vicinity like bees to the flower head.

As we approached, we saw that each nobleman was engaged in the same task. He would point to those of us traversing the road and one of his soldiers would immediately force his horse between the milling crowds to approach the man who had received the noble's attention. The soldier would bend down and speak to the traveller or labourer who would then follow the soldier back towards the noble.

One such pointed finger of fate came my way and I saw a mounted soldier head towards me.

"You there." He announced on his arrival in my vicinity. "You, with the sword and brown sack."

"Me sir?"

"Yes, you sir." He continued "My lord, Gustav of Bamberg, invites you to join our company of soldiers in the Holy War of Reclamation. Will you accept?"

"I should be delighted if his pay is reasonable." I responded.

"He pays slightly above the average, sir, but for this he insists upon absolute loyalty." This seemed a reasonable condition to me and I was enthusiastic to respond positively. However, it did occur to me that my new friends would be interested as well. Since I had already appreciated and benefitted from their prowess as warriors, I was desirous that they support me similarly on my quest abroad.

"I travel with two companions each of whom are excellent fighters. May they join me?" It was worth asking.

"They may as long as they have weapons." Both qualified as the French had learnt to their cost.

"They do, sir. Each is an accomplished swordsman and carries their own weapon."

"Come then. Let you all stand behind my lord, Gustav." He wheeled his horse around with a firm reign and trotted back from whence he had come.

The three of us, begging pardon constantly, forced our way across the two-way tide of humanity towards our new commander.

"That was easier than I thought it would be." commented Conrado.

"Gustav of where did he say?" Enquired Alfonso.

"Bamberg, I think he said" I replied.

"Where is that?" Alfonso was none the wiser from the name I had offered.

"I believe it is part of the Rhineland." I was able to reply to this enquiry because one of my private tutors had come from that part of the world and the sound of the place rang some sort of bell with me.

We quickly reached our destination behind our new master and stood as part of a group of some twenty other fellows. It quickly became obvious that nationality had played no part in selection since several foreign languages were heard from this select and selected crowd. Our swords had proven to be our passports. There were just two men who apparently had mere staffs to wield but the enormous size of those men were authority enough. I, for one, would not go up against them even with a sword.

As the crowd of passing voyagers and workers began to thin, our commander, Gustav, turned his horse to face us.

"You have been selected to become soldiers in my company. This decision will instantly be overturned if I or my officers perceive any wilfulness or disobedience. For such transgressions you will be punished and then dismissed. I pay fairly and expect you to fight for the causes I decide upon with devotion and without question. In exchange for this loyalty you shall be rewarded by a tunic bearing my crest which I expect you to bear proudly." At this one of his mounted escorts puffed his chest and raised himself in his stirrups to better reveal an image of an erect and attacking eagle outlined in red on the white background of his tunic. This image of the bird of prey was surrounded by a deep and not displeasing dark green border. We three looked at each other displaying our approval.

Our benefactor continued. "You will receive one substantial meal each day. For those of you without exceptional skill with weapons, you will be allocated to tasks befitting your condition. If a comrade should fall in battle, the first to recover his weapon may then present himself as armed and be promoted to a fighting role."

My lord, Gustav, continued. "I have commissioned a vessel to carry us and our supplies to Constantinople. It leaves by first light. You will all be boarded immediately and assist the crew in the loading and stowage of this craft."

His voice then began to rise to a crescendo. "My company shall play an historic role in subjugating Palestine in the name of God. Be proud that you are elected to serve both God and me."

A cheer rose up from the assembled company which we found ourselves prompted, by enthusiasm, to join.

So saying, he again turned his horse towards the water's edge and kicked it into a slow walk. His officers, for such I perceived them to be, moved on their mounts to the back of our number and shouted for us to follow our new master. They continued to bring up the rear ensuring no stragglers would be lost or allowed to stray from our number.

We travelled on the ship which was itself part of an impressive convoy. None of us knew what to expect when we landed but the enthusiastic babble aboard indicated the level of excitement common to all.

Finally, we arrived at Constantinople, a place up to now, that I had read about but never truly envisaged. Whatever my imagination had conjured up had not come close to the reality of this thriving city.

"Look at that!" exclaimed Conrado as we pressed our bodies against the side of the ship as it entered port. "That building is an amazing colour. Whatever materials did they use to build it?" He was looking at a structure which would, in size, have fitted the centre of Castille, but in colour might have been seen in a circus. It was a hue of what I can only relate to as a gentle pink; whether that was caused by the way the sun hit it, or the nature of the stone, I could not say. Never had any of us seen the like.

"It has a domed roof. How amazing is that?" Responded Alfredo. "I thought this was the uncivilized part of the world." His surprise at the sophistication we were witnessing clearly evident in his voice. A sentiment shared by us all.

"What are all those thin towers?" I ventured to throw the question open to any listening. "We do not have anything similar in the whole of Spain." This may have been a rash statement on my part since I had only really travelled in the area surrounding Aragon, but I felt sure I was right nevertheless. Murmurings, uttered by several men around me who were also pressed against the guardrails in attempt to see our destination, showed that none knew the answer.

The ship, having pulled roughly level to the dock, had its crew throw ropes to a small army of men waiting on land to receive them. These men formed chains and slowly pulled the ship until it lay in direct and close parallel to the stonework. Once the ropes were tied, off a plank was stretched from the ship to the shore, and we disembarked in orderly manner.

"It is so hot," observed Alfonso wiping his forehead with his sleeve.

"Indeed; no sea breeze to cool us now." Conrado agreed.

"What is that smell?" My nose turned up in disgust. I hadn't noticed it before but now standing on dry land the stench of humanity and its industries assaulted my senses. These were mixed in with aromas whose source I could in no way identify.

"Now I see why they say this country is uncivilized." Alfonso observed whilst protecting his nose from the smell. This was not a totally justified statement since I knew there were areas, even in my beloved Aragon, where ladies used various means, to disguise the surrounding smell in the street, when walking. But I must admit this aroma was worse than any I had thus far witnessed.

The next two weeks were a blur of agony, exhaustion and not a little regret. I counted myself as athletic until the torture we were put through disproved this. We ran. We jumped. We climbed. We engaged in sword, staff and knife fights. At night, aching in every joint, we would climb onto our makeshift mattresses and fall into deep sleep until the next clarion call rudely awoke us. We gleaned, thanks to Alfonso's talent for picking up gossip, that lord Gustav was waiting for an order as to where his company was to be sent. None wished that he receive that instruction more than me.

There were, thankfully, some odd days of respite. Whilst my two friends and I were mostly to be found together, my companions were more lured by drink than I, and oft times they would repair to the inn for ale on these days, whilst I amused myself in the town.

It was on one such solitary sojourn that I entered what appeared to be a well-stocked library. As I sauntered along a row of tomes, occasionally extracting one from its prison, then returning it having established its subject matter, I came across a Latin text which promised illumination into the geography we were set to explore. It was, unusually, a leather-bound volume and I was able to flick through the beautifully crafted pages; delighting at the dominant letter artistically decorated at the beginning of each section. The beauty of this work of literature and art blended in such a fusion of symbiosis prompted me to place the book on a convenient table top. From here I stood and leafed through the pages, drinking in the hand-drawn maps showing the layout of towns, one in relation to another. As I turned one page, which had shown me the surrounds of Jerusalem, I discovered a small slip of parchment incongruously secreted in the following page. I read the words on the slip.

First came a picture, if one could describe its insignificance as such. It reminded me of a slightly parted mouth. To describe it to you, the reader – if there be such in the future, - it might be easier to ask you to imagine a fish, as drawn by a child, whose tail part had then been erased.

(Tailless fish) The mouth of Ptolemy never spoke such wisdom.
(Tailless fish) But his guiding light illuminates the word.

The only thing I knew for sure was that this document did not belong in the volume I was viewing. Someone had no doubt slipped it in there at some time and for some reason. I decided to restore the book to its original unblemished perfection. Removing the slip, which I placed in my pouch, I closed the artwork with a satisfied feeling that I had, in some small way, restored order to its enchanting existence.

By this time, with Gustav of Bamberg, having recruited more men who had become separated from their original unit, and joined with other lesser companies, we numbered around four hundred as a group. Only senior soldiers rode whilst the rest of us walked in weary, humid and dusty lines or wore out our diminishing energy encouraging and assisting the beasts to pull the carts which accompanied us on our exercises.

One day our excursion into the countryside around Constantinople did not reach a conclusion. That night we lay where we had walked to. The next day we continued on the same path. We deduced that we were finally en route to a new destination.

"Have you heard any rumours as to where we are headed?" I enquired of my friends as we sat near a fire that night.

"I heard that one of the servants of Gustav heard him talking of Acre, or Akka, or Akk, or something sounding like it anyway." Alfonso was eager, as always, to impart this third-party gossip.

"Where is that? How far is it?" Conrado asked.

"I do not know. I do not even know if it is somewhere that the Popes army yet holds or is to be the site of our first battle - yet." Alfonso's words and manner indicated that he would make it his mission to find the detail of this unknown place in the days to come. I did not doubt that he would succeed.

It was several days later and after many miles that Alfonso sidled up to me during our passage and announced that he had found out all about our mission. I could hardly wait for camp to be struck so that I might learn our fate. Talk whilst on the march was not encouraged, although this rule did not apply to those mounted on steeds. Eventually my impatience was satisfied and as we sat with our food bowls on our laps, I pleaded with him to declare his revelations.

"I happened to be walking near a knight who was lecturing those around him as we journeyed", he explained. "Naturally enough I altered my path to draw closer to him until he was within earshot. I now know all there is to know about our destination." With this he sat up straighter and puffed his chest out in pride.

"Really", this from Conrado, "you know ALL there is to know, do you?" Whilst I detected amusement in his voice, I suspect that Alfonso's constant boasting was wearing thin with our companion as his weariness increased because of the traveling.

"Surely!" Alfonso was not as sensitive to the emotion behind the words as I.

"It transpires that we are indeed heading for a major port called Acre." Before another word could be uttered, Conrado interrupted.

"If it's a major port, then why are we walking? Why did we not find a boat and sail there?"

"Well I don't know, do I?" Alfonso responded defensively and somewhat aggravated.

"So, you don't know ALL there is to know then, do you?" Poor Conrado was really letting the journey spoil his usually good-natured humour.

"Do you want to hear what I have learnt or not?" Not that Alfonso doubted for one second that his listeners would respond positively to this rhetorical question. We both fell to silence and he continued after a small pause.

"According to this scholarly fellow, Acre is one of the oldest settlements and dates right back to, he believes, the Egyptian era of some 3000 years before our Lord.

"That can't be right", interjected Conrado angrily. "The Bible clearly states that the world is not that old."

Alfonso totally ignored this interjection, as if had not been spoken. "Acre, or Akko as it was then called, is actually mentioned in the Bible, this scholar assured me, when I put the same question to him." Alfonso *had* registered the question then. "He told me that it is stated in the book of Job that when God sent the great flood, He had said "Hitherto shalt thou come, but no further" and the line He drew was at Acre." Conrado made no response however I detected that he was thinking on this and would raise the debate again at some later date.

"To continue", Alfonso did not delay in expounding his knowledge. "The next stage in its history is that it was claimed by a Roman Emperor who, as was their way, renamed it after himself. It became called Ptolemais. Eventually the Muslims decided they wanted it, and the city fell to them. They renamed it again, to Akka."

"Obviously a city of some importance," I ventured.

"It is the port which is so valued, so sayeth the man I was listening to. He pointed out that it lies at the very gateway to the Holy Land." Alfonso paused for just a moment to allow his audience to digest this information.

"Anyway, our nobles certainly thought so, because apparently our army, led by King Baldwin, lay siege to it and it was only after four years that we were able claim the city and port as our own. That happened only last year. King Baldwin renamed the port at that time to Acre – and this is our destination!" He concluded triumphantly.

Neither Conrado nor I spoke. We just looked at each other, then to Alfonso, whilst this news was fully digested. One great question had been answered and that was that we should not have to fight in the near future. I am not clear whether this brought relief or disappointment to my heart.

Conrado voiced my very thoughts. "So, no battle then," he stated.

"No … and Yes!" Alfonso was back at the centre of attention, his natural place of comfort. "As I understand it, we are to stay in Acre only a short time … and then we are to march on Jerusalem itself." The emphasis he placed on the word 'Jerusalem' evidenced the adoration that we all shared for the city.

Having duly praised Alfonso for his diligence in attaining this critical information for us, the meal fell to silence, each of us wrapped in our own turmoil of emotions.

I had thought Venice a port of magnificence and Constantinople a port of astonishment. Neither exceeded my amazement at the port of Acre. The high walls, surrounding the narrow entrance to the shipping refuge, were of un-scalable height with the fewest of signs indicating battle damage. Throughout its battlements, which I later explored, slots were evident. These, I learnt, were to afford archers a clear firing range for any transgressors onto its territory.

The city itself was no less remarkable. It held the grandeur of Constantinople potted with its own unique architecture hitherto unseen by my eyes. My singular sojourns never ceased to enthral me as I explored this ancient and proud city over the next few weeks.

The languages of its peoples were represented by the whole of the Byzantine Empire from whence they had been brought. Fortunately, Latin in which I was comfortable conversing, usually granted me communication. I tried speaking Spanish once or twice but to no avail and soon gave up on speaking my mother tongue.

Just as our patience was wearing thin with being so inactive, word came that we were to join the mighty army by the city of Jerusalem. Our company was to swell its ranks. We set off overland always aware and alert for the Saracen bands which operated in the region.

"Saracens! Alarm!" The cry was raised by one of the outlying lookouts. We were just inside a narrow valley which cut through a small mountain range. We travelled alone, Lord Gustav's warriors, so our number was still around four hundred – those who had died already having been rapidly replaced.

"Archers!" Another warning cry just a moment before a cloud of angry projectiles darkened the sky before us.

"Make a shield", shouted the officer nearest to us. Those in the vicinity hunkered down in an artificial mound, with shields above our heads. This made us look like a giant beetle but at least we were safe, or mostly so. The arrows rained on our raised shields like Hell's rain and none were tempted to look out to see what was happening.

A second wave of ill-meaning arrows landed on our temporary roof. It was then we heard the next command shouted.

"Stand and defend!"

At this, as one man, we stood and repositioned our shields to the forward position thereby protecting our bodies. The sight which befell my frightened eyes was one which will haunt my sleep for the remainder of my days. Hurtling down the valley towards us was a cloud of dust which screamed with the voice of a thousand demons. We rearranged ourselves so that we less resembled a turtle and more a snake. Our stance, whilst imprecise, was at least a line of sorts, and thus we stood, inactive, watching in horror this oncoming, bellowing, dust cloud.

Far too quickly I was able to discern that the dust was merely the shield and that the real danger lay in what it covered. Horse after horse, rider after rider, became visible. As the first ranks drew close, I could see in the eyes of the riders' sheer, open, hatred. They held strange bow shaped swords aloft which more terrified me. Even the most accomplished of swordsmen required two hands to raise his weapon. These demons used just one hand to elicit a swinging action which more resembled a farmer scything, than a swordsman parrying or thrusting.

Onward they sped towards our frightened number. Just as I was sure they would ride right into our midst, the leading charge swerved to the side. As rank after rank of horseman approached us, they too came close and at the last minute took off to the side. It was chaos. We stood facing front but quickly found that the Saracens, for so we assumed them to be, were circling round behind us.

"Form circles!" This command was screamed by one of the seven mounted officers in our midst. We did not hesitate; being like children lost in a strange world obeying their comforting, all-knowing parent and trusting without question that they understood what we did not.

As we took up the posture of standing facing back to back, one of the officers dismounted from his horse and forced his way to our centre whilst sending his precious mount running off. In our circle, numbering perhaps fifty men, we held in our ranks; pike men and lancers as well as swordsmen like myself. These proved our greatest allies as they, unlike us, were able to extend their weapons to reach the circling attackers and occasionally unhorse one. Having become unseated the nearest swordsman would step forward and finish the demon.

All around me there were screams of agony from falling comrades as the evil scything cut them even through their limited chain mail. I remember thinking that I should never again be unfeeling for the corn of the fields when I saw a farmer gathering the harvest.

All the while those in our circle who were unarmed and had sought shelter in the middle, pulled any wounded comrades towards the middle to clear the path for those of us still ineffectually fighting. As I quickly glance behind me, I recalled a funeral pyre I had once seen of dead bodies gathered for burning during a plague. The scene behind me was only missing the flame.

I cannot say how long this attack by the Saracens lasted nor how many of them there were. It is impossible to count such fast moving and weaving targets but it seemed to me that they numbered many, many more than us. I had fairly good quality chain mail but whether this was a good thing or bad I could not determine. It protected me from more than one arrow but so raised my body temperature that I could barely stand from the heat. Thirst burnt my throat but there was no water except on a cart which I saw a small band of Saracens lead off.

The battle at last ended. I know not what signal the Saracen army had received but they withdrew as a body, suddenly, and along the path from which the screaming cloud had come. None of us moved for some time. We were all in a dream, or nightmare, and were trying to establish if we were now awake.

A comforting voice sounded in my ear at last. "Are you alright, comrade?" Turning my head slowly to the side I saw that it was Conrado. I almost laughed, incongruously, for he looked so pale, not from shock but from dust. As I scanned the men around me, I saw that we all looked the same – everyone covered in white powder. All variance of colour had gone. We were all one tribe at that moment - just men who had fought the battle of Armageddon against the demons of hell.

"Yes." I went to speak but my voice was dry and cracked. "Have you seen Alfonso?"

"No." We both looked at the men standing near us. Alfonso had been right next to us before the cloud had descended. Fearfully, we both turned to the pile of dead and dying behind us. Wanting to find him and yet dreading the thought of doing so.

"There." Conrado pointed to a prostrate figure to the edge of the funeral stack. We rushed over and knelt beside his bloody body.

"Alfonso. Alfonso. It's me, Conrado." There was no reaction as his eyes remained closed.

"Water! Someone, bring me water, for the love of God." Conrado looked around in pleading. A lancer who had been standing near reached into a carrier beside him and pulled out a small jug. This he passed to Conrado. No words accompanied this action. No words of sympathy were needed.

Conrado gently lifted Alfonso's head and allowed a trickle of the healing liquid to touch his lips. As water is the foundation of life, so this water restored life to our wounded friend. He opened his eyes and in a weak voice such as I had never heard from him before, he uttered "My friend. Thank you." Conrado fed him some more of the healing compound and then lowered his head gently to the ground once more.

"Did we win?" This enquiry of Alfonso's was so typical of his warrior nature and I loved him for it.

"Indeed, we did, comrade," I proudly announced. "We drove them off."

"Ah, good." At this he seemed to tire and once more shut his eyes. After a short time, he opened them again and looked directly at me.

"Do you believe in life after death?" I cannot conjecture why he should have asked this of me. We were all naturally raised in the Catholic religion, but I had never really given this particular subject much thought, nor ever discussed it with him.

The pleading look behind his eyes left me feeling inadequate to answer this question with conviction.

"Of course, I do, my friend. Our Lord shall raise each of us in His hands and bear us to Heaven. This I believe."

He looked at me with the intensity of someone who could read my soul on my face. With this, his eyes seemed to glaze over and I knew, I just knew, that my friend was no longer here. I stared back at his empty shell. Decency made my hand move out and gently close his eyes. I knew he was no longer looking at me.

Conrado was squatting with head bowed as in prayer - but I felt unable to pray. I just stared at Alfonso's body. It was hard to comprehend that such a vibrant life could be so cruelly and quickly stubbed out. Never before had death seemed such a close companion.

As we walked aimlessly around the field of battle, more truly described as the field of the massacre, the silence was the most dominant feature. The ground was spotted everywhere with the harsh red or brown of blood lost from friend and foe alike. Looking at the patches of discoloration there was no way to discern from whom it had come. As our faces all looked of the same hue, so our blood removed borders too. Be we knight or Saracen we were all human with the common fluid coursing through our veins and, in death, there was no difference.

Our numbers had been so culled that Gustav had decided not to continue on to Jerusalem; so we made the long, slow journey back to Acre. Conrado and I were near the back of the column of silently trudging men. Two of the officers, and Gustav, had found mounts, but the others were either dead or walking, having lost their horses. Another difference between men removed.

I had sustained a minor gash on my upper arm which had, at first, not bothered me. However, as the days progressed this became inflamed and the pain seemed to increase with each step. Eventually, Conrado pointed out to me that a fever had taken hold and I was delirious. His words only vaguely impacted upon me. As a true friend, he aided my progress and ensured that he always carried a little water with him to quench my rising thirst. One night the fever was at its height and I was vaguely aware of a stranger speaking to Conrado as I lay by a fire.

"If he lasts the night the worst will be over. Keep him still and take this water to cool him as needed. Use it sparingly though because our ration is limited. We should reach Acre tomorrow and he can be more properly treated there."

Oblivion of this world swept over me. Experience of another world became dominant.

I saw myself clearly standing in a warm, sunny meadow wearing nothing but a simple man's coverall. A gentle breeze washed over me and the delight I felt was tangible. Time itself was no longer relevant for it held no dominance here. As I looked around, the grass was even greener than that of my home ground; the sky was a clear blue; no other people were there but I was not lonely or afraid. I was alone and delighted in that. As I wallowed in the thrill of this heavenly place a light drew near. It was a light with more depth than any of earth. It had no edge to it nor did it hurt my eyes in spite of its brilliance. It encompassed my field of vision. There was no fear in my heart but, rather, an overwhelming feeling of peace and love. I was looking, I knew, upon the form of God Himself. It felt right and natural for me to fall to my knees and this I did taking up the simple, supplicant posture of a child at prayer.

Then a vision came into my mind as clear as if I was looking at it on the day I had found it.

(The tailless fish) The mouth of Ptolemy never spoke such wisdom.

(Again, the fish) But his guiding light illuminates the word.

I immediately remembered the slip I had removed from that beautiful, bound book. Next, I heard the voice of Alfonso exactly as he had related our destination details so long ago.

"The next stage in its history is that it was claimed by a Roman Emperor who, as was their way, renamed it after himself. It became called Ptolemais." I instantly knew that Ptolemais had been named after Ptolemy and that this place was now called Acre – our destination.

I wept at the joy which overwhelmed my spirit. It went so far beyond hope; it had become knowledge.

I slept then. When I awoke, I was lying in the shade of a building on a mattress and my strength, I felt, was fast returning. My vision, for I shall not debase it by intimating that it was a dream in delirium, was as clear to my mind as it had been at the time. It remains so even to this day and will remain so for the whole of my life.

My thirst for adventure had been satisfied and my lust for battle quenched. I had tasted death but not been consumed by it. I escaped from the ranks of Gustav and remained in hiding until his company, much swelled in ranks, again set out to reinforce Jerusalem. My parting with Conrado had been bitter but I knew that, unlike him, my hunger for fame and fortune had been sated.

Having established that the location was Acre, it had taken but a little thought to realize that the clue on the slip indicated that something was hidden here. With just a little more thought I recognised that the light, warning of the harbour entrance, must be the exact location. Whatever it was, would be found near, or under, the cautionary light afforded by a brazier and used to warn vessels.

One night I set out, with a small shovel in hand, to explore this area. I carefully moved the brazier a few feet nearer the edge, with a yoke I had bought that day. I began to dig under the spot. Some little distance down I found a leather satchel. With a feeling of awe, I lifted the precious carrier. I filled in the hole again and using the yoke returned the light to its resting place.

On returning to my humble digs I carefully opened the bag. Eagerly I read the testaments contained therein.

My life now took a new direction. Tired of fighting and challenge I still needed to earn a living and had few skills to offer an employer. My ability to write was an asset held by few and I hoped that this may in some way be utilized. Frankly, at this time the thought of a quiet collegiate lifestyle appealed. I made my way, using the last of my money, to Cyprus where I felt safe from Gustav's clutches.

With nothing left with which to pay for board or lodging I hung around the port where I had landed by day and climbed the nearby hill each evening to feed on wild growth, oranges and olives. At night my head rested under sheltering tree branches. On several occasions I was able to procure a day of work from one of the fishermen. Never before had I gutted fish but this was soon a skill I added to my portfolio. The money earned from this, such as it was, enabled me to bolster my diet with bread – which simple food had never tasted so good.

One of the more dominant fishermen had a contract for his catch with a market trader of equal importance. The trader operated in several towns on Cyprus and provided a network of transport to each location daily with the haul as well as produce such as oranges and olives. In order to co-ordinate this thriving business the trader demand a written listing of the fish caught overnight. Unfortunately for the fisherman he had never mastered the written word and relied upon a kinsman for production of the daily list. The kinsman, to my advantage if not his, fell ill. Thus, by an act of fate, I stepped in whilst his kinsman was incapacitated and created this nomenclature. The trader, noticing the superior quality of the lists, made enquiry of the fisherman as to their author. He sought me out.

"I understand that you are the one writing these lists?" he enquired having approached me on the dockside and waving several of my lists in his plump hand. By his stature this was not a man who had known hunger.

"Yes sir."

"Are you employed full time I ask?"

"No sir. I am just doing this task whilst my employer's brother-in-law is unwell."

"Ah, ha". His inflection indicated that this had given him a new idea. "So! What is your normal employ?"

"Whatever I can, day by day, sir." I must confess that my hope was rising that this might prove to be a benefactor who might offer a more permanent solution to my constant battle for money.

"Good. Then I wish to make you an offer. I run a trading business across this side of the island and have need of a scribe. Are you interested in filling this position?"

I was not of a mind to argue or barter. "Sir," I responded. "I should be most grateful for the opportunity."

"Right, then that is settled. You begin immediately." He looked smug or was that my imagination?

"Sir, respectfully, I cannot begin yet. May I ask your indulgence that I begin once the kinsman has returned to work?" I knew I was chancing his impatience but honour is all to a knight - even one who wished to be one.

There was a pause as his plump jowls formed a shape akin to distaste. Then a smile broke on his pouting face as he spoke. "I admire a man of integrity even more than a man of letters. Indeed, you may join me once the fisherman's kin is returned." He held out his hand to seal the contract. I accepted in acknowledgement of the deal struck and he departed, rolling his way out of the dock area.

It was a happy four years that I spent in the employ of this trader. He was a firm man who demanded the highest standards in everything at all times but he was also fair in his dealings. I made many acquaintances during my tenure, of tradesmen from all corners of the globe, or so it seemed to me. We dealt in an increasing variety of products as the wealth of Cyprus and her peoples increased. More luxury goods arrived from a wider range of provinces. These I recorded carefully and in my best hand, all clearly marked as to their cost and the price for which they would be sold. At the end of each week, I would add up the amount spent and the sum of the income and present this to the trader in a purposely devised statement. He and I were both pleased with our arrangement.

As the four-year mark approached, I had found feelings arising in me of wishing to move on, journeying with the trading partners with whom we intermittently dealt. A ship came all the way from Spain and thoughts of home returned to me. Another came from France; some from even further into the Holy Roman Empire; yet others came from the South, in the area of Africa. As each took their leave, I found myself wishing I could be going with them. It was not that I was unhappy it was just that I wanted to explore.

Herr Pelzer was one whom I had met before and welcomed on his return to our island. He was, he informed me over ale, originally from an aspiring town called Bamberg, far, far away. I missed the other information he continued with, because the name of Bamberg had alerted me to the fact that this was where Gustav had come from and my concentration on the present was diverted to remembrances of the past. I was deeply intrigued to learn more of his home town and especially whether Herr Pelzer had come across Gustav. He did not personally know him but he assured me that, of course, he had heard of him.

I bought my companion another refresher and explored with him exactly what was involved in his journey. It was in the back of my mind to, perhaps, accompany him on his journey. As he related the length and challenges of his travel, rather than being put off as any of right mind might be, my sense of adventure increased.

"This is to be my last voyage," Herr Pelzer offered. "My eyes are not sharp enough now and my bones weary at the constant challenge of the seas."

I was surprised. "What will you do?"

"I have built a sound trading route with many contacts for goods. When I get to home port, I shall sell the ship and its route, with contacts, to the highest bidder. Then I shall enjoy the pleasure of again coming to know the personality of my wife. The money I raise should be enough to raise a small-holding and there, she and I, will live in peace. This is my dream."

My mind raced. Here my companion was in thoughts of settling down whereas mine were in thoughts of moving on. An idea came into my mind and I decided to explore it further.

"How will your route be valued?"

"I must keep note of goods bought and sold on this passage. The profit of this, reduced by the crew share, will determine that value," he informed me.

"Herr Pelzer. As you know I am employed to use my skills to perform this exact function now."

"I have heard nothing but praise for your diligence". I was gratified to hear this, no more than now.

"Sir, may I suggest that I be crewed on your craft to carry out this odious duty?" There. I had made the commitment.

Herr Pelzer went silent. Just picking up his mug he took a leisurely draft from it. Slowly he put it down on the table again and his eyes turned to seek mine. "What would you want for this service?"

"I am able bodied, sir, and can act as crew in all aspects. The duty of maintaining records of your purchases and sales I willingly undertake as an additional task. It is my belief that an accurate recording of your wealth generation may buy you some extra livestock for your small-holding with no added work for yourself." There I had made my plea.

Silence again descended upon our table.

"Most of my crew earn bed and board with a small share of profits on arriving at my home port. Will this suffice you? You shall only be entitled to half share of that of the crew since you are merely making half of the journey." My spirits rose considerably.

"I should be more than content with that. My greatest wish is to earn passage."

"You are a man who carries luck with him, sir," my new employer offered. "Luck is essential to the life of a sailor and so I value this trait fully."

"How so?" I was confused by this assertion of his.

"I took aboard a young lad on the outward journey but on arriving here he informs me that he wishes to disembark. For some reason he intends to settle in this unholy region of the world." He was silent for a time as he obviously tried to grasp why any would exchange the lush civilization of his home area for the heat and blandness of this land. I decided not to interrupt his reverie.

Eventually he continued. "So! Your luck. For had he not disembarked then there would have been no birth available. It is settled! You may crew on my ship with the added duty of presenting a healthy account of my takings upon reaching our destination. Shake and the deal is sealed my lucky young friend." My hand shot out from my side and the smile I felt on my face seemed attached to its movement. I was to voyage again.

Whilst I was sad to leave my current employer I was thrilled at the prospect of once more being on the move. I shall not recount the details of our six-month journey but suffice to say we harboured in many ports, traded, and moved on after restocking our supplies. Diligently I recorded all transactions, taking pains to record operating costs in a separate column to those of the trading, thus highlighting the value of the trade contacts. We faced and conquered all the challenges of Neptune and delighted in the beauty of his domain when he and time allowed. My captain and I would oft talk in the late evening over rations. Using his memory, he thrilled me with tales from his home of Bamberg and its rich aspirations. This was a place I planned to see.

Herr Pelzer was delighted at the price his trader fetched at the auction. Not a little of which was due to my record keeping which inspired other movers in commerce to desire his route. I was excited to be on new, unexplored territory and he and I parted most amicably; he to his new life – I to mine.

It was nearly two months before I arrived in my destination town. I would work at whatever was needed by the local landowners or farmers as I travelled, rest in the countryside, and then continue on. It was only on looking back that I realized how very far I had come.

Sitting on a newly formed hay bale I was speaking with a fellow farm hand one evening whilst we tore hungrily at our bread.

"Where you off to then?" He enquired. He knew I had just secured two days' work.

"I am aiming for Bamberg," I replied.

"Bamberg, eh?" He took another tear of his bread, flavoured it with a small chunk of cheese and devoured these whilst apparently deep in thought. When his mouth was again unoccupied, he made an announcement. "I know a bit about Bamberg. My sister's husband comes from there."

"Really? What can you tell me?" I was eager to swell the knowledge my captain had imparted and a local seemed the ideal teacher.

"It's all to do with the Pope. Bamberg. Did you know that for a time Bamberg was the centre of the Holy Roman Empire?" My look of incredulity obviously amused him. He continued. "Yes. Not many know that. Ha! The centre of the Holy Roman Empire. Bamberg." He obviously thought this worth repeating and he was right to do so, since I was so stunned at this revelation that I was not sure I had heard aright.

"Oh yes. There's an abbey there which is well over a hundred years old. Benedictines got it. Yes. And a cathedral! Now that's worth a visit. Indeed it is. Yes." They reckon that was built by King Henry. The second one. My brother in law says it's packed full of treasure. All gold and the like."

"Really?" I was overwhelmed at the importance of this place which I had thitherto thought to be some minor town of little or no renown. It crossed my mind that maybe Gustav had been of greater standing than we, in his company, had assessed him. We had just thought he was the spoilt, rich son of some minor noble or other.

"Yes. Really." He took another tear of bread and morsel of cheese. This partaking of repast precluded any further conversation since his mouth was henceforth too full to speak. We did not converse on Bamberg again nor anything else for that matter as the work was not inconsiderable and the two days, which stretched to three, proved very long.

Some few days later, the path of my journey crested a hill. Ahead of me lay a valley, formed by seven such hills, in which nestled the proud town of Bamberg. It was with amusement that I recalled that Rome also stood in the vale of seven hills and the thought passed my mind that maybe that is why it was suggested that this place be the centre of The Holy Roman Empire.

Luckily, (perhaps my captain had been right and I was indeed lucky), I obtained work at a local hostelry and staging post. One of my duties was to keep the barrels of ale replenished in the dark and poorly stocked inn. My other duties were likely to be whatever needed doing that did not involve handling Hans', the proprietors, money. Greta was the large, middle-aged wife of the owner who served the customers at their table and cooked whatever the daily offering of stew was to be – or reheated it if some remained from the previous day. She was a delight to be in the room with and her jovial attitude lit the otherwise dim interior. I slept above the barn, ate well not least assisted by extra morsels that Greta would secretly hand me, and was contented.

After a few months of this ideal relationship between Hans, Greta and myself, Hans came to the decision that I was worthy to also tend the bar occasionally. I am certain that it was Greta's insistence that allowed me this less strenuous position. Hans, at first, kept very close to my side and repeatedly counted the coins I was collecting but, as time passed, he seemed to satisfied himself as to my honesty and would commonly join his friends at a table or even leave the inn completely.

One night an older man entered our poor surround and found a seat at an unoccupied table in a dark corner. Since Greta was in the back reheating the stew for another local, I went to his table to find out what we could provide for him. He wore an all-encompassing cloak, gathered around him loosely and his cowl raised to further hide his face. When I spoke to him, he slowly looked up and the sight that befell my eyes shook me to the very core.

A gaunt face appeared, with an ugly scar which stretched from his mouth, across his cheek and up into the folds of his cowl. It was not this alone which had so unnerved me. I instantly recognized him to be Gustav. But he looked so old and so ill. He was not much older than me and yet he looked more as I would imagine my father to have been. Whatever could so suck the years from a man?

"Ale." His one-word hoarse response to my enquiry provided no hint that he recognized me. Nor should he for I had been a lowly swordsman in his company and as such had not been worth a second look or thought. I fetched his beverage with a hundred questions bombarding my mind – none of which I dare ask.

I placed his mug on the table and waited for just a moment wanting to speak but not daring too. He made no acknowledgement other than to reach for the ale and take long, thirsty swallows of the draught. I withdrew. Not long after I heard a disembodied cry of "More ale" from the corner where my noble sat. I retrieved his mug, refilled it and returned it replenished. I did not speak but he did.

"I know you," he ventured almost suspiciously.

"Yes, my Lord. I had the honour to serve with you at Acre."

"Were you at the fight on the road to Jerusalem?"

"Yes indeed, sir. I was wounded there and had to leave your service rather than try again to reach Jerusalem with you." I declined to indicate that I had deserted. He took another long drink.

"So, you were not involved in our defeat?"

"No, sir. To my regret." Having begun the deception, I decided to give it strength.

"Sit," he commanded with a wave of his hand. I knew that my current allegiance was due to Hans and his customers so I looked around and was gratified to see that Greta had now returned to the public area. I sat.

"You are not from Bamberg. What brings you here?" A small gentleness had entered his gruff tone.

"You, sir." That was the truth of it. "I knew you to be from here, and on meeting a trader also calling this his home town, I decided to find where such noble men were born."

"Rubbish, sir." Fury rose in his voice. Both his hands reached onto the table as if he were about to use their leverage to stand. "Do you mock me?"

"No, sir. Really." I was agitated in my defensive attitude. "Truly I do not. I have the heart of an adventurer and it seemed too much a coincidence to meet two such fine gentlemen from one place not to explore that place. Truly, I do not mock, but admire."

"Hmph! I choose to believe you." His voice had once again donned a gentler mantel although there was great weariness in there too. I detected that whatever had befallen him had removed his will to fight. His left hand returned to his lap whilst his right one reached for his mug.

"Sir. Please forgive my presumption but did you happen to come to know a worthy knight in your employ called Conrado?" I knew this to be a vain hope but I would never forgive myself if I did not ask.

"I know the names and faces of the survivors – not the fallen." His shoulders slumped even lower. "There were far fewer of them." He looked as if he was deep in thought for a moment whilst absently taking a swallow of his ale. I remained silent, willing him to name Conrado in this collection. "No. I know of no Conrado. He must have fallen. One of the nearly four hundred men I lost in a single day at Jerusalem." Silence again. "God forgive me."

My heart fell and my head with it. First Alfonso and now Conrado gone. How rash youth are and how invulnerable we had felt that day we defeated the Franks together on the dock? For the first time I felt the pangs of loneliness. I arose and without further conversation returned to my duties. My heart was heavier and as Gustav had aged, I felt that I too had aged greatly from that brief meeting.

I owned very little. What few possessions I had, fitted into my small but faithful carrier. The meeting with the fallen Gustav had awakened in me a desire to reconnect with my past for the first time in many, many years. It was thus that, having finished my duties, I returned to my cot and with trembling hands, explored the meagre collection contained in the carrier. I withdrew the testaments which I had read so long ago. Then, they had held little meaning for me. Now, I wondered if there was something in those words which might rekindle some purpose in me, for my spirit had indeed been lost. I reread the tale of the Jew in Jerusalem and the adventures of the Italian. Finally, I reread the sayings and deeds recorded by the Jew.

It was if a light had been put before me for the first time. As I absorbed the words, which I truly believe to be of our Lord, I came, during the course of that sleepless night, to a personal revelation. As a Spaniard I was raised as a Roman Catholic. I had attended church each week and confession every two weeks. A very young man does not have a lot of sins to confess, I had thought, or rather I did not think so at the time.

What I now realized on that lonely night, reading these accounts, was that I had never really thought about what my belief meant. It was just something that one did, like eating or drinking. As these two functions perform a life sustaining service to my body, without me understanding how, so too it was with my religious discipline. I carried out the function of my religion without ever giving thought to how it served me.

I recalled the memory of Alfonso, at his last, asking me if I believed in life after death. My response was aimed at comforting him rather than being a statement of my belief. For the first time I clearly understood that this was the case.

I contemplated the numerous sermons I had heard and the prayers I had, with others of my faith, chanted. I understood for the first time that they were meaningless. They, if the writings were to be believed, were a misconception of the truth. I was wracked with anguish. It is inconceivable to a Catholic that the Pope was not infallible and yet … what was written here was simpler than any edict of my religion.

Should I make known these writings? I dared not. As Gustav was so clearly weary of the world, I came to realize that I too had no taste for arguments and unrest. If I were to go to the Cathedral and show these to a Priest I should be cast out as a heretic. I could not bear that prospect; even though I now understood that some of the lessons were complicated beyond their original simple message. I no longer had the rash certainty of youth nor the bravery of a Knight of God. I was content to remain a simple man and invisible to the world.

That night, or more truly as dawn broke, I made the decision to protect these testaments but at the same time not be the one to face the outcry of revealing them. I would bury them for a braver soul than mine and let whoever that was, be the one to decide their fate. I had enough faith in God to know that if He wanted them found, they would be. If they were a trick of the devil then they would remain hidden. It was not my decision.

The decision I was left with, however, was what to do with them. How would I keep them secure and yet allow my successor, if there be one, to find them?

My answer came one day when I was walking in the countryside surrounding my new home. The city, for now it was defined as such, is marked by being very close to the confluence where the River Regnitz flows into the River Main. At this very point an ancient tree stands in defiance to the water. As I sheltered under this tree on that fine, sunny day, I noted that there was a crack near its roots at the base of the stout trunk. The scar was just tall enough that the leather pouch containing the ancient documents could pass through. Here they would be protected from the elements, hidden from the casual eye and at most intruded upon by a sheltering squirrel.

The irony of the proposed hiding place did not escape me either.

The confluence of waterways perfectly expressed the situation created by the documents. A single channel absorbed by a larger canal. It perfectly illustrated the words of Our Lord being swept up and contained within my religion. The Main containing the waters of the Regnitz but the latter swallowed up by it so as to be absorbed to the point where the original waters are indefinable from the larger watercourse.

For me, it seemed that the tree symbolized the Tree of Knowledge, or the Tree of Good and Evil as described in the Genesis account of the Garden of Eden. The tree is a strong creation, which had been born without mans' intervention, and remained permanent as generations of humanity passed through. Its roots were widely and securely set and no amount of nature's interference would cause it to move. It would still be observing us long after I had joined Alfonso and Conrado.

So decided, I then set to puzzle what hint I might devise to alert the chosen one of the package whereabouts and where this clue must be placed.

I thought of the previous slips left by the others who had placed the bundle securely. The symbol used by the ancient Jew, of the form representing a mouth or the word, sat comfortably with me as still being appropriate. I decided that the location of the text would be revealed by the following clue.

(Tailless fish or mouth) In the city of the second Rome two ideas join to become one.

(Tailless fish) In the growth which conducts this union find the first.

I was contented with this clue and now set to thinking where best to place it. Memory allowed me to clearly recall how I had found the Italian's clue integrated incongruously into what was otherwise an outstandingly beautiful work. The memory of my enchantment at the book was never forgotten. My finding and keeping the texts had been mere happenstance brought about by its very incongruous nature. Thus, the hiding place of my choice must illicit similar emotions.

I had already decided to make the city of Bamberg my home and did not envisage travelling again from here. Where then to place the clue so that it was distant from the hiding place of the treasure? I mulled on this for some time – long past the single afternoon.

As a regular worshiper I attended the Cathedral frequently and knew one particular Priest quite well. He was truly a man of God. I further knew that the diocese was occasionally visited by Fathers from Rome. If I might devise some method of having one of these visitors carry my clue to that great city, without knowing what he transported, then my mission would be accomplished.

Fate stepped in some two weeks later whilst I was still contemplating this quandary.

I was tending bar, whilst Hans was visiting his mother with Greta, when a stranger entered our hostelry. Having satisfied both his thirst and his hunger (which was considerable) I engaged him in conversation, the public area being empty of locals.

"Hail friend. You enjoyed that," I observed when collecting his empty platter.

"I was truly hungry I do confess," he responded amicably. "I have been on my journey for two days without a morsel to eat. I was very glad to see your place I can tell you."

"Do you come far?" It seemed a reasonable question.

"I have always come far!" He laughed. "I barter my trinkets to earn a small living and delight to remain a rover, always on the move."

"Trinkets? What is it that you sell?"

"I am a whittler." He seemed to believe that this would offer some illumination. It did not.

"A whittler? What manner of trinket is that?"

Reaching over to recover his bag he opened it and brought forth the results of his mysterious trade. From his carrier he removed carefully and lovingly a small, but highly decorated box, wrapped in cloth, the quality of which I had never before set eyes upon. As he handed it to me and I turned it over in my hands I was dumbstruck by the fine detail carved thereon. It was truly a magnificent work of art. I held it up to the candle to better determine the patterns.

"That's just a sample," he continued, seeing the delight in my face. "I have much more in the bag still on my horse." At this he stood and quickly disappeared through the door. It never even crossed my mind that he might not return to settle his dues. My faith was justified. Within moments he re-entered the inn with a large sack. Placing it carefully on the table he began to bring out items which continued to amaze me. There were wooden statues of thoroughbred horses; figurines of ladies; cups, so beautifully decorated that it seemed a shame to hide them by holding the cup; and many, many more smaller trinkets. The only thing his variety of wares seemed to have in common being that each was carved from wood.

"These are truly outstanding!" I was awed by his obvious artistic skill. "Who can afford to buy such wares?"

"Some are more expensive than others. I confess I assess the price according to whom I am showing them." He laughed again. "A lady dressed in finery will pay more for a trinket than the lowly wife of a farmer. It also depends how hungry I am at the time." His eyes shone mischievously.

"Let me show you this. I think you'll like it." He picked up the box I had seen first from the table. He placed his finger on a fleur-de-lis and, moving the rest of his hand so I could clearly see what he was doing, pressed. The bottom of the box detached itself from the square and protruded slightly. He pulled gently on this and revealed, to my utter amazement, a small drawer.

"Let me try." My enthusiasm caused him to again burst into laughter as he handed me the magical box. I gently pushed the hidden drawer until it was in perfect alignment with its main form and invisible from the whole. Then, just as he had done, I applied pressure to the same flower and the drawer again protruded. "How does it work?"

"Treat me to another ale and I'll tell you." Never had I been so eager to refill a mug. I placed a small coin from my pocket in the box behind the counter in payment. On returning to the table with his beverage he continued.

"What I've done is whittled the flower such that it retains a piece of itself on the underside like a solid finger of hidden wood." He turned the box carefully the better to demonstrate. "Next, instead of whittling the flower from the main wood piece I inserted a perfectly fitting hole into which I placed the detached flower with its finger. Do you see? Here! The drawer is a separate piece again but carved in decoration as one with its main box which, of course, has its own base." He placed just the very tip of his finger on the flower. "Now, as I press, see how it descends slightly? That in turn causes its attachment inside to flick and behold, causes the lower draw to move outwards." He looked at me exuberantly. "Clever huh?"

"Truly astounding! I am mighty impressed. And how much might a piece like this fetch?"

"That depends who I'm selling it to. At a fine house I might get the value of meals for up to a month. But if it is for some young newlywed so she can hide some precious letter without her husband being aware, then she might only have enough money for a week of meals."

An idea was slowly forming in my mind. "How much for a poor and lowly assistant in a hostelry?" I put on my most pathetic face in attempt to raise sympathy.

He looked into my eyes, smiling with just the sentiment I had wanted to elicit showing on his face. "You? Tell me what you can afford."

I quickly thought of what I possessed. The truth of it was I had nothing. A few coins only and nothing of value beyond that – except - I still owned my sword. Many times, on my journey, I had almost discarded it but something had made me hold onto it. It was the one connection I still had of my home and family, having been a gift from my father. It was wrapped in cloth under my cot where it had lain untouched since my arrival.

"I have a fine sword. It travelled with me to the campaigns in Acre. It is worth many good meals I am sure."

"A sword you say? Let me see it." So invited, I ran as fast as my legs would carry me to my cot, retrieved the now dusty package and ran back to the waiting tradesman.

"Here." I handed the bundle to him. Whilst he inspected it, memories flooded back of the sights that sword had seen. Alfonso and Conrado seemed very close to me in those moments. Even my father, for whom I had had no great love, seemed to join me in that room as I remembered his lecture as he presented it to me. "Be an upright man and always ensure that you do not disgrace this family" he had said. To my elder brother he had used the term of "bring honour to the family". I was, in his mind, not capable of bringing honour and the best he could hope of me was not to bring disgrace.

"This is a good piece and I can certainly exchange it for many meals. Are you sure you want to part with it?"

"Sir. My days of travel and exploration are passed. I am now content to remain here in quiet solitude and honest work. Please, if you will accept this sword as payment, I would be most gratified to exchange it for this masterful box."

"You have a deal, my friend. Here, let us shake on it." We shook hands by way of sealing the exchange and I took possession of the means by which I would get my clue to Rome.

I wrote this account of my adventures and explained why I have decided not to announce the testaments of the old Jew. These I have included in the pouch which I have hidden where I said I would in the tree. The small box, containing my clue in its secret drawer, I passed to my friend the Priest.

(Tailless fish) In the city of the second Rome two ideas join to become one.

(Tailless fish) In the growth which conducts this union find the first.

He accepted it as a gift for the palace of the Pontiff and assured me it would be carried by the next visitor from Rome. He is unaware of the secret drawer. I have complete trust that he will honour this agreement.

My Dearest Cousin,

I should be most interested to know what you made of the tale by the Warrior? Do his adventures seem likely? Do the wise men within your University concur that his tale is, at least, feasible?

Please find below the account written by a man purporting to be from the 4th Century. Likewise, having read this, I would ask for your confirmation, or not, of the likelihood of it being a genuine record.

Yours in anticipation,
Beattie
(Encl.)

Dear Beattie,

Again I find myself, with the assurance of my colleagues, confirming that the potted life of the Warrior passes all tests on its plausible likelihood.

The 4th Century you say? I am fascinated. I shall return with my conclusions as soon as I have finished reading the enclosed.

Yours, in confirmation,

Jackie

The Heresy

4th Century A.D.

My name is inconsequential when compared to my tale. To remain anonymous is also a vocational requirement as an outward display of my humility. However, my status is relevant and so I beg to regale you with how this unsettling revelation began.

I am Italian by birth, but nation-less by choice, following a fateful meeting with a man in a piazza in Florence, the city of my birth. This man was devoted to the worship of God and a dedicated disciple of Iēsous. He stirred something in me and I took the decision to also answer this calling.

I believe in, and follow the teachings of, Saint Paul. To this end was determined to one day visit the the small tomb, built by Emperor Constantine in Rome, it being the buriel place of that most saintly and Blessed of men, Saint Paul.

Saint Paul had advocated that in order to not be distracted by the temporal things of life, one should remain unmarried and without worldly possessions. An example he famously practiced himself. This sponsored a devoted trust in God to supply my needs. This is an action which I have resolutely followed and a philosophy that has never disappointed me. Additionally, since we are to form the army of God, when He brings His Kingdom to the earth, any attachments would merely distract us from the impending and imminent battle against evil.

In order to more properly become a desert father, I set out for Antioch to make the land surrounding this historically important town, my center. The journey was long and arduous and it seemed, when I finally arrived, as if I had travelled to the other end of earth. Everything was so different from my native land that no *rapporto* (comparison) could justly be drawn.

The preference for community living of such as myself had recently reached this forsaken corner of the world and so, unwilling to fully embrace a life of wondering in this unknown desert, I joined such a conclave.

The Father who held leadership in our area was, to my mind, a cruel taskmaster who had little patience for those like me who were new to the Holy Ways. I remember clearly beatings that I suffered "for the purity of my soul" as he would put it.

He was, however, a man of some influence with connections to many bishops of the churches of Iēsous. It was in this capacity that he learnt that our Emperor Constantine had decreed that a Council be convened of all bishops at Nicaea. The Emperor, a recent convert had I understand, decided that if this new movement was one he was to lead, there must first be unity on the beliefs of the various sects.

Since Saint Paul (and others) had established many roots, each assembly had tended to take one or two lessons and concentrate their knowledge around this alone. In this way, it was not uncommon for one area to know every detail of, for example, the signs of the coming Kingdom of God, whereas the area next to it may not even have heard of these. Some communities had concentrated their learning on one text but given no heed to another. Some travellers had told some tales, whilst others were ignorant of certain spoken instances. Such was the oral tradition and its failings. It was only Holy men, such as myself, who devoured the entire testaments and all related texts. We were then in a position to contemplate their cohesion in conjunction with the prophecies.

As a preface to this great Council, messengers were dispatched by Constantine, for some years before, and throughout the Empire, instructing that all texts relating to Iēsous be gathered and delivered to the slowly gathering bishops at Nicaea.

I was tasked with searching in Antioch for any such relevant material. There was only one main *biblioteca* in Antioch but it contains a *bibliografia* (bibliography) of great repute; with the books and scrolls held therein reflecting in detail the rise of Christianity – and indeed the naming of it as a religion.

Antioch is the venerable city in which the Gospel of Matthew had been written; it was from here that Paul set out on his missionary work; it was here that the first Gentiles were baptized.

It is still one of the most important cities in Christendom and had even entertained Saint Peter himself at one time. As such it was no surprise to me that so many important writings were contained therein. So important was the town that the Emperor actually visited Antioch in the same year as the Council. I didn't get to see him although there was great excitement in the town I understand.

The next few weeks were spent in a blissful state of discovery and excitement. I was gathering so many key documents that it would surely take two mules, or even three, to carry the pouches from Antioch to Nicaea. I carefully recorded the title of each document selected, cross-checking this list before adding another text, to prevent un-necessary duplication.

On about the twenty-second day of my information gathering I came across something unexpected wrapped inside another rolled scroll. It was a single, small slip of hide on which was written the following:

(A fish, like the newly rising Christian symbol, but with no tail) Beneath the mouth is the true spoken word.

(The same fish symbol) Above the three-tiered palace the garden of the king blooms rarely.

To this day I don't know why I picked that small document up because I certainly already had enough to carry, but pick it up I did and placed it in my pouch, aside from the collection I was collating. I failed to add it to my list.

By the time I returned to the conclave that evening I had forgotten about the slip. The leading father met me at the evening meal and, as usual, asked if anything of importance had been discovered. I related the new additions to my list which seemed to satisfy him.

It was not until a few days later that I had occasion to inspect my pouch. I looked at the slip and tried again to fathom the significance of these few words – to no avail. I would see if the father had any idea of its significance tomorrow at supper once speech was permitted.

After the evening meal the father, as usual, asked me what I had found at the *biblioteca*. I regaled him with the newest additions to my list. Then, remembering the slip, reached into my pouch for it and pulled it out. I was just about to pass it to him when he said the following which halted me in my action.

"You must show me each document before entering them into the carriers for dispatch. I insist that only the most Holy relics be passed to the bishops. I shall not tolerate any deviance or contradiction to the direct teachings of Iēsous."

"But I thought that anything which mentioned Our Lord was to be examined by the Holy men?" I replied.

"They are not as wise as me. They do not live in the solitary manner advocated by our beloved Saint Paul. I shall be the judge of what may be submitted for their deliberation."

"Yes, father." I submissively responded, slipping the paper back into my pouch surreptitiously. This was no man to involve in a mystery. I withdrew into the sanctity of silence once again.

This short conversation had indeed unsettled me.

It was my understanding that the gathering of bishops, who were the leaders of the followers of Iēsous, were to be the ones to judge the worthiness of all texts. They, I had understood, were being convened to establish the truth from the fable surrounding the life and teachings of Iēsous. Most importantly, they were to use the powers of the Holy Spirit to be guided in their task. Yet, here in my own small community, I saw a pre-judgement being made, which by its very nature, was interfering with the God inspired task. If this was occurring throughout the country, then the texts upon which the bishops would decide would already have been culled.

It was at that very moment that I began to doubt that God's Will was being carried out by his followers.

Do not *fraintendere* (misunderstand), I did not doubt that the leader of our small community was a good man. Rather I saw for the first time that the Will of mankind sometimes overshadows the directed path of God's Will.

Orgoglio, pregiudizio e l'ego (Pride, prejudice and egotism) are powerful enemies, as indeed, Iēsous and Saint Paul had been at pains to point out.

During the next few years *ero fondamentalmente contenuti* (I was fundamentally contented). Each sunrise I awoke and spent some hours in prayer. It was then my joy to tend to our planted foodstuffs, all the while in quiet contemplation of Our Lord, Iēsous. As evening meal arrived each mouthful tasted so wonderful because I knew that my hand had been used by God to grow this fodder.

As time had gone by our senior father had encouraged us to remain distant from those around us who dwelt outside our community. This he had explained was to lessen their impact on our desires allowing us to concentrate on our awareness of God and commune more closely with the Lord, Iēsous.

An exception to this practice was when a fellow follower and desert father arrived to beg sustenance. At such times we welcomed him into our small community. I must confess on such occasions there was always an excitement in the air as we gathered for evening meal. I love my brothers dearly but was *rinvigorito*, invigorated, at the prospect of speaking to someone new.

Such a father arrived one evening in early first planting season. During supper he talked of his journey. I suspect he had not spoken to any for some time since his voice was rough at times especially at the start of the meal although his enthusiasm for speaking slid easily from his lips.

"I travelled then from Jerusalem to Masada on my pilgrimage. Later, having returned from the ruins of King Herod's Palace at Masada, to Jerusalem, I begged passage on a trade vessel. This took me along the coast of the great sea until I landed here, having finally navigated the river Orontes." He told us.

"Why did you go to Masada if it is only ruins?" I could not help myself asking.

"Why? To be truthful I do not know. I heard of the place in Jerusalem and since I was so close, I felt that a pilgrimage there would afford me time alone with My Lord to contemplate."

"What was it like? What was there?" The enthusiasm in my voice elicited a scowl from our leading father. Enthusiasm, in his eyes, was the sole property of worship to Our Lord. Taken out of context it was an expression of the Devil.

"Masada is the sight of a palace and fortress built for King Herod the Great about four hundred years ago. It was erected in defense against either a Jewish uprising or the designs of Cleopatra, Queen of Egypt, to depose him. It is only three or four days travel from Jerusalem. Its greatest claim to fame though, is that it was here that the last of the Jewish Zealots committed mass suicide." (Here he crossed himself by way of atonement for their great sin). He then continued. "These were the Zealots who had escaped from Jerusalem and chose their own way of death rather than submit to the judgement of the Romans. This great sin happened just three years after the destruction of their Temple and Jerusalem by the Emperor Titus.

I was greatly impressed by the method the Emperor had employed for water collection. He had great stone cisterns dug out of the rock which collected any rain water. Those are still evident at the sight.

The palace was built on three distinct levels of the rock. It greatly surprised me that the King's garden was on an outcropping *above* the palace."

My mind was instantly alert.

"Above?" I enquired.

"Yes. Before I have witnessed gardens below such structures to afford the occupants to view them from the palaces, but in this case, it was clearly above. Of course, there are no flowers or desert blooms there now – just dust."

"Was the destruction of the palace great?" one of my companions asked.

"Utterly destroyed." Replied the pilgrim. "I have to admit that the Zealots conviction on life after death must have been a shock to those pagan Romans on discovering so many bodies following the siege. Such was the faith of the Jew that they had automatic admittance to Heaven whilst they remained deaf to the teachings of Our Lord. I pray for them in their ignorance of salvation."

The Father then brought this tale to its end, by prompting for the closing prayer to be delivered. He was obviously unimpressed by the history surrounding this ruined site. He only had interest in the words of our Gospels and the more ancient history relating to the Hebrew texts.

That evening, after the meal was finished and the usual evening service of prayers duly made, I rushed to my bed area to find the slip of hide. It was with a feverish agitation that I searched for it and found it where I had hidden it so long ago balanced on the slat of my cot.

(A fish, like the newly rising Christian symbol, but with no tail) Beneath the mouth is the true spoken word.

(The same fish symbol) Above the three-tiered palace the garden of the king blooms rarely.

My memory had served me well. Above the three-tiered palace the garden of the king ….

Surely this must mean the King's palace at Masada? It could not be anywhere else. I fell to my knees in supplication.

Every fiber of my being wanted to follow this enigmatic clue to discover what the writer had been referring to. Now, suddenly, the first step in solving the riddle had arrived at our community and told me the site of exploration. But how would I get there? I had no means. The pilgrim had either been very lucky or very skilled because traders who ploughed the sea were not known for their generosity in granting free passage. Overland the journey was perilous and beset by bandits eager to steal even the clothes from a traveler's back.

Never-the-less I was a man driven by passion. By night my dreams centred on this mystery. As I sat in silent contemplation or prayer my brain refused to concentrate but kept imagining what might lay behind the writing. It was as if I was possessed and nothing would quiet my soul but a conclusion. Finally, I realised I should never again find the peace to devote myself quietly to God, until I had solved this mystery which was eating me alive like leprosy. It was a topic upon which I was *fervente*.

Some days later I begged to speak in private with my senior. He granted me an audience and I entered his room in trepidation.

"Father. Thank you for allowing me this time." I began by adhering to the etiquette of such a meeting, with my head bowed low and hands in a supplicant posture.

"What is it my son?" His response was kinder than the one I had expected since I knew I had never been a favourite of his.

"Father. I wish to be granted your patience and permission to embark upon a journey of pilgrimage."

He could not have looked more alarmed if I had confessed to some sin I had committed. His mouth opened and then closed again as if his instinctive utterance had been withheld and was being redesigned.

"You wish to leave our sacred community?" He enquired in a challenging manner.

"Oh no, father. I would just like to take some time alone in the desert, to greater increase my communion with Our Lord, Iēsous. To walk where He walked... To visit the places where He went... To spend time in the desert alone as He did."

"I will admit that you are not a model disciple of Our Lord. You never have been." He went silent for a moment as if recalling all the times he had felt the need to beat my spirit into submission.

"It is this very aspect of your character which troubles me and stops me from granting you leave from this conclave" he continued.

As this last was uttered my heart fell as I realised that I was not to be allowed an absence. The disappointment quickly underwent metamorphosis into anger. I suppressed it with difficulty. Instead I feigned humility, being the better tactic to get my way.

"Father, I know more than any, of my failings. They are brought about by a distance in my heart from the teachings of Our Lord. It is this very inadequacy which impels me to spend time alone, in the manner of a true desert father, and commune with God."

The old man was silent. He stared into my eyes as if looking through them at my soul. I also remained silent and stared back at him willing him to see my ardour.

"I shall pray for an answer from Heaven. You may leave me now." He concluded our meeting. I bowed low and silently left his presence.

For over a week the matter was not mentioned again. At each evening meal the old man seemed to avoid eye contact with me.

Then, after supper one evening he finally spoke as we rose.

"Son. I would speak with you." He announced. "Come to my room after prayers this evening." My heart leapt in my chest and fear burnt my innards.

After prayers I, with trembling legs, made my way towards the father's room. As I stood outside the fear was so great in me that it was only by extreme self-control that I did not turn and run away. *Tremavo.* I entered.

The old man looked up and rose from his knees to sit on his cot. He gestured for me to join him. I sat.

"I have given much thought and prayer to your request. It is because of this that, on reflection, I feel that you, above all others in our community, will indeed benefit from coming to know Our Lord more closely." My heart leapt with joy. The insult which he had delivered did not even impact on me until many days later.

He continued "An acquaintance of mine, a trader from Rome, runs a caravan via Antioch down to Jerusalem fairly often. I have sent word to him and he has replied granting you allowance to travel with him. You leave tomorrow."

I could have kissed this previously cruel man. The passion, inherent in me of my Italian birth, required expression and was not to be sated without touch. I grasped his hand and kissed it with fervour and pressure. He recoiled and pulled his hand from my grasp.

We briefly discussed preparations about the provision of which food I should be allowed to take from our store and the meeting arrangements with his trader. He commanded me leave him as soon as he had transmitted this information; obviously unwilling to enter into the excitement he detected in me.

"Grazie. Grazie." I enthused as I bowed and reversed myself from his room in manner of a supplicant.

So it was that some days later I found myself on passage from Antioch to Jerusalem.

My benevolent trader went by the name of Antonio. He led some eight camels and two mules on this dangerous journey, all of whom were loaded to near capacity with wares and subsistence. As both helpers and protectors, he employed five other men to accompany him. Each was armed and seemed in a permanent state of readiness to repel any fortune hunters.

It was after we held left Damascus and once again entered the wilderness of the desert that a small mountain range stood before us. Our protectors seemed more than usually alert. Antonio explained to me that recently there had been many raids in this area and we must be extra vigilant. *Banditi erano vacini.* There were bandits here.

That night as we made camp I noted that, unlike on previous occasions, no fire was lit. We sat instead nearer to our animals and talked in hushed voices. It was agreed amongst the warriors that the youngest amongst them, a boy name of Matteo, remain awake and keep first watch. When we had dined on dried meat and hard bread as usual, I pulled my hood up over my head and lay down where I sat to sleep huddled to protect against the cold.

Had I been awake the decision that faced me of fight or flight might have been easier. As it was, when I was suddenly brought from slumber by the anguished cries of my fellow travellers, my first instinct on witnessing the horror was one of fight. Bandits, about five of them, were attacking our camp. They rushed at us from the darkness of death with rods and knives. One of them was already atop Matteo, the youngest of our party, whose cries I had hurried from slumber to respond to. He was beating the lad with his fists like a man possessed. As I watched, frozen in terror, this assailant withdrew a knife from his belt and plunged it into the innocent boy.

At this sight the monster within me rose and took over my body. I was enraged and beyond all reason. I grasped my staff and springing to my feet aimed a swing at the head of the demon. I struck him with such force that his head moved to an angle unnatural, which I witnessed clearly, as time itself had slowed almost to a stand-still. The robber's body followed his head and he was thrown off Matteo. He did not move again.

Looking around me I saw that the other would-be thieves were being attacked successfully by my fellow travellers. They were in no need of my help. I bent down to assess how wounded the boy, Matteo, was. From his side the life blood of his existence was draining away. Instinct made me press my hands against his wound as if by will alone I could quell the tide.

I do not know how long I remained in this position because time was still at an unnatural passage. The monster who had taken over my body once again returned to his dark place and slumbered. Instead I was overwhelmed by a sense of love and caring for this injured young soul. My brain raced to try and remember any useful tips it may have stored on what best to do for him. All the while my hands grasped his wound and clung to it ignoring the blood which leaked onto them in an unstoppable flood tide.

I was aware dimly that Antonio had approached us. I looked up and for the first time realised that there was no sign of the robbers. Our guardians had obviously overwhelmed them and they had disappeared back into the darkness from whence they had come. Except the one who lay dead to the world near me.

"How is he?" He enquired looking at Matteo.

"I do not know. I am just trying to stop the bleeding." My response held an air of despair.

Antonio disappeared from my vision but quickly returned with a length of cloth.

"Here" He said. "Wind this around him. It will put pressure on the wound."

We set too, and whilst Antonio carefully and caringly raised Matteo from the waist upwards, I wound the cloth tightly around his mid. The blood disappeared as if by magic under the cloth with only the residue remaining on his garment. Antonio and I sat back on our haunches and viewed the unconscious ally.

It was as if Antonio for the first time noticed the bandit. I also had forgotten that he was to our side.

"You gave him a good knock." Antonio remarked with not a little amusement in his voice. "He will have a mighty headache when he wakes. And here, I thought you Holy brethren were gentle folk." Laughter broke from his lips.

At this moment I saw for the first time the damage I had inflicted on another human being. I had broken one of the most important Commandments of both God and Iēsous. I had allowed the inner animal of my anger to over-ride the most basic principal of my chosen path. I moved across to the man and inspected his wound. A gash split his head from the top of one ear to nearly the back of his skull. Blood poured from it.

"What have I done?" I cried to the Heavens.

"Do not worry, brother. He attacked us not the other way around." Antonio continued in effort to quell the tangible distress in me. "I'm sure he will survive."

I was not to be pacified. I tore some of my outer garment from the sleeve and carefully wrapped the man's head much as we had tended to Matteo's cut.

"We cannot stay here, brother." Antonio said. Looking into the sky he then added, "It will be dawn soon. We must hurry onward. We need to clear these mountains before nightfall or the same fate may befall us again." He quickly rose from his spot by Matteo and went off to talk to our other protectors, congratulating them on doing a worthy job.

For the next two days I cared for Matteo as if he was my own *bambino*. Antonio had cleared some carriers from one of the mules which had allowed just enough room for Matteo to ride. The protectors did not seem to mind accepting the added bundles since it was one of their own who benefited.

Matteo had regained knowledge of this world by mid-morning on the first day when we had been travelling for some few hours. Whilst he was at times unable to hide the pain of his stab wound, he donned a stoic attitude which encouraged a sense of pride from me on his independence and fortitude.

We arrived without further incident at Jerusalem. By this time Matteo was much stronger and able to dismount from the mule unassisted, if slowly. Blood had appeared on the binding cloth but it had ceased spreading after the first day. The remedy which Antonio had devised had been sound.

For myself, my pain was expanding. The pain caused by knowing that I had injured a fellow human being. We had left the poor unfortunate where he lay, for his brethren to recover and care for him, after we had left the area. I prayed to God that they had done so. Part of me wanted to return and assure myself as to his safety but a greater part of me knew this would be a useless and foolhardy move. The anguish of my sin spread until it bound my soul in its terrible grasp.

After a mere eight days I decided not to linger in Jerusalem, amid its ease and pleasures, but rather to punish myself in penitence by undertaking more solitary desert travel. My destination, only vaguely formed, being towards Herod's ruined temple. It was the journey which was to be my punishment.

As I exited the gate nobody could have been more surprised than me to find Matteo waiting there for me with a travel bundle slung by a rope over his shoulder. As I approached, he smiled with a beam which wrote in itself *"Grazzie."*

"Matteo. What are you doing here?" I asked.

"Signore" He smiled with gentle eyes. "Signore. You saved me and I wish to travel with you to learn more."

"Learn more what?" I enquired a little confused.

"Signore Antonio tells me you are a Holy man. A follower of one called Iēsous. I know nothing of this person. I wish to know more for, if you follow him, then he must indeed be a man out of this time. I would know more."

Had Matteo used any other reason to accompany me then he would have been denied for I am not worthy to follow. However, as one who follows The Way, at least when it suits me judging from my recent lapse into sin, it was my duty to teach any who wish to know of Our Lord. For this reason, and this reason alone, I allowed Matteo to join me in my penitent journey.

As we travelled, I talked of the words and actions of Iēsous. Matteo was like a starving man feeding on every word. He questioned, what I had a long time ago accepted as just factual, and nagged at things like a dog with a cloth rag, unwilling to let a point go until he felt he had conquered the lesson with depth of understanding. I had heard men say before that the best way to learn something is to teach it. This was true for me. As I struggled to explain why I believed something, or what Our Lord had meant by some statement, I found myself reviewing my own faith.

The more I came to re-evaluate the words of our Master for Matteo the more I found that I understood and took new meaning from them. It was as if I was being taught for the first time. In the past if something had been unclear to me, having been rebuffed many times, I came to accept that some things "just have to be taken on faith", to quote my community father.

With this personal growth on the lessons of Our Lord came also greater despair at my past sin. In a strange way, as I drew closer to Him, I also grew further away. By the time we reached

Herod's palace I felt so ashamed and unworthy that I dared not even pray to God – such was the shame at my outburst of anger resulting in injuring a fellow being. I was truly in despair but carried out my duty to teach Matteo with diligence. He was without such a grave sin and I must pass on the teachings of Our Lord so that he might follow where I had failed.

We arrived and set camp on the lowest ruins of the structure. I knew not what to do next. For several days Matteo and I satisfied ourselves with the business of survival in such a hostile place whilst continuing to increase our understanding of the Teachings.

Some days later it rained. This is not an unknown occurrence I understand but neither is it common. The joy of standing, with face upturned, allowing the refreshing and cleansing liquid to invade our being was exhilarating. If any had spied Matteo and I at that moment they would surely have believed we were simple or besieged by a demon of madness. Matteo in his youth ran and spun and danced like a woman. I was sorely tempted to follow suit and in a moment of rejuvenation, did.

Once the fall from Heaven had stopped, we both felt cleansed. Wet; but cleansed. We laughed, perhaps for the first time, that evening as we huddled by the small fire with gentle mists rising from our sodden garments.

It had become my practice to walk each day to the topmost layer of the palace whilst trying to summon up the courage to pray to God. As I rose in altitude my humility became deeper. Only as I reached the top layer of the ruined garden did I venture to beseech God to forgive me. I would then descend to our camp slowly. Never had I felt forgiven. I was tolerated, but at the same time so insignificant, that I was ignored by His Almighty Majesty. I deserved such soul rending agony and accepted it.

The day after the rain I had, as usual, made such a metaphorically significant journey. As I reached the garden level my eyes were opened wide in surprise and my soul filled with a joy unknown to life. The garden had suddenly taken on a coat of many colours. Everywhere I looked the blooms of Heaven waved in the gentle breeze to welcome me. I was so taken aback that I fell to my knees.

"Lord, God, Almighty." I prayed with my hands clasped and my head low. "Dare I believe that this is a sign of your forgiveness and blessing?"

I waited as if I truly expected a voice to thunder in reply. I felt such an overwhelming outpouring of love, both from and too me, that I wanted that moment to last forever. I remained like that for some time thanking the Almighty for His manifest miracle. I felt as if the rain had cleansed my body and the Lord had cleansed my soul.

Finally, I opened my eyes again and drank in the beauty of such a sight in such a previously barren landscape. All manner of shades displayed before me. I carefully stepped between the blooms speaking to many of them in welcome. It then dawned on me that I was being selfish in not revealing this living miracle to my companion and I went to the edge of the plateau and shouted in the loudest voice for Matteo.

"Matteo. Matteo. Come up here quickly. God has sent us a miracle. Matteo."

The startled boy ran toward me. When he saw what I had been so inspired by, he too, fell to his knees in prayer. It was as if the Truth, of which Iēsous had spoken, was being revealed to him. From that moment he was a true believer in the validity and power of Our Lord.

As he and I wandered through this little piece of Heaven, suddenly adorning the earth, I recalled the slip of hide that I had secretly protected for so many years. With trembling fingers, I carefully pulled it out from my pouch.

(A fish but with no tail) Beneath the mouth is the true spoken word.

(The same fish symbol) Above the three-tiered palace the garden of the king blooms rarely.

For the first time I realised what "…. the garden of the king blooms rarely" meant.

Perhaps, dare I believe, perhaps the first riddle is also now to be answered.

I showed the slip to Matteo his being the first eyes to read it since its discovery other than my own.

(Tailless fish) Beneath the mouth is the true spoken word.

It was as if the lad had always known the answer to the riddle. In an excited voice he begged me to search for a bed of blooms in the shape on the script; the shape of a mouth or tailless fish. We looked at each other as only a true companion can, in a bond of understanding, and began walking, eyes down, in separate directions around the garden.

I found it. Though I can barely believe it even today there before me, about midway towards the rear wall of rock, was a ring of white blossoms in the unmistakeable shape of a mouth. How nature had devised such a shape is known only to God.

"Matteo." I called. "It is here. I have found it."

Matteo came running over, carefully choosing his steps so as not to dishonour any of the blossoms. In doing this, his movements more resembled a dance than a run. We both looked down on the spot. Neither of us moved. We just stared.

It was Matteo who eventually broke the spell. "We should dig," he suggested.

I did not move. All I kept thinking was "the true spoken word." Whose word? What words? My mind was a fever of possibilities. All the while I dared to hope …

Matteo bent and with his bare hands tore at the hardened ground. Had it not rained recently nothing would have been achieved but the shredding of his fingers. But it had rained and the ground was softer than normal. I joined him and my fingers added to the makeshift shovels. We dug down for a good distance.

Then we felt something which was unexpected. A smooth surface was hidden in this compacted ground. We dug with even more vigour, using our sense of touch as our guide. The side of a jar was slowly and carefully unearthed. We continued until able to free the receptacle from its premature grave.

I stood with the jar in my hands as if I was holding a new born baby. Matteo stood beside me patiently. Neither of us spoke fearing any words would prove inadequate and break the spell we found ourselves under. The lid was still attached so whatever was inside was as the burial master had intended. We carefully descended to our makeshift camp with Matteo watching my steps as if guiding a blind man across rough ground.

As Matteo and I sat on the ground near our fire bricks I took courage and carefully prized the lid from the jar. Images of snakes, scorpions and other deadly apparitions shot through my mind as my hand tentatively entered the darkened interior. My sense of touch, heightened by fear, my brain on full alert to withdraw the hand at lightning speed, I quickly realised that the contents was a bundle of texts. Having identified our new companions, I grasped the parchments and slowly withdrew my hand.

Looking up at Matteo I could not help but clearly see the crestfallen look upon his face. The poor lad had, undoubtedly, believed in his heart that treasures such as gold would be his reward. Writings held little allure for him. To confirm his fading expectations, he turned the opening of the jar towards him and peered inside. This was eagerly followed by his hand which performed a circular motion within the container to be assured that no golden piece had been overlooked. His shoulders slumped in disappointment as he fully appreciated that another day dream of his had been shattered. Such had been the history of his short life. I felt sorry for him but, for myself, I welcomed the treasure I had found and valued it more than gold. To a man used to reading sacred texts the lack of such in his life is a form of starvation. I loved reading and this cache was to satisfy that hunger admirably - whatever the subject matter.

I quickly determined that the language of the documents was Greek. This would be a little challenging for me but not insurmountable. During my investigations in the *bibiotech* of Antioch I had come across many texts in this language and honed my skills in the field. Luckily it was a gift of mine, I had discovered, to see meaning in foreign writings and, with little effort, determine their content.

Matteo and I spent several uneventful months at this location. He busied himself daily with gathering stones and rocks from the surrounding area and building us a shelter of sorts. He was a skilled artisan we were both pleasantly surprised to discover and his creation soon took on a reliable shape. He was unable to assist me as reading of the written word, in any language, was not one of his many skills. Schooling had never been an option for Matteo.

Meanwhile, having made the long trip to Jerusalem and back to arm myself with ink pressed from berries and several nibs, I began the slow and arduous task of translating the documents from Greek into Latin. I determined to perform this translation on the underside of the original documents so that scholars could, in the future, confirm the integrity of my conversion.

It was with a trembling heart that I slowly was able to decipher the writing of the Jewish trader. As his tale unfolded, I came to know the subject matter of the other texts and it frightened me. The possibility that the words recorded therein might differ from that taught throughout the land was a possibility which filled me with dread. I recalled the culling of texts undertaken by our community leader and the fears I had had at the time, that the fathers in Nicaea might not have access to all information. This was proving to be no exaggeration. Nightmares invaded my sleep on the content of the remaining Greek notes and the implications for mankind.

As I neared the end of the trader's tale my translation grew slower. It felt as one did when nearing the final lines of a beloved story. I was eager to learn the conclusion but, at the same time, not wishing it to end because it would mean I was to lose this new found friend. I felt that, through his writing, I had come to know this gentle fellow of old. By way of procrastination Matteo was more and more assisted by my seeking and finding stones to his very exact specifications.

Too soon the dwelling was ready and there could be no more excuse not to begin translation of the various documents recorded by my Jewish trader friend.

As Matteo and I stood admiring the outer walls of his creation before declaring it completed, we both bathed in satisfaction.

Matteo as the architect had, perhaps for the first time, achieved a dream he had set out to undertake. Whereas I, by some instinct, knew that this little building was to become a focal point for followers of Our Lord. As we entered the small doorway, Matteo first and then me, I prayed for blessing on this offering and it became a chapel of worship, a hermitage of peace.

Over the next several weeks I spent my days sitting in our central spot outside our chapel and painstakingly translating the recordings of the trader into Latin. Matteo meanwhile created traps and tilled the earth for meagre offerings, which we supplemented with offerings from the local Christian community and passing travellers. He carried out the work of a slave for his master. Each evening, as the sun set and the cold night air drew down, we would retire to the chapel. Shedding the self-imposed slavery of his daily toils, Matteo would take on the mantel of a student to his master, as we talked of the events in the life of Iēsous. I was careful to talk only of the decreed statements.

However, for myself, as each new record exposed itself to my understanding, I became both satisfied on some points and confused on others. By the time the whole had been written in Latin I was a mind and heart in turmoil.

There was heresy here. What I had no way of knowing was, who was committing this heresy. Was it the establishing church or the author of these records? The teachings, on which I had been fed during my life to now, were from wise and good men. These lessons had been further strengthened and clarified by the gathering of fathers at Nicaea. For the most part, what I had understood as the words of Iēsous were as the recordings of the trader's – but not wholly. Some passages I had never come across before; whilst some others were, apparently, spoken differently to those I had inherited.

Our Lord, Iēsous, had taught that only He was worthy to judge. I never felt more unworthy than now as I faced the dilemma of trying to decide on the source of the heresy. I prayed for enlightenment. None came. I was like a man without a country - lost in an exile of indecision.

The final verses of the old Jews letter played over and over in my mind:

It was the plea of the old man which finally swayed me as to the course that must be taken. God was not speaking to me, "*loudly and clearly.*" He was silent. Therefore, the time could not be now that this revelation should be made known. Once I had determined that the criteria for making known these works was not now, my heart immediately settled, my mind cleared and my soul felt peace once more. Now was not the time. The decision was not mine, but Gods, and He had not told me to allow their discovery.

My only remaining duty was to safely hide the treasure again. For now that hiding place, I decided, would be the same spot where we had found it. Placing the documents carefully back in the jar and resealing it with the lid I placed it back in the ground. The desert flowers had again disappeared back into the earth but I knew the spot and carefully removed the topsoil to relay the treasure below. The slip I hid behind a small rock in a corner of our dwelling.

During the next few years our life remained peaceful. Together Matteo and I took enormous pleasure in laying a pattern of mosaic on the floor of our hermitage. We had spent long evenings discussing the picture to be portrayed and finally decided that neither of us had the artistic skills to create one. The final decision was therefore, naturally, a pattern only; artistic in its way but undemanding when taking into account our lack of drawing ability.

Towards the end of one season, Matteo went happily to Ptolemais, it being the nearest settlement to us. It would take just under a week, at a comfortable pace, to journey there and about the same back. I confess I missed his company and looked forward to his return.

It was nearly three weeks before he returned and I was beginning to worry remembering the dangers all too ready to pounce on the unwary. After the second week one of the first things I did upon waking was walk to the edge of our home plateau and scan the horizon for any sign of the lad. This practice I repeated several times each day.

Finally, one afternoon, my patience was rewarded. Far in the distance I spotted a lone traveller coming from the direction of Ptolemais. My heart leapt in delight. It had rained, in one of the infamous flash floods not too long previously, so the enormous vat we had semi rebuilt from the ruins, was brimming with water. Matteo would be pleased. He could refresh his body as well as quench his thirst.

That evening I stood by the pathway leading to our site in readiness to welcome the traveller home. Even before he was within earshot, he waved to me and I to him. The smile on his face assured me that his journey had been a safe one. I had prepared supper so, having grabbed one of the two shoulder sacks he was carrying, we repaired to our chapel.

"So," I enquired "How was Ptolemais? What was it like?"

"It is an amazing place. I learnt that it is one of the oldest cities in the world. The port is spell-binding. Ships from everywhere dock there and the town is full of sailors and traders. There are so many stalls, full of wares I have never seen before, that I hardly knew where to look first." He took a sip of water then continued.

"There were big ships as well as the smaller, island and coastal, craft." His mind was seeing the sight again as evidenced by the faraway look in his excited eyes. "I have never seen so many different types of craft and so many different designs for them."

He was silent for just a moment reliving his recent discoveries and then he seemed to suddenly remember something and jumped up to retrieve one of his carriers.

"I bought you a present." He declared rummaging in his sack.

"How did you manage that? You had so very little money." I was surprised by this revelation.

"There were many, many ships in the port so that finding a job as a loader and un-loader was easy. Each morning I went to the docks and within minutes would be snapped up by someone wishing to hire me for a few hours." The sense of pride at his ingenuity was evident in his voice.

He pulled from the carrier a bundle wrapped in cloth. Carefully undoing it, he proudly handed me a whole sheaf of papyrus. From another much smaller bundle he extracted both a container of ink and a dozen nibs.

"Here." His pleasure at giving me a gift was written all over his face.

"This is wonderful, Matteo. Thank you so much. Grazzie. Grazzie."

"Now you can write your own story and add it to the one we found." He had obviously thought this through. Without ever declaring to Matteo just what the texts had revealed, I had told him that they were the records of a citizen of Jerusalem, some three centuries before, which might prove of historical significance one day. He had obviously decided that I too should add to the text history that I might also one day be of "historical significance."

Hence this humble record of my minor part in what I believe will one day be a revelation – be it heresy or not.

"Saint Paul visited Ptolemais." He suddenly declared incongruously. This I already knew from my studies on the book of Acts but it was reassuring to hear it confirmed.

"I understand that there is a large Christian community in Ptolemais. Did you find this?" I asked.

"Everyone I spoke to, traders, sailors, stall holders, all seemed to know of Iēsous. There are icons on most stalls; some selling them, others with just the one, for blessing." He confirmed. I was pleased, and not for the first time, blessed the Emperor Constantine for his conversion to Our Lord.

Matteo suddenly seemed to collapse with tiredness. The sparkle in his eyes dimmed and a yawn issued from his mouth. Solicitously I recommend that he sleep now. He did not argue but went immediately to his makeshift mattress where he seemed to fall to slumber instantly as his head lay down.

I have written this account of my discovery over the last year or so, in my beloved language of Latin. I am now at a time where it is my belief that the "treasure", if such it be, find a new home. Matteo and I are coming to the mind to move soon, to a place more populated than this desert outcropping. He, still being young, is thirsty for adventure and I detect my own approaching ill-health. My eyes are not so sharp now and a whitening of patches on my skin might indicate the early onset of the curse of our time, leprosy.

Ptolemais is a favoured destination. Legend recalls that Hercules found healing herbs in this town. I hope that this may be more than myth and that, indeed, herbs and remedies may be found there to at least slow the progress of this ravishing and debilitating ailment. I had briefly considered returning to my previous community but had come to terms with my still rebellious nature, enough to know that I would not again settle peacefully there. It would merely serve to agitate my disquiet about where the heresy might lie.

It is now some months since we arrived in Ptolemais. We have found shelter in the home of one of our Christian brethren. Matteo is employed as a carrier at the port and I fill my days tending the gardens to grow food for our brethren. Whilst we all live in different dwellings, our Christian brethren seem to have formed into communities, which are called assemblies. In this way one family may trade; one may labour; one farm vegetables and grapes; one tends animals; and all manner of other diverse skills, which are then shared amongst their assembly. It is a system which works well and plays to the strengths of each of us.

Late one evening whilst sitting outside our dwelling, watching the still bustling crowds pass on the narrow street, Matteo raised a matter which I had been giving deep thought to recently.

"I really think it is time to find a secure place in which to hide our treasure" ventured Matteo.

"I agree, my young friend. I too have been giving this matter some thought."

"I was working late at the port and an idea came to me which I would like to put to you." He made the suggestion. "It struck me how clearly the brazier beacon on the end of the harbour wall shows during both the day and night. This made me think that it might be a suitable place for us to bury the texts."

I was immediately enthusiastic about the idea. "Indeed; a very fitting place for the burial of the documents. For here an illuminating clue may be devised for what may prove to be an illuminating script.

He looked at me in question and saw the twinkle in my eye as I appreciated the humour in my unintended wit. We both laughed heartily and it felt good. Once we had both regained our composure, we agreed that this would be the ideal resting place for the precious bundle.

My mind made up about the soundness of this spot I continued "I will leave you to devise a method of hiding the package beneath the beacon without attracting attention and I shall try to devise a clue as to its whereabouts which only the faithful will pursue." With this, the plot had been set.

(A drawing of the tailless fish) The mouth of Ptolemy never spoke such wisdom.

(A tailless fish sketch) But his guiding light illuminates the word.

We have just spent a whole week of Matteo's wages on a leather pouch in which to wrap this precious bundle. I have carefully folded each document in a manner designed to preserve them and with trembling hands placed them into the pouch. Matteo takes my humble letter and the other writings to the beacon tonight.

I intend to hide this parchment clue in a collection of papers being carried to Constantinople soon by my good friend Anastia. He has strict instructions to ensure that it is hidden in the folds of any book contained in a *bibioteca* there. I know this gentle fellow well enough to know he will carry out my wishes without questions. He is a faithful friend and a good Christian whose word is his bond.

All is now in the hands of God and under his protection. My part is done. The Jew's legacy is again safely concealed. I have to trust that it will only be opened by one chosen by the Lord.

Blessings, my friend, to whoever is reading this because know that you have been chosen by God Almighty to fulfil His word.

La benedizione di Dio e di addio. (The blessing of God and farewell)

Dearest Cousin of Mine,

I hope that the tale of the early Christian monk proved worthy of your time to read.

Now, we come to the document written by the 1st century Jewish trader.

I make no comment as to its veracity but trust that you will honour me by reading it with an open mind.

Yours in friendship,

Beattie

(Encl.)

Dearest Beattie,

It is with the greatest gratitude that I received the latest tale in this saga.

As far as I can tell, the encounters of the previous script writers all shine with the light of truth. I have little doubt that this, your latest enclosure, will prove just as realistic.

My impatience knows no bounds and so, this note must be short, since I can wait no longer to explore the enclosed document.

Yours, in excitement,
Jackie

The Text

1st Century A.D.

They say that before a man dies a record of his life may be shown to him in an instant. Whilst I am near death, as judged by my age, I find that I think clearly of events and achievements from my past which I may present to my God on His inquisition.

When I began this deliberation, I was going to offer Him the evidence of my children. I have five who survived. I am proud of them all and consider them to be the culmination of a lifetime of sacrifice, learning and moral standards. I have instilled in each of them the values placed upon a man and the duty placed upon a woman. They will, Elohim willing, survive me and continue to live by the morals which I have instilled in them and by which I have lived my life.

I could offer my Lord the evidence of my prudence and sound judgement. Having inherited the small trading business from my father, my being the eldest surviving son, I turned this trade smallholding into a well renowned name throughout the lands.

These achievements, I will offer Him, will outlive me and allow me to have left my mark upon history.

However, perhaps the thing for which God will most favour me, and find appeasement for the destiny of my soul, is my recording of events surrounding a certain man.

In hindsight, I find that this was, most likely, my greatest worth to mankind and the thing for which I shall be remembered. This may be the mark I have made which will last the longest and matter the most. I pray the God of Israel will credit me, with believing that in this duty, I honoured Him. And so look gently upon this poor mortal, soon to face His Almighty presence in justification of my life.

My story begins when I was but a young man of just 14. I had recently been raised into our most Holy belief in and acceptance by Abraham, Moses and the Great Prophets. These great

Prophets are the messengers of the Lord God Himself. Finally, I was old enough to be admitted to the most sacred ground of The Temple in my home town of Jerusalem.

How many years had I stared at the outer walls of this magnificent Temple to Shaddai and longed to pass its sacred portals? I still remember the feeling of yearning and isolation before I was allowed to be admitted. Even as an old man, tears still well up in my tired eyes when I recall those emotions. Tears then fill my eyes the more as I remember the feeling of pride and joy as my ceremony of admittance was conducted and I was fully accepted as a member of the sacred house of God.

Once my admittance to such Holy ground, the very site where Almighty God lives, was confirmed, I spent every spare moment I could within the outer walls. The sages teaching there in the outer sanctum fascinated me. My hunger for knowledge exceeded any other desire I may have had. My dear father often found himself having to remonstrate with me, for neglecting other duties, in favour of being within the hallowed walls. How he must have suffered with my wilfulness of youth? May Our God grant him peace now that he has passed from this troubled world.

It was on such a visit that I saw a boy, not much older than myself, talking with the Elders. I wandered in his direction. It seemed to me that the very questions I had always wanted to ask, but was too shy to voice, were the very same ones which this outspoken and obviously more brazen boy was asking.

I remember that I was also thinking that when I listened to the teachers and their disciples, they all had more knowledge than I. They spoke in words I could barely understand; about concepts which I thought of as 'other-worldly'. It is hard for the young to contemplate the next life when they barely understand this one. I was hopeful that this boy would ask and be answered in a simpler manner more suitable to a child's level of instruction.

However, on this point, I was to be disappointed.

As I drew closer, and sat amongst the other listeners, it soon became clear that the boy's understanding of the Torah far exceeded my own. For that matter his knowledge and understanding, of even the concepts, exceeded most of those around me; boy or man.

It was then that I realized there was something very special about this person. He was not a Rabbi and yet he spoke with them with the same authority as one. He was not a Scribe or a Pharisee, both of whom were highly schooled in our Sacred Texts, and yet he spoke to them, reminding them of and quoting some of the more obscure elements, from those most Holy words of God.

Whilst the teachers became frustrated, as he questioned their conclusions on the meaning of some point, the boy remained calm throughout and humbly suggested that the meaning was being misinterpreted. It was fascinating to listen to him make his point whilst, at the same time, succeeding in not arousing fury from our most learned and superior tutors. I had never before seen, or even imagined that, our Temple Priests could be rendered speechless; and yet this boy succeeded in doing that time and again.

The next day and the next I returned hopeful that the boy, whose name I had found upon enquiry to be Yeshua, would be in the courtyard. I neglected even my most basic duties to spend every moment listening to this protégé. On one bitter occasion I was punished by being denied my evening meal by my infuriated father. Luckily my mother, a most gentle and kindly soul, slipped me some bread so my stomach rumbling did not keep me awake that night. God keep her soul in peace.

On the fourth day I again, upon rising, ran to the Temple. Search as I might I did not find the boy again; nor ever did I see him again; at least not until decades later.

However, the seed had been sown. I knew, as it were by instinct, that this boy was something special and that I would come across him again one day. I understood, somehow, that he was to become important to me although I could not imagine in what way.

As I sit today, I believe that his influence is the offering I can make to God for my very existence and the factor that will weigh heavily in my favour as I suffer His Righteous Judgement.

As, by midlife, I had established a network of agents for trading around the Mediterranean, it was common for me to hear news from all areas of our domain; albeit with some delay. It was the messenger from one such agent who informed me of a phenomenon gripping the outlying areas of Judea. Apparently, a Rabbi, named Yeshua, was teaching of an impending end to Roman dominance and the dawning of a new age for my oppressed people. Who could resist such a claim? It is the dream of my people to truly know the taste of freedom. Our God of Israel had promised it. Our faith believes it. For who could doubt the promise of the One True God?

This messenger sat with me for evening repast, as is usual during his journeys. For once the 'conversation' was not as the word implies, but rather an exuberant monologue from the messenger on the words and actions of this unusual Rabbi.

I had no doubt that his relating of the tales was enhanced for dramatic effect. After all, healing, which this Rabbi performed, was not uncommon; preaching on the Torah, was regularly conducted by our own Priests at the Temple; even our own Emperor claimed to be related to some god or other; but this Rabbi claimed to call our supreme God, Yahweh or Elohim, as his Father. There was something new and refreshing in his teaching rather than the somewhat dusty approach others took to passing on the will of God.

Every few years some prophet of doom or dominance appeared amongst our populous and, in the normal way, I should have paid little heed to this young messenger – but the name Yeshua alerted me to the possibility that this prophet was indeed the one I had heard speak as a child. My curiosity aroused to establish the Rabbi's identity, I instructed the messenger to inform my agents throughout Judea, to report to me whatever they heard this man say. A similar message I sent throughout my business empire to every agent who worked for or with me.

As each trade representative visited with their wares and list of trade goods required, I interrogated them on the Rabbi's teaching. Each responded with what they had heard him say. It surprised even me how many of them had heard him in person. Each and every word I recorded in writing having first been satisfied as to the veracity and accuracy of the recital, often through the Torah confirmation of witnesses.

The life changing event for me, and the spur to continue my recording, was when I heard that Yeshua was preaching within walking distance of Jerusalem. I decided to hear him for myself. It was without doubt the most powerful delivery I had ever heard, even from the greatest speakers at the Temple.

Although I was in the company of a multitude, I felt he was addressing me personally, which I know to be the most powerful tool of a public speaker. He was truly spell-binding and I was happy to be caught under his spell.

He spoke to me of peace, love and the promises from God made directly to me. He said, and I believed him, that if I had trust in God, he would ensure that I should be blessed with everything I needed. Yeshua taught me that day how to speak to God without using outward symbols or declarations and yet it would, he assured me, please Our Most High Majesty, our God of Abraham. He gave me hope that this suppression by our conquerors was not to be loathed, but rather, tolerated. He taught on the Laws of Moses, clearly and without conditions.

He spoke all day on so much, about which my soul had been troubled, by listening to the dry academic, or unreachably mystical, teaching of the Elders. He had awakened in me a new clarity on the wishes of God which had formed and settled, for the first time, upon my soul and has remained with me to this very day.

The first time I heard him speak I returned home that evening bathed in a new sense of hope. Certainly, I was hungry; but it was a hunger in my spirit, to allow the Kingdom of which he spoke to settle there. I was thirsty; but with a thirst which could only be truly quenched, by the outpourings of this amazing teaching. I was a little tired; but it was a tiredness forged from realizing that the interpretation of the Elders was not the whole Truth. My mind and body both felt rejuvenated as if I had been reborn. The past seemed irrelevant as I had a whole new outlook upon life and relationships. I knew with certainty, that any past transgressions were from the old me, not the newly inspired me, and that these misdemeanours were already forgiven.

Whilst he was in the area, I went to listen to him several more times. My enthusiasm for recording, after verification, any words from this magnificent speaker was set alight with a degree of fervour I had never experienced before. My humble recording had suddenly taken on a new importance. I did not know why, but I knew that it was a task allotted to me, in humility, by my God, who is the God of Israel, and I was not going to disappoint Him.

This gathering of his precious sermons and sayings continued for what must have been a little over three year. Each evening, having devoured the words related by my messenger or agent over the meal, I would sit at my desk and record in writing, what they had overheard him say. Often quotes were included in the letters I received from my agents and these too were added to my growing anthology.

Also included is a physical description of the man and a little detail, which I gleaned over time, about his personal life. I did not if know the description would be relevant but it aided me to read and write about him if I could visualize him speaking. His eyes. Oh, I so remember his eyes. They were dark and deep. As he spoke, it seemed as if he looked directly at, and into, each one of us. Even if there were tens, or hundreds of us, afterwards each person swore that he had addressed them personally; no matter how far apart they had sat.

I had decided, at the beginning of my God given task, to complete this record in my trade language of Greek, rather than my native language of Hebrew. I believe this thought was put to my mind because, somehow, I knew that it would become universal property, not a uniquely Jewish one, and the language of Greece seemed to fulfil this requirement. However, in deference to my heritage, I shall also include a Hebrew account of the same.

I dared not, nor desire to, publicize this growing work. I held too much business with the occupying forces to allow anything to blot my sound reputation with them, which had been a hard-fought battle over many years. Neither did I make it known to any at the Temple that I was so fascinated by this man's mysterious but simple teaching. They would surely curse me if they knew that I was bothering to record his words for later reflection.

However, I did inform two of my closest friends and we would oft, after eating together, close the door and shutter the window to then discuss, covertly, some statement I had recorded. My friends and I relished these sessions since they were a departure from the concerns of our daily lives; did not involve the idle chatter of gossip which we liked to think was the domain of our women; and yet, somehow, instilled in us a feeling of hope, something sadly lacking as we looked around Jerusalem.

I was unsurprised when I learnt that Yeshua had finally decided to re-enter Jerusalem and been arrested for his troubles. Our conquerors had no tolerance for our God of Abraham. They preferred instead to hedge their bets by appeasing all the gods of their culture. Anything which is likely to cause unrest, or worse, revolution, within our unhappy peoples was to be stamped out with force and not a little violence.

I learnt that shortly after his arrival here the Rabbi had been put to death. I did not attend since the penalty for my being seen at the scene might well have caused the demise of my business. I sent one of my newly employed carriers to spy from a short distance though, with strict instructions to be close enough to hear any spoken word, and report them back to me for my final record. This he did.

It was perhaps some ten years later that a knock was heard at my door. Upon opening it I found a stranger standing there. He had the look of a traveller since he carried the unmistakable staff common to those on a journey. This is carried as both an aid to walking the rough terrain and as an armament. The dust from the road clung to his garments. My first thought was that he was a messenger from one of my agents and so I invited him in and offered him some wine as refreshment. It transpired that he was not whom I had believed him to be.

He introduced himself by claiming to have been a close friend of the executed Rabbi, Yeshua. This raised in me both a memory from my past and, at the same time, a reflection of my present. His business was equally surreal in that he had heard that I had been making a record of the words spoken by his master and desired, most fervently, to borrow them.

My first reaction, not surprisingly, was to deny the existence of any such writings. The Romans (and even the Temple authorities) were renowned for using the most underhand methods of finding and persecuting any that deviated from the approved path. The approved path being an uneasy agreement believed to exist between the High Priest and the Roman Governor which placed the onus on the Temple for keeping the peace amongst the people if allowed to conduct their religious duties.

The stranger, however, quoted to me some of the words of the Rabbi which immediately struck a chord as those which I had heard for myself some time before. It was on the subject of trust and God's will. I cannot say why, but I felt at ease and even dare I say, at peace, to acquiesce to this stranger's request. It just 'felt right' to allow him access to my unusual collection. This I did. He thanked me for my trust as I handed over the precious documents. With a promise to return them by the following season, he departed with my treasure.

He was as good as his word. Towards the end of the following season there was once again a knock on my door and there he stood clutching a travelling sack containing my treasure. I naturally offered him food and lodging for the night, which he declined to my great disappointment, and he departed as if he had never been.

In the following months I felt like a man whose purpose in life had been removed. Often, after supper, I would look towards my desk and long to be granted the task of writing a new saying from the Rabbi. Looking back, I felt that that time of writing, when each word had been so diligently noted, had been a chapter in my life of total fulfilment. I hadn't realized it at the time but I saw it for its consuming power only upon reflection.

Then came an unsettling period; caused by a friend relating to me the words of Petros who was retelling the lessons he had heard in the company of the Rabbi, Yeshua. He was in Antioch at this time which is where my friend had heard him. The quotes that my friend studiously recited were similar, but slightly different from the words I remember recording and reading so many times. My friend and I recovered my treasure and found the relevant passage. Indeed, there was a very small discrepancy in the Petros translation. Not major admittedly, but just enough to slightly dull the meaning.

I tried to put this niggling worry from my mind but it hung there like a lamp, or menorah, which refused to be extinguished.

Some seasons later another friend recited part of a sermon given by Paulus, another of Yeshua's confidants; although I understand he never actually met Yeshua. Again, there appeared, upon investigation and substantiation, a small, almost insignificant, difference between what Paulus was preaching and the words of Yeshua as I had recorded them. On this occasion Yeshua's words had been added to for illustration. Not in itself, one might think, a problem but I found the original script to be very simple and clear, whereas the Paulus explanation somewhat pandered to the Gentile attitude.

My first reaction, having had this second example of small discrepancies on recollections, had been to assume that I had recorded the messages incorrectly or that my informers had been mistaken. However, a nagging doubt remained and grew. Over the years I had taken so much care to ensure accurate recording using, on more than one occasion, witness substantiation, (which is the Jewish way), that I could not help but have confidence in the integrity of the writing.

It was these small examples of discrepancies which pressed upon me the importance of the written word.

We, as a people, have a history of oral tradition for the maintenance of our customs and doctrines. This has the great advantage that the relaters of our traditional history put great stock in accuracy of the oral story. A key factor in this relating, is that the teller has no vested interest in convincing the audience as to the veracity or worth of the tale. In this way no explanation is offered for why something happened; it is simply recited as learnt.

However, those passing on the words of the Rabbi are dedicated to convincing the ears turned in their direction of the value and unique status of this most venerable prophet. As such they respond to questions raised and may, in some cases, expand the actual saying beyond its original rendition. That, I believe, is where the value of my recordings lies.

As I mentioned at the beginning, I am in the latter part of my allotted time now and death is a constant companion waiting to spring and guide me into Gods Kingdom. It is therefore a matter of some urgency that I decide on the method of preservation for my writing.

My eldest son is a Zealot and has been since he was in his early teens and found influence from his circle of friends. He is, however, married to a delightful girl of good heritage whose father, like me, once heard the Rabbi speak. My daughter-in-law was so much influenced by this sermon related to her by her patriarch, that to this day she counts herself amongst the "converts to The Way" who quietly gather momentum. She had mentioned to me that she and a number of her friends meet often and discuss his words, much as I used to do with my friends. She is therefore like a gift from God for me, as I find I am confident that she will correctly value my treasure and protect it respectfully, unlike any of my own children.

I declared the purpose of the small scroll collection to her one day and the light which appeared in her eyes confirmed my assessment. She quickly agreed to take up the mantel of keeper of the words. Whilst I was sad to let them go, I knew it to be the correct path.

Some several seasons later she and my son have returned on a visit and she confidentially indicated to me that she had found the perfect storage place for the writing in view of my insistence for their secrecy. She had noticed that only at rare times, following rain, a patch of desert wild flowers bloomed for only a two- or three-day period. When they did, the blossoms formed the shape of a barely open mouth. Even more miraculous, when this plumage happened, it formed the shape of the Hebrew letter for mouth, word, or speak, in our language.

Having found this small area, she had decanted my writings into a jar and very carefully buried it beneath this unusually apt spot. Little could be more significant, nor more secure from ignorant eyes. That is where my treasure is securely stored and where it shall remain until Elohim selects a worthy man to retrieve it and make known the contents.

She had further designed a clue for genuine seekers which safeguards against both her death and mine which would, as consequence, cause the treasure to be lost.

(The mouth shape) Beneath the mouth is the true spoken word.

(The mouth letter) Above the three-tiered palace the garden of the king blooms rarely.

This clue she had concealed in a collection of texts from the Prophets relating to prophesy on the coming Messiah and stored in a hoard, assembled by converts of the Rabbi, which she knew had eventually found its way to Antioch. It was there secure.

As my daughter in law prepares to take her leave with my son and return to Masada, I have given her this letter and asked her to bury it with the treasure when she may, so that when they are revealed an explanation is found also as to their source.

I now feel that my life's work is complete and I shall spend my remaining days in prayer to Our God of Israel that He acknowledge that I have fulfilled His purpose.

I humbly beseech the one in possession of this treasure, to reflect upon whether now is the time to make these documents known; or whether the more prudent action is to keep the contents secreted until God speaks, loudly and clearly to the heart, that the time of revelation is now.

For, from my knowledge, I know that God's voice is, like Yeshua's, clear and simple when it comes to His commands.

To whoever reads this, may God guide your heart and influence your mind.

My Dearest, Cherished, Cousin and Confidant,
Is it Time?

Now comes the time to disclose the writings of the Jewish trader and display the spoken words of Jesus which the old man so diligently recorded.

Whilst I am happy for you to look upon them, I remain in doubt as to whether now is the right time to allow them to become common knowledge? It seems to me that the world is already in turmoil and these sayings can only cause even greater disharmony.

It is now several days since I first composed the start of this letter. So seriously do I contemplate this dilemma. My inclination, after much thought and even, dare I admit, some prayer, is that now is NOT the time.

I have devised a clue, with the same identifying symbol at the front, and placed it in a city remote from my home. The parchments and writings I have encased safely in a new box and hidden safely miles apart from the clue. This to follow the example of the, shall I call us, 'Caretakers', who came before me.

If, however, you demand to see the old trader's records, I shall send them by secure delivery. This would mean that you take full responsibility for them. The choice I leave to you.

For now, this fictional (?) novel hides the story behind the secret.

On a different note! I have recently been approached to become an illustrator for some books. How exciting! This was prompted by my sketches of the people in the accounts being spotted by a visitor to my home. I had formed them into a, necessarily, anonymous collage. The board I had hung above my mantlepiece.

This newly acknowledged skill earns me a good and reliable income whilst being a task which I thoroughly enjoy – especially in the cold, Winter months. I still dabble in object d'art but sketch animations are my new and rewarding primary income source.

Reggie is still my devoted companion and I get his approval before submitting any of my artwork.

Yours in trust as to your wisdom,
Beattie
(No enclosures)

My Darling Beattie,

I agree. Do not yet publish, even to me, the historic sayings as recorded. I do, however, love that you have formed the tales of the 'Caretakers' into a novel. An inspiration indeed.

It is too much responsibility for me to undertake even though my curiosity is at a peak. I must admit, while my head longs to know the content of the last parchments, my heart says that it is not meant to be.

Like you, I am content to allow God to decide the date of the full publication.

This novel of yours will be read by many I have no doubt. Perhaps then, the heart of someone will be moved to recover the lost treasure?

Yours, contentedly ignorant,
Jackie.